RANDOM HOUSE
LARGE
PRINT

ALSO BY NICHOLAS SPARKS AVAILABLE FROM RANDOM HOUSE LARGE PRINT

Counting Miracles
Dreamland
Nights in Rodanthe
A Walk to Remember

REMAIN

NICHOLAS
SPARKS

with

M. NIGHT
SHYAMALAN

REMAIN

A SUPERNATURAL LOVE STORY

RANDOM HOUSE
LARGE PRINT

F

Published by Random House Large Print in association with
Random House, an imprint and division of
Penguin Random House LLC, 1745 Broadway, New York, NY 10019,
randomhousebooks.com, penguinrandomhouse.com

Original cover design: Flamur Tonuzi
Design adapted for Large Print
Cover photographs: Getty Images (background), Arcangel (house)

The Library of Congress has established a
Cataloging-in-Publication record for this title.

FIRST LARGE PRINT EDITION

ISBN: 979-8-217-29035-2

Printed in the United States of America

1st Printing

The authorized representative in the EU for product safety and compliance is Penguin Random House Ireland, Morrison Chambers, 32 Nassau Street, Dublin D02 YH68, Ireland, https://eu-contact.penguin.ie.

For Theresa Park,
who has been with me every step of the way

REMAIN

CHAPTER 1

Cape Cod in May stirs hope in the hearts of previously frozen New Yorkers, its verdant lawns and ocean breezes holding the promise of summer days just around the corner. As I rolled down the window of my car, breathing in the scent of growing things, I marveled at how distant the chilly gray skies and rain-flooded gutters of city life felt. Here, at least, winter had long since retreated and the dream of slower, sun-drenched days felt close enough to touch.

I had visited the Cape a few times before, but never this particular town. A quieter, smaller cousin to the nearby magnet of Provincetown, Heatherington seemed to revel in its classic 1950s vibe. Cruising down its main thoroughfare, Pleasant Street, I took note of the quaint, upscale stores selling antiques, gourmet ice cream, wooden toys, and brick oven pizza, as well as the parents pushing expensive strollers on brick-paved sidewalks. Day-trippers ducked in and out of shops, while beneath a large old-fashioned clock, a pair of older gentlemen in baseball caps conferred on a wooden bench. Idling at an intersection to allow some musicians with guitars strapped to their backs to cross, I spotted a retro-style pharmacy and soda shop on the corner; inside, a group of teenagers sat at a counter, sipping shakes out of long straws.

I smiled, thinking the scene was almost too perfect to be real, but upon reflection it made sense that my best friend, Oscar, the offspring of immigrant parents who'd run a deli in Boston, would seek out a slice of the mythic American ideal. As traffic began to move again, I caught glimpses of neatly kept Colonials and clapboard homes with white picket fences on the side streets to my left and right. Heatherington **was** picturesque, I had to admit, and as if on cue, the clouds overhead suddenly cleared, giving way to a blue sky so intense that it made me squint.

It was Monday, the typical beginning of a new workweek, and I was in town to help Oscar and his wife, Lorena, design and build their vacation home, although until now I'd only seen photographs of the plot of land they'd bought. I was looking forward to hearing what they had in mind, as today would be our first real conversation about the project. Following the directions they'd given me and keeping an eye on my GPS, I turned off Pleasant Street, heading for the house's future site, where we planned to meet. On the outskirts of town, I passed a sprawling fairground with performance stages in various states of construction. Dusty pickup trucks filled the gravel parking lot while workers toiled in the distance. It was a hive of activity, frantic preparations under way for the upcoming Mask and Music Festival on Memorial Day weekend at the end of the month. I'd heard about the festival while trying and failing to find a place to stay; in the end, I'd had to enlist Oscar's help to find accommodations. Apparently forty or fifty bands would be descending on the town for the long weekend, and as many as twenty thousand people were expected to attend. When I asked about the kind of music being showcased, Oscar had merely snorted. "How would I know? It's probably weird Gen Z music."

A few minutes later, I turned off the road onto a grassy track that climbed to what I assumed was a bluff overlooking the ocean. I drove slowly, following the tread marks of previous vehicles, my Aston Martin bouncing and shimmying as the grass gave way to dirt. On either side, arching birch and elm and maple trees formed a canopy overhead until I emerged into a clearing at the top.

It was a flat and grassy plateau, ringed with majestic oak trees and a panoramic view of an ocean the color of dark sapphires. Butterflies floated above a small patch of dandelions, and the air was briny, conjuring my own memories of summers at the beach. Over the sound of the engine, I could hear vibrant bird-calls drifting from the trees, and when I looked up, I glimpsed a Cooper's hawk circling. I marveled that this lot had somehow escaped development.

Soon a substantial wooden structure came into sight: a city-size playset that looked as if it had been dropped from the sky, complete with swings, hanging bars, sandbox, multiple slides, and a fort crowned with a multicolor awning. All five of Oscar's kids swarmed over the structure while he and Lorena watched from a nearby picnic table. As usual, Oscar was wearing a throwback football jersey from the early 1960s, this one from the Cleveland Browns.

Not long after graduating from NYU, Oscar had secured funding to purchase franchise rights from the NFL, NBA, NHL, and MLB for the purpose of manufacturing and selling apparel. His concept was to put current players' names and numbers on vintage-style jerseys. He was meticulous about design and quality, making sure each garment felt ultra-soft and appeared appropriately distressed. He was also extremely savvy when it came to promoting and marketing on social media, and while the jerseys were popular from the start, sales exploded when a prominent rapper began wearing them at concerts and trendy influencers began posting regularly about them. Eventually, private equity firms started sniffing around and Oscar sold the company for nearly a billion dollars. It was the ultimate success story. His parents, whom I regarded almost as foster parents of my own, could barely contain their pride and wore matching jerseys whenever they went out, bragging to their many relatives in the U.S. and back in India about their son's success. Oscar humored his parents, but the money hadn't fundamentally changed him or Lorena.

I parked next to their matching Cadillac Escalades, which made my car look like a toy, and Oscar approached with his arms opened wide for a hug. Like the rest of his family, he was a hugger, and I'm pretty sure he hugged everyone, including grocery store clerks, the guy who cleaned his pool, even IRS auditors. I'd long given up any WASP-like resistance and embraced him in return. He slapped my back before we separated.

"You made it," he said, with a wide grin. "What do you think?"

"It's incredible," I admitted. "Even better than the photos you sent."

Oscar looked around with a faint air of wonder. "I still can't believe I was able to close on this place. I was bidding against one of those hedge fund bros and you know how much they hate to lose."

He nodded in the direction of the picnic table. "Come on. Lorena has been asking about you nonstop."

As we started toward her, I tilted my head at the playset. "What's with that?"

"I had it installed last week. I figure that once we

start building, it'll keep the kids occupied when we visit the site to check on the progress."

"Remind me how old they all are now?"

"Leo is seven. Lalita and Lakshmi are six. Logesh is five, and Luca just turned four. I know it's a lot of Ls, but on the plus side, I get to say things like, 'Get the L out here!' or 'Shut the L up!' or 'Sit the L down!'"

"I'll bet Lorena loves that."

"Not so much," he said with a chuckle. "But the whole their-first-names-should-start-with-L thing was her idea, and they think it's hilarious."

By then, Lorena was standing. She shook her dark bangs out of her eyes and hurried over. A gregarious Italian American dynamo, she possessed unyielding strength and stamina that even Oscar couldn't match. Like him, she was a hugger, and her embrace felt like being enveloped in a down comforter. After pulling back, she continued to hold my hands.

"How are you doing?" she asked, her expressive brown eyes searching my face. "I've been so worried about you."

"I'm better," I answered with what I hoped was a reassuring smile.

"Did you get my care package?"

Halfway through my recent stay at the hospital, a giant basket had arrived filled with snacks, candy bars, and Jolly Ranchers, and accompanied by a rather large plush toy penguin. For some reason—

maybe because I'd once enthused about the documentary **March of the Penguins**—Lorena believed that I was particularly fond of emperor penguins, and I'd never bothered to correct her.

"I did. Thank you. I hope you don't mind that I shared those goodies with some of the other patients."

"Not at all," she said, finally letting go of my hands and appraising me. "You look good. More . . . rested than the last time I saw you."

"I feel more rested," I agreed. "How are the kids?"

"Wild as ever." She sighed, waving in the direction of the playset with a rueful smile. "I never should have let Oscar talk me into a fifth. All standards and rules had fallen by the wayside by the time Luca arrived. He gets away with murder."

She laughed good-naturedly. An economics major whom Oscar had met at NYU, Lorena had helped him build his business until the twins arrived, at which point she stepped back to tend to their growing brood. Their home, like Oscar's had been, was messy and loud, a constant buzz of energy coursing through the walls and hallways. Yet Lorena took the chaos in stride. Never once had I seen her frazzled or impatient.

"How long will you be able to stay?" I asked her.

"Just until Friday night," she said. "The kids have recitals and exams next week. But once their break starts, we'll be here the rest of the summer."

"Let the L go!" Oscar shouted, and I couldn't help

smiling when Lorena rolled her eyes. "Hold on," Oscar said to us before marching toward the play area. Leo had Logesh in a headlock but was doing his best to act innocent on the off chance Oscar had been yelling at one of the other kids.

"I don't know how you two do it," I said. "It's always impressive."

"What? Raising kids?" She feigned innocence. "The nanny helps, but really, it's just like taking care of Paulie. You put out bowls of food and water in the morning along with a litter box and forget about them the rest of the day."

I smiled. "Thank you for looking after her while I was in the hospital. Where is she?"

"She's still in the cat carrier in my SUV," Lorena said, "the one next to yours. Don't worry—I left the windows open, but I wasn't sure how she'd react if I brought her outside. I know she's an indoor cat."

"She is," I confirmed. "Aside from visits to the vet and staying with you, she's never left my apartment. How was she?"

"It took her a few days to come out of hiding, but after that, she was sweet and happy, except when the little ones were chasing her around the house. She spent a lot of time on the back of the sofa near the window, where they couldn't reach her. At night, though, after they were in bed, she'd curl up on my lap."

"Sounds like she took a liking to you."

"I always thought of myself as a dog person, but

she totally changed my mind," Lorena declared. "I have to ask, though: why did you name her Paulie?"

"What do you mean?"

"She's a girl, and Paulie is a boy's name."

"I loved the movie **Rocky** when I was a kid."

"Then why not name her Adrian?"

"Because she looked like a Paulie."

Lorena laughed. In the meantime, Leo had released Logesh, who continued to rub his neck, while Oscar rejoined us.

"He said he was trying to show Logesh what to do if bullies ever went after him," Oscar explained.

"And you told him that instead of putting someone in a headlock, he should tell a teacher or come to us, right?" Lorena asked.

"Yeah." Oscar nodded emphatically. "Of course I did."

She gave him a skeptical look before clearing her throat. "I know that you and Oscar have some catching up to do, so I'm going to take the kids into town to get something to eat. They're probably starving by now. What can I bring back for the two of you?"

"A salad with grilled chicken would be great, thanks," I said. "Or whatever you can manage—I know you'll have your hands full," I apologized, nodding in the direction of the playset.

"Can you bring me a double cheeseburger and onion rings?" Oscar chimed in with a hopeful look. "And a chocolate shake?"

Lorena lifted an eyebrow in amusement. "Uh,

yeah . . . That'll be two salads with grilled chicken coming right up," she answered.

"But, honey, I'm hungry . . ."

"Then I'll bring you an apple, too." She turned toward the playset. "Kids?" she called out. "Let's go get some lunch!"

The kids ignored her.

"Time for grub, so get the L in Mom's car!" Oscar boomed.

With some reluctance, they climbed down from the playset and slowly jogged toward Lorena's car. The adults followed, and Oscar opened the back hatch to pull out the cat carrier. Taking it from him, I peeked in at Paulie, who stared back with wide, frazzled eyes.

While Oscar and Lorena helped the kids load up—some were still in car seats—I brought the carrier to my car. Putting my fingers inside the cage, I murmured greetings to Paulie, but she was still too nervous, or discombobulated from the drive, to approach me. I let her be, and after rolling down my windows, I retrieved my laptop, as well as a notebook and a pen from my backpack. Lorena waved at us as she backed out of the driveway.

As soon as we sat down at the picnic table, Oscar leaned toward me.

"Okay, now that we finally have some peace and quiet, fill me in on your last couple of weeks at the hospital. I gotta say, the place looked more like a country club or a small college campus than a psychiatric facility."

"They went well." I shrugged. "And yes, the amenities were pretty fancy, although it wasn't just a bunch of spa treatments."

Though we'd chatted by phone occasionally during my stay, I briefly described the program again; it emphasized DBT, or dialectical behavior therapy. DBT, I explained, focuses on the importance of behaviors as opposed to feelings or emotions, which are transitory.

"Okay." Oscar nodded. "But was the food really as good as you said?" he persisted.

"Yes," I assured him. "On the weekends, if the weather was good, we even had barbecues."

"It sounds like **White Lotus** with therapy."

"It's not a bad place," I admitted. "But I also got to explore some aspects of my life that I'd spent a lot of time trying to ignore."

"You mean your Richie Rich childhood and the wacky parents who messed you up?" Oscar cracked.

"Something like that."

Oscar folded his hands in front of him and studied me, serious once more. "You have to promise to call me if you feel that darkness creeping up on you again, Tate." He looked away for a moment before solemnly meeting my eyes. "I was scared for you."

Moved by his words, I nodded, both of us silent at the memory of those harrowing days. But

Oscar's expression soon turned mischievous again. He leaned in, his eyes alight with curiosity.

"Did they ever help you decode those little bombshells your sister dropped right before she died?"

Recalling what she'd told me, I shrugged again. "The doctors speculated that Sylvia was experiencing neurological anomalies as her organs were shutting down."

"But you believed her?" Oscar pressed.

I hesitated, choosing my words carefully. "Sylvia never lied to me, which means she believed everything she told me. But let's talk about it when we have more time. After all," I said, opening my notebook, "we have a house to design."

located in the lush countryside of Connecticut. During the course of my four-month stay, I saw him three times a week, in addition to participating in group therapy and sessions on emotional skills building. While most of the patients were struggling with addiction, a smaller subset, like me, were there for other reasons, and I'd checked in voluntarily with the knowledge that I could leave at any time. These days, I'm relieved to say that I no longer feel as though I'm living in a darkened tunnel, although I sometimes wonder whether I'm really cured.

I'm still me, after all: Tate Donovan, a thirty-eight-year-old architect who lost his only true family with the death of his sister. In the wake of all that happened and many months of physical and mental absence, I finally allowed my partners at one of New York's premier architectural firms to buy me out. Thus, I found myself for the first time in my adult life entirely at loose ends, alone and uncertain of what kind of future was still possible for me.

If you'd asked my parents, they probably would have expressed little surprise that I ended up this way. Then again, nothing I did ever seemed to please them, and while I may not be alone in feeling that I was neglected or unloved as a child, Dr. Rollins helped me understand that I didn't need to allow those feelings to define me forever. Still, even he admitted my childhood had been unusual in its circumstances.

My father had been the CEO of a conglomerate

that made money in a variety of industries. Mining. Farming. Pharmaceuticals. Oil and gas. Aerospace. Despite the fact that I was still one of the major shareholders, I'd never paid much attention to the business, other than to glance at the monthly statements when they arrived in my inbox. The company had been started by my great-grandfather, expanded by my grandfather, and eventually built into an empire by my father. Real go-getters on that side of the family, at least when it came to creating generational wealth. My mother, on the other hand, was a Romanian beauty who spoke several languages fluently and had appeared on the covers of magazines. She'd been working as a model when my parents met, and I suspected they had children for no other reason than that people of their station were expected to make heirs. But I'm just guessing. I don't really know.

What I do know is this: We lived in a penthouse on the Upper East Side of New York, but my father was seldom around. He traveled extensively, usually for business but other times—as I eventually learned—to enjoy the company of his various mistresses. My mother started drinking every day after her morning workouts, picked at her salads instead of eating them, and spent many evenings at charitable events. My sister and I were raised by nannies, and the staff included housekeepers, assistants, a chef, even a lady who came in twice a week to wrap gifts. I was driven by chauffeurs, flew on private jets, and like Sylvia, was educated by tutors during my early life, which kept me isolated from other children my age. We spent our summers in an oceanfront mansion in the Hamptons, where every other night my parents hosted cocktail parties, which my sister and I were forbidden to attend. Instead, we would watch movies upstairs or sit on the beach while drunken guests reveled by the pool. On the rare night that the four of us were home together, I had the sense that whenever my parents glanced at Sylvia and me, they were baffled by who we were and where we had come from.

If my parents had one redeeming feature, it was their appreciation for the value of a good education, which explained the endless string of highly paid tutors. After surgery led to an improvement in her health, Sylvia was finally allowed to attend Brearley, an elite all-girls school just blocks from our home. A few years after that, when I was twelve, I was shipped off to Exeter.

My years at boarding school had a profound effect on me. While I missed my sister, dorm life and distance from my parents finally gave me a chance to make friends. Over time, I learned the art of small talk and casual conversation, even if I continued to keep my inner world private. As my confidence grew, I joined the soccer and lacrosse teams, and was a natural enough athlete to pick up the sports

I hadn't played as a younger kid. I excelled in math and developed a knack for drawing. I even had a bit of luck with girls, eventually dating Carly, a pretty girl from Newport, Rhode Island, for much of my senior year. Most significant, I became best friends with a scholarship student named Oscar and spent occasional weekends with his large and lively South Asian immigrant family in Dorchester. They joked and talked over one another, laughing loudly. When I gathered with the nine of them at the table for dinner, watching as they grabbed at the platters of aromatic food while telling colorful stories, I couldn't help feeling that I'd suddenly landed on another planet. It was Oscar who taught me what it meant to be a friend, and with him, as with my sister, I was able to relax my defenses and simply be myself.

Because I seldom saw my parents—I went home only in summers and on holiday breaks until I graduated from Yale—they remained mostly strangers to me. I do remember that in the tumult of my high school graduation, my father pulled me aside to tell me that he wanted me to follow in his footsteps and major in business at college. Nonplussed, I stared in silence, then pretended to see a friend in the crowd and rushed off. Following my own inclinations and openly defying my parents' expectations for the first time in my life, I majored in architecture instead. The summer after I received my diploma, I moved into my own apartment in the city and started work as a lowly draftsman at an Upper East Side architectural firm. Eventually, after returning to school a few years later for a master's degree, I became a partner at that same firm, attracting newly wealthy clients who were intent on building their dream homes.

Sylvia, meanwhile, attended college in the city, graduating from the New School with a degree in environmental science. She was working for a nonprofit and living in the East Village when she met a man named Mike through friends and fell in love. My father insisted on a prenup—Mike taught music at a tony prep school near our home and was as poor as we were rich—but it was clear that Sylvia and Mike truly adored each other. After our parents' jet nosedived into the Atlantic when I was twenty-nine, Mike held my sister while she wept at the funeral and supported her with patience and understanding through her grief. He was, and remains, a genuinely good guy.

Sylvia took their deaths harder than I did, but then again, she'd never felt alienated from or unloved by them. My sessions with Dr. Rollins helped me accept the idea that they might have been different with her because of her health issues; that the neglect I felt may have been at least partially the result of their anxious focus on Sylvia. Still, in my heart I believe that Sylvia's innate goodness simply skewed her perceptions. She was kinder than I, more forgiving and inclined to assume the best about people.

Unlike me, she believed in God and the mysteries of the unknown, including the existence of ghosts and the afterlife.

I wouldn't understand just how deep those beliefs ran until much later.

CHAPTER 3

At the picnic table, I turned to the first page of my notebook.

"You and Lorena have discussed the basics of what you want, right?"

"Somewhat," Oscar answered. "We've always dreamed about having a summer house, and the kids love the beach."

I cocked my head. "Do you two have a style in mind? Like a traditional Cape Cod? Or something more modern?"

"We were going to wait to see what you might recommend."

I nodded, unfazed. Many of my previous clients—all of them highly successful in all sorts of ways—had difficulty at the concept stage of the process. The challenge usually lay in their desire to build something recognizably better and different and more attention getting than their equally wealthy neighbors' houses, but I knew that neither Oscar nor Lorena thought in those terms. They were less interested in building a status symbol than in having a place that would truly feel like a home.

"Do you want to wait until she gets back? Before we start getting into it?"

"Nah. She won't mind if we go ahead."

"All right," I said. "But before we jump in, I wanted to take a minute to thank you."

"For what?" Oscar looked puzzled.

"For giving me the opportunity to design and oversee the building of this house."

"Tate—"

I held up my hand. "I know that you threw me this project because you felt like I needed something concrete to get me back on my feet, especially because I left my firm. And I'm in a better place now—thanks in large part to you. I'm excited to start working for myself." I faced him squarely. "But I want you to know that I'm determined to build you and Lorena the most beautiful house imaginable."

Oscar smiled. "I know you will."

• • •

After hashing out some basics—among other things, Oscar guessed they'd need twelve bedrooms to accommodate not only the kids but extended family members, in-laws, and friends they intended to host—we walked toward the bluff. The sun had begun to warm the air, making the sea breeze feel almost balmy. The Cooper's hawk continued to circle, tracking our progress across the property. At the edge, the bluff sloped gently toward the sandy beach below.

"The property stretches halfway down," Oscar said, pointing. "It's public land from there to the beach, but as you can see, there's really no way for the public to access it except by boat. And the view is unbeatable."

"You're going to love it here."

"Is it anything like your place in the Hamptons?" he asked, referring to the house I'd inherited from my parents.

"No," I answered, "but it's just as beautiful."

As I continued to study the rhythm of the waves below, I noticed movement off to the left, near my car, a familiar flickering at the very edge of my peripheral vision.

These flickering "visions," referred to as peripheral oscillopsia, had begun shortly after my sister died. Neurologists at New York-Presbyterian had checked me, wanting to rule out possible congenital defects, disease, or injury unrelated to my depression. They'd run every test imaginable, no matter how expensive or time-consuming, before concluding there was nothing physically wrong with me. They'd theorized instead, as Dr. Rollins later would, that it was a symptom of stress associated with the loss of my sister and that the incidents would subside over time.

But they hadn't, and as the oscillopsia continued, I felt a sudden tension in my neck and shoulders. **No,** I thought, **not again.** I reminded myself that there was nothing off to the left. And yet . . .

The movement intensified, insistent in its urge that I find the source. Unable to resist and knowing there was only one way to stop the flickers, I finally turned and searched for a possible cause. A swaying branch, for instance, or a hiker who'd lost his way, or even a squirrel bounding across the earth. The scene, however, was perfectly still.

"You okay, Tate?" Oscar asked, interrupting my thoughts. "You just went pale."

"I'm fine," I said with a forced smile, but when I faced the ocean again, the flickering resumed, bringing with it a nagging sense of unease. I tried to ignore it, but again, wanting the movement to stop, I finally turned and saw nothing that could have caused it. Oscar followed my line of sight before glancing at me.

"Did you see something?" he asked, frowning in concern. "That flickering thing you told me about?"

"I'm probably just tired from the drive," I said, not wanting to answer his question. "I'm sure I'll feel better after a nap."

CHAPTER 4

People found Sylvia's expansive, almost mystical vision of the world irresistible, and she collected friends the way I collected lint on my clothing. In her twenties and thirties, her calendar was filled with lunches, dinners, and outings with so many different people I stopped trying to keep track; whenever I visited, her phone would beep with texts and ring with calls until she finally turned it off so we wouldn't be distracted. Years later, when her heart weakened and she was in the hospital awaiting a transplant that would never come, even the doctors and nurses gravitated toward her like planets orbiting the sun. At one point, she had so many visitors that Mike resorted to scheduling appointments.

Because I'd never made friends easily, she often worried about me. While I was away at Exeter, she regularly called, emailed, and even sent me handwritten letters. In my dorm at Yale, her care packages—stuffed with goodies from Eli's and Russ & Daughters and Dylan's Candy Bar—were legendary. Despite her heart troubles, and unlike my parents, she made an effort to visit me a few times during the school year. After the death of our parents, over time, she effectively became the mom—not mother—I'd always wished I'd had. As I settled into my career, she celebrated my accomplishments but also chided me gently about my personal life. She knew that aside from her and Oscar, I kept most people at a distance, shielding myself with the excuse of work. She often urged me to take time off to travel, like she and Mike did. They went on safaris and visited Machu Picchu; they loved southern Spain and Central America, sometimes staying there for weeks during the summers, when Mike had time off. She traveled to Rome, London, Paris, Amsterdam, and Berlin, and saw polar bears when she and Mike journeyed by train through Alaska. Upon her return from such far-flung adventures, she would show me photographs and videos, hoping to convince me to join her on future trips.

Despite my outward success, my childhood still cast a pall over me. Suspecting I was depressed, she often asked when I recalled last having a sensation of wonder or awe, emotions she experienced regularly, and I never knew quite how to answer. For the most part, I lived my life as though I were checking items off a to-do list: I spent long hours at the office, exercised and ate healthy food, fed my cat, kept in touch with Oscar, went out on the occasional date, and spent as much time with my sister as I could. Sylvia, however, wanted more than that for me. She wanted me to imagine a wider realm of possibility and was convinced that falling in love—and fully surrendering myself to its wonder—could provide the antidote to my loneliness.

Not that I didn't have opportunities in that regard. In my twenties and even into my thirties, I flitted through relationships, some lasting longer than others, but none ever evolving into anything serious. Like many men, I was a sucker for beauty but was also self-aware enough to realize that genuine relationships required a vulnerability I'd never been entirely comfortable with.

"You're too closed off," Sylvia observed after I'd explained why yet another girlfriend had proven incompatible.

"No, I'm just picky," I said, half joking.

She laughed, but behind her smile, I could see her sadness.

• • •

Perhaps because Sylvia's health issues had always been part of our lives, I never truly believed I would lose her. As the years passed, however, her heart condition took its inevitable course. After a series of increasingly desperate medical interventions, she was admitted to the hospital for the final time. Every detail from our last visit together remained as vivid as if it were happening in the present.

"Hey," I said to her.

Beneath fluorescent lights and surrounded by flowers, Sylvia had been sleeping for hours. Behind her, medical equipment beeped in rhythm with her heartbeat. Her skin was gray, her breathing rapid and shallow. She'd been growing smaller with every passing day, and sitting at her bedside, I raged inwardly at the unfairness of it all. How could a lifetime of unfettered joy and generosity lead to this? Although she was only forty-two, she'd been on the transplant list for more than a decade. Her blood type was AB-negative, the rarest of all, and in all that time, no donor had been a match.

"Hi, Tate," she whispered, before turning toward Mike.

"Can I talk to my brother alone for a few minutes?" she whispered.

"Of course," Mike said. "I'll get some coffee and be back in a few."

When he was gone, I slipped my hand into hers.

"How are you feeling?" I asked.

"Dumb question," she said with a wry smile. "Ask me something real, something you've been too afraid to ask before."

I closed my eyes before opening them again. "How am I going to live without you?"

"You'll find your way," she answered. "I've been praying about it."

"Don't you mean **your** way?" I joked.

"Same thing." Her eyes crinkled in amusement, and my stomach filled with lead.

"I hate this, Syl."

"Me, too." Even now, her tone was soothing, as if she needed to support me instead of vice versa.

"Are you scared?" I croaked.

"No," she answered. "I worry about Mike, and I worry about you, but I'm looking forward to whatever's coming next."

"How can you say that?" While I had always tried to humor Sylvia's otherworldly beliefs, I felt a surge of incredulousness verging on anger.

Despite her exhaustion, her voice was firm. "Because I know there's something more out there."

I said nothing to this, but Sylvia, who knew me better than anyone, squeezed my hand.

"I have a surprise for you, Tate. Actually, three of them."

"What are they?"

"Messages," she said.

"What does that mean?"

"You'll see," she said. "But first I want to tell you something." She waited until my eyes were fixed on hers. "I know you're not going to believe me, but I want you to pretend that you do. Can you do that for me?"

When I nodded, she went on.

"Mom and Dad came to see me today," she announced. "They sat in those chairs, and we talked, just like the two of us are doing now."

I said nothing, but really, how was I supposed to respond? She tried to frown, but it was more like a squint.

"I asked you to pretend, remember?"

"Fine, okay. What did they say?"

"They told me that they were happy to see me again, and that we'd be together soon."

"Uh-huh," I offered.

"Try harder."

"That's . . . nice?"

She choked out a laugh, which eventually gave way to a coughing spasm. When she recovered, she tried to catch her breath, but even that effort taxed her body. It was a few long seconds before she was able to go on.

"You're bad at this, so let me just come out with it. It's not the first time they've visited me. And I've seen others, too. Do you remember when we were kids, how I would watch people in the park for hours from my bedroom window? Well, I wasn't watching only living people. Sometimes, people who had already passed appeared to me as flickers of movement at the corners of my eyes, like figures I barely registered in the background, nagging me to look again. At other times they were opaque, or resembled shadows." Her sunken eyes gleamed. "But once in a while, Tate, they looked completely real, right up until they vanished into thin air."

It took a moment for me to grasp what she was saying. "Are you telling me that you see ghosts?"

"Or spirits. Or maybe they're just souls that haven't departed yet. I'm not sure what to call them. I do know that each of them seems to be bound by different rules, and that most of them are visitors, here and gone in a matter of minutes, like Mom and Dad earlier."

I could only stare at her in stunned silence.

"But some of them," she continued, "can't find a way to move on. They're troubled, sometimes even in terrible pain. Maybe something about their death was traumatic, or there were unresolved issues when they died, but whatever the reason, they remain here." She paused, searching my eyes with almost feverish intensity. "If they stay too long, the good part of them fades away until only negative energy remains. Then they're stuck here, forever tormented by anger and grief. Those are the ones I always wished I could help, but I never knew how."

I swallowed, unable to formulate any kind of response. She seemed lucid, but how could I accept this as anything but the product of a delusional, dying mind?

"I know you don't believe me, but Mom knew I could see them," she added. "She said that her mom had the same gift. I want you to do something for me—please try to pretend it's a reasonable request, and don't ask any questions." She gave me a beseeching look. "Promise?" When I nodded, she lifted a papery hand and waved me closer. "Lean forward and open your mouth," she instructed.

This is crazy, I told myself, but I did as I was asked. She blew into my mouth, her breath as light as a feather. Oddly, it didn't smell sickly at all. If anything, I thought I detected a licorice-like scent, gone as quickly as it registered.

"Thank you," she whispered, collapsing even farther into her pillows.

"Can I ask what that was about?"

"I don't know. Just now when she visited, Mom told me to do it." She released my hand and studied my face with doting affection. "Never forget that I love you."

"I love you, too," I whispered.

Her voice was growing hoarser, but her words were clear. "You're going to fall in love, Tate. And when you do, it's going to change your life forever."

Mike rejoined us, holding two cups of coffee. He offered one to me, but feeling shaky, I declined. Instead, I left the room so they could have some time alone together.

I half stumbled to the end of the corridor and collapsed in a seat near the elevators. Closing my eyes, I felt a tidal wave of memories wash over me—Sylvia ruffling my hair when I was a toddler; staring with fascination out the window of her bedroom; gazing with pride at me as I pointed out a home in

East Hampton that I had designed. I recalled the joy of her wedding day and the wild delight of her laughter. When it struck me that there would be no more memories to come, I felt the weight of an unbearable future descend on me like an anvil. How long I sat there, sobbing quietly into my hands, I do not know.

• • •

On my last day at the hospital, I recounted that memory to Dr. Rollins.

"You've told me about your final visit with Sylvia before." He leaned back in his chair, hands interlaced over his belly.

"I know," I said. "I just can't stop thinking about it."

"Do you think there's a reason you brought it up again today?"

"It's appropriate, don't you think? Since today is my last day?"

"Because it was the precipitating event that led to your stay here?"

"Maybe." I shrugged. For a moment I struggled to identify what I was feeling. "I don't know. I guess I thought I'd have a greater sense of closure by the time I left here, although I do feel better than I did when I arrived."

"You did a lot of good work here, Tate. But processing grief—and a lot of the questions Sylvia raised in her last days—takes more than a few months." He watched me with the patience and compassion that had coaxed forth so many of my own revelations. "I've given you the names of several therapists with whom it would be worth continuing your work. Prozac and inpatient treatment are only a first step," he reminded me gently.

I nodded, promising to follow up.

"Any problems with sleeping?" Dr. Rollins continued.

And just like that, we were back in our regular, if final, session. He asked about my specific plans for the next few days, and I went through the basics—that I planned to catch up on mail and email, meet with my accountants, and make some calls to contractors in the Cape Cod area to start the process for Oscar's construction. Otherwise, I intended to take it easy until I left for Massachusetts. Dr. Rollins asked if I had any regrets or negative feelings about my departure from the firm where I'd long worked, and I assured him again that I didn't. And so on and so forth. My answers to such questions hadn't changed during the last few weeks, and I assumed that was a good sign.

On the way out of his office, I shook his hand and agreed to call him after I settled back into real life to let him know how I was doing and whether I had connected with the therapists he'd recommended. It wasn't until I was almost out the door that I heard him clear his throat.

"Tate, by the way—are you still seeing things?"

I kept my expression steady. “No,” I answered.

His gaze was unwavering but neutral, and I couldn’t tell whether he believed me.

• • •

Oscar and I were waiting at the picnic table by the time Lorena returned. While the kids went back to climbing on the playset, he and I ate our salads before we all settled down to business. Fortunately, Lorena had done a lot of thinking about what they would need. To my surprise, she agreed that twelve bedrooms was the right number, even if it meant the home would be larger than they’d originally anticipated. I walked them through a wide sampling of photographs and drawings of summer homes and various interior rooms on my laptop; some of them I’d designed, and most of them I hadn’t. I noted their likes and dislikes before we all began to zero in on the idea of a large, shingle-style home. I spent another hour going over what to cxpcct as we moved forward, including various stages of design and construction, approximate time lines, and what to consider when choosing a general contractor.

As I wrapped up the final items on my checklist, we rose from the table, discussing times to get together over the next two days. I reminded them that I’d already arranged meetings with three potential contractors later in the week on Friday, but since Lorena planned to take the kids to the beach on

Thursday, we decided to leave that day open. Oscar told me he'd figure out something for the two of us to do instead.

"You know how to get to the place I booked for you, right?" Oscar asked, smothering me in one of his bear hugs.

"I wish you were staying with us in Chatham," Lorena said, elbowing Oscar out of the way for a hug of her own. "But I don't blame you for choosing a more peaceful environment than our house. Even on the best days it's bedlam."

I gave her arm a reassuring squeeze. "I like being closer to the site," I assured her. "Besides, from what I saw of it, Heatherington looks incredibly charming."

"That's why we picked it," Oscar agreed. He looked at his watch. "Hey, you'd better get going—aren't you supposed to check in soon?"

"Yeah, I don't want to be late," I said with a last wave. "Thanks again for finding me a place to stay."

"No problem," Oscar said. "And, Tate?"

I stopped and turned as Oscar put his arm around Lorena.

"Get some rest, okay?"

CHAPTER 5

In the kitchen, she stirred sugar into her cup of tea, absently watching a pair of cardinals perched on a branch of the old elm tree she used to climb when she was a girl. It looked like a beautiful day, but oddly, the idea of venturing outdoors felt daunting. She generally loved being outside. Just the other day, she'd ridden her bike into town, and the breeze in her face and the familiar swish of her ponytail beneath her helmet had relaxed her in a way she hadn't felt in ages.

Even the out-of-towners arriving early for the town's music festival hadn't bothered her, though many of them drove as if sharing the road with a cyclist was merely optional. She'd spotted dueling musicians playing on opposite street corners near the park, no doubt hoping to be discovered by powerful music executives. Sadly, talent scouts didn't bother visiting their little festival, but the performers and the crowds added a little spice to their ordinarily sleepy town.

After taking a sip of her tea, she drew a long breath, hoping to clear her head of the dark thoughts that had haunted her all these long months. Her grandma believed the old superstition that bad things come in threes, but she'd decided that her grandma was wrong. Instead, hers came in fours or sevens or even twelves. Then again, she supposed it all depended on how far she went back in time and which of the bads were big enough to count, but the fact remained that she'd cried more tears in the last three years than in the first twenty-seven years of her life combined. She'd sobbed at her grandma's funeral and for weeks afterward, of course, then fretted incessantly during the pandemic lockdown when tourism evaporated and Heatherington's businesses, including hers, went into free fall. Lately, in meetings with her attorney she'd sometimes become so angry she hadn't been able to sleep at night. Moving back home and falling out with her once-closest friends prompted even more tears, all of it making her question whether she'd irritated God somehow.

Oh, she knew it wasn't God's fault. Not all of it, anyway. No, most of her problems were of her own making. She was, she decided, a poor judge of people, the only consolation being that her mistakes hadn't yet broken her. But she was weary, and recently she'd taken to surfing Airbnb listings in Rome and Paris and Barcelona, picturing herself wandering open-air food markets and learning how to make artisanal olive oil. She knew it was a fantasy, but she longed to live a carefree existence—preferably in one of the exotic capitals she'd always dreamed of—at least for a little while. Why shouldn't she have a little **Eat, Pray, Love**?

Grandma Joyce would have snorted in disgust at the idea of running away, observing that only a fool would believe life was supposed to be easy or fun. She was a hard, practical woman, who'd lost both her husband and her only daughter before deciding to start a business while single-handedly raising her young granddaughter. She never once seemed to dwell on what could have been. Instead, when confronted with adversity, she'd straightened her shoulders and hitched up her canvas trousers before getting back to work, confident that she could handle whatever happened next. Grandma Joyce wouldn't have been out of place in the pioneer days or even as one of the original Massachusetts Bay colonists. Tough enough to endure a lifetime of harsh New England winters, she referred to March and April as mud season, planted and maintained her own garden, and up until she was in her sixties, occasionally smoked a fragrant tobacco pipe.

That she ended up running a hospitality business seemed as unlikely as her developing the ability to fly, but Grandma Joyce was a woman of contradictions. She hunted and fished but had been known to tear up at the sight of a cat or dog that had been struck by a car. She spoke in short, clipped sentences and favored salty aphorisms but sang in the church choir with a clear, sweet soprano that belied her weathered face. She often walked to town wearing rubber boots and an old flannel jacket but had taken her granddaughter to Saks Fifth Avenue in downtown Boston to buy a dress for her senior prom. The old woman had few close friends, but she was unshakably loyal and discreet with the ones she had, never betraying a secret. Everyone figured she was stubborn enough to reach the age of a hundred, but she had died three years earlier, leaving a hole that would never be completely filled.

• • •

Depositing the tea bag in the garbage, she pictured the townspeople reveling in another exquisite spring day. When she'd last biked through the square, she'd seen Steve and Kenny, the twins who worked as mechanics at their dad's shop, throwing a football while the Dobson toddlers' mom pushed them on the swings. Doc Harbison and Clayton Jones were sitting across from each other at a small table, playing chess; they'd played for years, though when the weather was cold, their games took place inside Doc's antique store, usually by the window, so any passersby could watch if they were interested. Near the edge of the park, she'd caught sight of Ethel

Lampier holding court in her lawn chair; beside her Ellen Jameson was whispering something, no doubt about her husband, Tommy, whom everyone knew was sleeping with Marge, the teller at the New England Credit Union. Elmore Barden had stopped sweeping the sidewalk in front of his coin shop to wave at her, and in front of her restaurant, Dianne Mills was scrawling the daily specials onto a chalkboard. The specials were strictly for tourists; as all the locals knew, Dianne concocted them from items in the refrigerator that were about to expire.

That was the blessing and the curse of being a lifelong resident of Heatherington, she thought. She knew almost everyone in town, and those she didn't know personally, she knew about. There was predictability and comfort in knowing her neighbors, but in a town this small, it also was impossible for people to leave the past fully behind. Once, when she was a teenager, she'd TP'd Mrs. Torkelson's house with some friends. Mrs. Torkelson was notorious for handing out Bible pamphlets instead of candy on Halloween, and a little toilet paper in her elm tree was a small price to pay in most kids' reckoning. Unfortunately, they'd been spotted by a nosy neighbor, who informed Grandma Joyce before she had even made it back home. Grandma hauled her straight back to Mrs. Torkelson's house, and in addition to apologizing, she'd been forced to clean everything up. In a larger town, a childhood prank would have been long since forgotten, but even now, when she was checking out at the drugstore, someone she knew would sometimes jokingly ask whether she was gathering supplies for her next victim.

Okay, maybe she'd had something of a reputation as a wild child—she'd caused her grandma some sleepless nights for sure—but she hadn't been a **bad** kid. It was just that like every child who ever existed, she'd been bored every now and then, because let's face it: there really wasn't a whole lot for teenagers to do in Heatherington. Frankly, there wasn't a whole lot more to do now that she was an adult, the Mask and Music Festival excepted. It was yet another reason to take the plunge and move away for good, if, of course, she could summon the courage.

She'd made a grocery list for that last trip to town but hadn't needed it. Only when she was expecting a guest who was vegan or lactose intolerant or allergic to certain foods did the list vary. For the most part, breakfast meant eggs, pancakes, bacon, sausage, fruit, bread, and Danish. For the last two items, she preferred to visit the Rolling Scones, which she had patronized for years because Eileen was a wizard when it came to baking. During the summers Eileen would prop the door open, and tourists, led by their noses, would inevitably find their way to the counter.

After that, she'd swung by Let's Meat, owned by Sal Ferrenzi, whose great-great-grandparents, he claimed, were the first Italians to make Heatherington their home. She'd picked up the bacon and sausage he'd set aside for her, put them in her bicycle basket, and was soon on her way.

Ordinarily, she would have taken a few minutes to stop by her **other** business downtown—but that hadn't been the day for it. Even the thought of doing so had darkened her mood, so she'd pedaled past without a second glance, heading for the farmers market. There, she'd purchased eggs from Ralph Montrose, who owned a small farm near Provincetown, and picked up some juicy-looking berries from Lucille Kowalski, who didn't actually grow any of it but sourced her produce from the same high-end suppliers used by Whole Foods. She'd set out for Kevin Tiernan's stall, with the intention of stocking up on his delicious clover honey, but it was not to be.

Instead, as she'd pushed her bike through the throngs of shoppers, she'd caught sight of Dax, his wife, Tessa, trailing behind him. She could remember ducking over her handlebars, praying neither saw her. Dax was someone on her growing list of people to avoid, so she'd decided to forgo the honey. Instead, she'd squeezed between two poultry booths and escaped into the next aisle. She'd told herself that she wouldn't look back, and for a while, she hadn't. But just as she reached the street, she'd peeked over her shoulder and saw Tessa scowling at her with her hands on her hips.

Shaking off the memory, she looked down at her mug and noted that her tea had gone cold. Dumping it in the sink, she washed the cup and set it in the dish rack to dry. Surveying the kitchen with a critical eye, she began a mental to-do list.

After all, guests would be arriving soon.

CHAPTER 6

Following the directions on my phone, I turned at the second intersection downtown and slowed to inch past an SUV and a pickup truck, both illegally parked in a no-standing zone. As intent as the town planners had been on creating a Norman Rockwell ideal, they'd apparently ignored the reality that people also needed places to park. I turned onto Fairview Lane, and eventually the homes petered out, giving way to farmland. The road became a gravel track that curved back toward the coast a few miles down from Oscar's property.

Rounding a bend, I saw the house for the first time. Oscar had mentioned in passing that it once operated as a bed-and-breakfast, but it was far grander than I'd expected. It was a massive Victorian, likely constructed around the turn of the previous century, with four turrets, large bay windows, and a porch that spanned the front and one side of the house. It was gray with white trim, and while the paint had begun to flake in places, it appeared otherwise in good condition. To the left of the house stood a smaller cottage, and behind it I could see a pair of sheds, one larger than the other; on the right was an overgrown formal garden sporting a large fountain filled with stale, algae-choked water.

A sturdy-looking couple in their forties was waiting on the porch to greet me. They were both dressed simply, with the exception of a small heart-shaped locket that hung from the woman's neck.

"Mr. Donovan?" the woman said, descending the stairs as I climbed out of my car. "I'm Louise Gaston, the caretaker here." She extended a hand, and we shook before she gestured at the broad-shouldered man beside her. "And this is my husband, Reece. He's the groundskeeper."

I introduced myself before she went on. "I hope you were able to find the place easily enough."

"I did."

"How about I show you around?"

Reece unloaded my suitcase from the car, but I slung my backpack over my shoulder and toted the cat carrier myself as we followed Louise up into the house.

The front door opened onto an airy wood-paneled foyer, with a parlor to the left and a staircase directly ahead, leading to what I assumed were the bedrooms. Tall windows provided ample natural light, and a large ornate marble fireplace divided the parlor into two seating areas. I took in patterned sofas, overstuffed chairs, an armoire, a gaming table in the corner, and on the far wall, bookshelves bracketing a large-screen television. Oriental rugs, elegant coffee tables, and delicate lamps with colorful shades completed the tasteful yet comfortable décor.

As I set down my belongings, I saw Louise's eyes alight on the cat carrier.

"Is that a cat?"

"Yes." I nodded. "Her name is Paulie."

Louise looked worried. "Pets aren't typically allowed in the house."

"When the arrangements were made, I wasn't aware of that. Will it be a problem?"

"Hmmm," she said. "I suppose if we keep it between us, it should be okay. She won't scratch the furniture, will she?"

"Of course not," I assured her, thinking, **Of course she will. She's a cat.** "But if there are any damages, you have my word that I'll take care of them."

"Okay," she said. "But don't tell Mr. Aldrich."

"Mr. Aldrich?"

"The trustee of the estate that owns the property."

"I won't."

• • •

We started the tour upstairs, where the odor of freshly applied stain suggested that the floors had recently been refinished. There were six bedrooms in total, Louise explained, each with its own bathroom. From the top of the stairs, I saw three doors on each side of the hallway, with one door at the end. Halfway down the left side of the hallway, a small sign hung by a chain from a doorknob that read, THE COAST IS CLEAR! Louise stopped in front of the door, mentioning that it was the only one that swung outward into the hall, rather than inward into the room. She added that even though all the rooms had their own bathrooms, this was the only bathroom with a tub, and it could be used by anyone.

Curious, I pulled the door open, flinching at the hinges' loud, long squeak. Turning on the light, I was surprised at how modern and spacious it was, with high-quality Italian marble tiling, an elegant antique claw-foot tub with ornate metal hardware, a Villeroy & Boch sink, a gilded mirror, and even a pair of matching velvet chairs that echoed the color scheme of the tiles. **Nice,** I thought, though as someone who seldom took a bath, I doubted I would use it.

"Which bedroom is mine?" I asked, closing the door and straightening the hanging sign on the doorknob.

"The suite at the end of the hall has been readied for you," Louise said. "It's the largest room and has an ocean view." She hesitated, a reluctant expression crossing her face. "I'm sorry if the house feels . . . un-lived-in. Mr. Aldrich only informed us last week that he intended to allow you to stay here."

Reece briefly exchanged glances with his wife, then stared down at his feet.

I nodded, sensing the decision had been a little unsettling to Louise and Reece. Thinking it better to avoid the subject, I made a noncommittal noise and proceeded to the bedroom at the end of the hall. Opening the door, I indicated that Reece could leave my suitcase just inside as I poked my head in, took a quick peek, then closed the door.

Louise led us downstairs again, sharing the Wi-Fi password and guiding me through an old-fashioned country kitchen with an open ceiling and rustic beams. The gas stove didn't always ignite, she warned, hence the jar of long matches on the counter. In the pantry, another door hid steps descending to the cellar. There, Reece pointed out the location of the circuit breakers in case the lights went out, the furnace in case the heater went on the blink, the water heater in case my shower was ice-cold, and a valve to turn if one of the pipes burst. He walked through instructions, making those situations sound almost inevitable, and I nodded along, not really paying attention, mainly thinking, **Got it: I'll call you if anything goes wrong.** They showed me the washer and dryer, along with detergent, bleach, and an iron, before pointing out a sturdy wooden table built into the wall that I could use to fold and press my clothes. Since I'd never done my own laundry or ironed anything in my life, I simply continued to nod, knowing I'd find a place in town to do it all for me. In the pantry, Louise pointed out the broom and a flashlight while Reece fidgeted in the background.

On the way back through the kitchen, I made sure she showed me where to find the microwave, the toaster, and the coffee maker, which were the only appliances I generally used.

In the closet near the front door were umbrellas, two black rain slickers, and an oversize pair of rubber boots I was free to use. Reece also mentioned that there was no back door. I commented that that sounded like a fire hazard—especially in an older wooden home like this—to which he shrugged, saying the house had been granted an exemption to certain modern building codes because of its importance as one of the most historic homes in the area. He did assure me that there were rope ladders under every bed upstairs, which didn't entirely comfort me. He added that the house creaked and groaned in the wind, and the pipes tended to squeal when water rushed through them. Finally, I learned where the thermostat was located and was told it controlled the entire house, not individual rooms. If it was hot upstairs during the night, there were extra fans in the cellar; if I was cold, there were extra blankets on the bench at the foot of the bed.

"It's an old-fashioned house, so why not do things the old-fashioned way, right?" I said good-humoredly.

Louise gave a polite smile. "I'll come by twice a week to dust, vacuum, and tidy up. I'll exchange your sheets and towels, but other than that, I'll try to honor your privacy, so it feels like your home while you stay here." She motioned toward the foyer. "Please keep in mind the front door locks automatically, so if you go outside, remember to bring your keys. If you need anything else, you can usually find me in the cottage." And with that, she was gone.

Outside, Reece walked me through the formal garden, remarking apologetically that Mr. Aldrich hadn't released any funds for spring replanting, but that he was trying his best to get him to change his mind. Same thing with the fountain, he added; the pump had broken, but he was hoping for funds to repair it soon, especially now that the house was going to be open to renters again. We visited a gazebo and a bench near the edge of the bluff before starting toward the woods, at which point I asked him how long the tour was going to take. When he explained that the property was twenty acres, I asked if we could do it another time. To me, that meant never, but Reece simply said, "Of course," and we returned to the porch, where we said our goodbyes and he handed me the keys.

As soon as I reentered the house, I opened the door to Paulie's carrier. I didn't try to take her out;

instead, I walked away, suspecting that she'd prefer to navigate her new environment on her own terms. By the time I'd set up her litter box in the kitchen and filled her water and food bowls, Paulie had exited her carrier and, after the mandatory pit stop, begun to explore. A white-and-gray tabby with a little M on her forehead, she investigated the kitchen and other rooms, sniffing everything and occasionally looking back at me as I followed. When her tail went up and she started doing zoomies from the kitchen to the dining room and back again, I took it as a sign that she was going to be okay.

Climbing the stairs again to the room I'd been assigned, I paused just inside the threshold. It was huge, spanning the entire width of the house and incorporating two spacious, light-filled areas. In the larger of the two, sunlight poured through three windows, illuminating a king-size bed with a lovely walnut frame and a rounded, padded headboard. As promised, there was a bench at the foot of the bed heaped with extra blankets; matching end tables flanked the bed along with brass lamps. A sizable walnut wardrobe stood opposite an antique, well-used rolltop desk and chair. In the smaller section of the room was a seating area with a sofa, coffee table, and two comfortable armchairs. In the far corner, a door led to the bathroom.

Once I'd unpacked and organized my belongings—setting aside a framed photograph of my sister—

I booted up my laptop and spent half an hour organizing photos, video tours, and renderings of outdoor living areas, game rooms, bedrooms, and foyers into files to export to Oscar and Lorena for their review. I hoped that the images would spur ideas about what they might want in their new home. I'd always loved this dreaming stage of a project more than any other—anything felt possible, and expense wasn't yet a factor.

Closing my laptop, I stood and stretched, moving to the windows to take in the view. Like Oscar's future home, the house had been built on a bluff, although a bit farther back. Drinking in the sight of the ocean's dark expanse beneath an increasingly threatening sky, I decided to open the windows a few inches to air out the room, which I accomplished with a few solid whacks to the sticky frames.

Downstairs, I smiled at the sight of Paulie lounging on the sofa in the parlor, already beginning to make herself at home. After placing the photograph of Sylvia on the mantel, I examined the books on the shelves, noting various classics and an extensive collection of poetry. Opening one of the books at random, I found a highlighted excerpt from **Leaves of Grass** by Walt Whitman with notes in the margin beside it.

Not I, not anyone else can travel that road
for you,

You must travel it for yourself.
It is not far, it is within reach,
Perhaps you have been on it since you were born and did not know,
Perhaps it is everywhere.

I paused, reflecting on my own journey in the wake of Sylvia's death. In the margin, in a young girl's loopy handwriting, was the sentence **Our life's journey IS our own, but wouldn't it be better with someone by your side?**

I closed the book and set it back on the shelf. I decided to lie down on the sofa, and a moment later, Paulie crawled onto my chest and began nudging my cheek with her head before eventually falling asleep, her purrs motoring softly.

I must have dozed off, because when I opened my eyes, Paulie was sleeping at the far end of the sofa and light was fading from the sky as sunset approached. Blinking the sleep out of my eyes, I glanced at my watch and was idly contemplating a trip to the grocery store when I suddenly realized I could hear someone humming, the sound coming from the kitchen.

"Louise?" I called out.

I rose slowly and walked in that direction, the sound growing louder as I approached. I thought I recognized the tune—it was a song by Bruno Mars—but when I reached the kitchen and turned on the light, the sound vanished, and I saw no one.

Confused, I glanced toward the dining room, but no one was there either. **Odd,** I thought, shaking my head. I figured it was likely a remnant of my nap.

Feeling a little foggy, I hunted around for my wallet and keys. Finally locating them between the cushions of the sofa, I shook off my inertia and drove into town, noting again the quaint local businesses, including a café with a sidewalk chalkboard listing some strange-sounding daily specials. At Star Market, I loaded my basket with the same basics I'd kept in my refrigerator since I was in college: coffee, bread for toast or sandwiches, butter, frozen vegetables, peanut butter, honey, a rotisserie chicken, and a few apples. I also tossed in several cans of cat food.

Dinner that night was a quarter of the rotisserie chicken with a side of microwaved corn. It wasn't that I disliked cooking; I'd just never bothered to learn how to do it. In the city, I often worked late, and in any case, it was easier to just order delivery from my go-to restaurants.

Later, I fired up my laptop again in the parlor with Paulie beside me, sifting through additional interior images and references for Oscar and Lorena to review. After a few hours, I turned out the lamps and headed upstairs, wondering if Paulie would follow or if she'd settle herself in the parlor. I hadn't made it halfway up the stairs before she bounded up after me, as if to say, **There's no way you're leaving me down here alone!**

I smiled, comforted by the return of our easy companionship. I'd missed her.

In my room, she leapt onto the bed as I undressed and tossed my clothes into a pile in the corner. I brushed my teeth, closed the windows as lightning flashed on the horizon, and crawled beneath the covers. Then, turning out the light, I fell asleep within minutes.

During the night, Paulie infiltrated my dream. I found myself standing near the top of the steps in the darkened hallway, somehow understanding that I was more of an observer than a participant in what was to come. The hallway appeared oddly distorted, almost like a carnival funhouse, and it took a moment for me to realize that all the doors were leaning slightly to the left. When I blinked, I realized I was mistaken. The doors were leaning to the **right,** but with a quick shake of my head, I saw they were suddenly back to normal. A light shone from my bedroom, where the door was open, and I watched as Paulie crept past the threshold, fixated on the hallway bathroom door. Suddenly, she lowered herself and pinned her ears back, as though sensing danger. I wanted to go to her—I wanted to pick her up and protect her from the unseen threat—but I was frozen in place.

Paulie rose slowly and took several tense steps toward the bathroom before crouching again, at which point I heard the unmistakable sound of a door latch releasing, followed by the squeal of hinges.

The sign draped over the doorknob tapped against the wood as the door slowly swung open. From my vantage point, the darkness of the bathroom radiated a forbidding intensity, and I sensed the presence of someone—or something—inside. Whatever it was, I knew it resided in that dark place. It **lived** there. It was **trapped** there, and it **wanted . . .**

Paulie hissed, and my neck muscles tightened while the hairs on my arms began to rise. My breathing came in shallow bursts, and my heartbeat thudded in my ears as Paulie crept forward before freezing again. She was moving like a hunter, but I feared she was the prey.

Go back! I shouted, but there was no sound. I could only watch the inevitable unfold. Paulie was growling, and then snarling. But the darkness—that **thing**—was luring her closer. She inched forward again.

I tried to move, but I couldn't. I felt the beginnings of panic, my heartbeat spiking as sweat broke out all over my body. Paulie was close to the bathroom door now, too close . . .

Time seemed to slow; each second stretched as I watched in growing horror. The darkness emanating from the bathroom seeped into the hallway, its cold shadow expanding toward Paulie, but just when I felt sure that something terrible would happen, Paulie's ears relaxed and her growling ceased.

Her fur settled, and the taut muscles in her limbs unfurled. She didn't turn and scamper off, though.

Instead, she rose to all fours and slowly padded to the bathroom's open door, more curious than afraid. But before she could enter, the door slowly closed in front of her, and I heard a click as it latched into place.

CHAPTER 7

When I woke the next morning, I felt the thrum of a light headache before the dream came flooding back. Once again, I heard the squeal of the bathroom door's hinges and felt dread wash over me at the darkness within; I saw Paulie exit my room and approach the door as if irresistibly summoned, at once hunter and hunted . . .

I rubbed my eyes, trying to clear away the images, but they were oddly sticky. I forced myself into a sitting position, which exacerbated the ache in my head. Checking the bedroom door, I saw that it was closed. Paulie dozed at my feet, untroubled.

Pushing back the covers, I got out of bed and found a bottle of ibuprofen in my Dopp kit, dry-swallowing two tablets before moving to the window. The sky was overcast, and the sheen on the stone pathway to the garden indicated that it had rained overnight. Strange that the storm hadn't awakened me, since I was normally a light sleeper.

Hoping that a shower would help me feel better, I stood under the spray of hot water for a long while, the pipes groaning and whining as the water coursed through them. Afterward, I dried off and caught sight of myself in the mirror, noting with irony that the hospital stay had done wonders for my physique; I was in my best shape in years. With little else to do, I had spent the mandated morning breaks at the gym, lifting weights and running on the treadmill.

I threw on a pair of jeans, a shirt, and loafers, a little surprised that Paulie hadn't yet stirred. Once I started moving, she usually took it as her cue to remind me that she was in dire need of food. She'd follow me around, meowing plaintively, to which I would inevitably respond in exasperation, "For God's sake, Paulie, you're not starving to death! Give me a minute!"

Cats.

I opened the door and stepped into the hallway, then backtracked when I realized I'd forgotten to bring my phone. Glancing at the screen, I was surprised to see a text message from Mike, my brother-in-law. I hadn't heard from him since the funeral and wondered why he was reaching out. I took a seat on the edge of the bed. Mike had sent a longish text accompanied by a video. Ignoring the text,

I clicked on the video, reaching down absently to stroke Paulie's sleepy head.

My sister Sylvia's face filled the screen.

"Hi, Tate," she said. The sound of her voice made my stomach drop. In shock, I closed the screen and steadied myself on the bed, trying to stop the room from spinning.

• • •

After a few deep breaths, I woke the phone again. This time, I clicked on Mike's text.

> Sylvia asked me to send this to you three months after she passed, but you were in the hospital then without access to your phone, so I held off. After your discharge I figured I'd wait a few days to give you time to get back on your feet. She told me that you were expecting the videos and that you'd let me know when to send the other two. (I'm assuming you know more about all this than I do.) Hope you're doing well, and let's grab coffee when you get back to the city.

I reread the text, vaguely recalling that Sylvia had mentioned messages in that last visit in the hospital but certain she hadn't said anything about videos.

I peered down the hallway to gather myself before playing the video. It was a selfie taken at the hospital, my sister's normally radiant face gaunt. In the background, I could hear medical equipment beeping; at the periphery of the image, I spotted the bouquet of lilies I'd brought her the day before my last visit.

Hi Tate,

I know you're surprised to hear from me but seeing you these last few days made me realize I wasn't ready for our conversations to end just yet. I'm sure you're struggling to maintain your stoic façade, but it makes me sad to think of you suffering now without anyone to console or support you.

I suspect you'll lean on Oscar as you have since your school days, but we both know Oscar has other responsibilities, so he won't always be able to be there for you. I'm afraid now that I'm gone, you'll withdraw even further into solitude. But loneliness, over time, is like an acid that eats away at you. You often teased me about my love of sunsets, but what went unsaid was that the sunsets I loved most were the ones I was able to share with people who meant something to me. I treasured every sunset you and I watched from the dunes behind our beach house, the two of us basking in all that beauty while Mom and Dad threw parties on the rise behind us.

By the time you receive this I will have been gone for some time, and I fear that you will be living on autopilot and feeling disconnected from the world. So I want you to do something for me. Sometime soon—maybe today, maybe later this week—I want you to strike up a conversation with a stranger. And as silly as it may sound, I want you to be open to the idea that the encounter happened for a reason. Every human interaction, after all, is seeded with infinite potential.

You may recall that I met Mike in my friends' coffee shop, but this conversation could just as easily arise at the gym or in the aisle of a grocery store. Sometimes the most mundane interactions create ripple effects downstream that we only decipher later.

I know your first instinct will be to ignore my request. You may not think you need anyone, but I promise you that there are people out there who need you. And being needed is often one of the most rewarding experiences of all.

Please, Tate. Trust me on this.

• • •

I watched the video two more times, trying and failing to hold back tears. The sight of Sylvia's depleted figure on screen instantly collapsed the months since her death, making her loss new and fresh again. As if sensing my distress, Paulie roused herself and climbed into my lap. I stroked her cheek, breathing raggedly, before finally wiping my eyes.

I left the room, descending the stairs on shaky legs. I was about to turn toward the kitchen when I glanced into the parlor and did a double take. I took in the scene, disoriented by the sight of a woman doing yoga in front of the fireplace.

I guessed she was in her late twenties, with long dark hair fastened into a messy ponytail, and wearing gray yoga pants paired with a loose pink athletic top. She was barefoot on the mat with one leg extended straight behind her, her body horizontal to the floor; a battered water bottle and a pair of shoes were set next to a white hoodie just off the mat. As I watched, she exhaled and slowly came out of the pose, lowering the extended leg to the floor, straightening upright, and bringing her feet together, her arms at her sides.

Confused, I remained in place, trying to figure out what her presence meant. Was she another guest that Reece and Louise had neglected to tell me about? I'd assumed that I'd have the house to myself, but maybe there'd been a miscommunication. All I knew for sure was that she seemed at home, her ease in the common room evident.

She must have heard me because she turned, her face brightening.

"Hey," she called out. "Good morning."

"Uh . . . hi," I managed, trying to hide my confusion. I hesitated before entering the sunlit parlor.

"I'm almost done here," she said with an apologetic

smile. "I didn't think you'd be up this early. I'll only be a few more minutes."

Again, I wasn't quite sure how to respond. She obviously knew that I was staying here, even if I hadn't known about her, so I said nothing. Instead, I watched as she slowly bent forward to place her palms on the floor, her hamstrings straight and fully extended.

"I'm sorry I wasn't here to greet you when you arrived," I heard her say, her face pressed almost into her knees. "I must have been taking a nap."

I blinked, feeling even more confused, before she went on.

"Have you ever done yoga?" she asked, straightening up, her cheeks flushed from being upside down.

"Once or twice," I said. "But I'm not very good at it."

"It takes practice," she conceded. "But it's a great way to start your day."

She lifted one knee and took hold of her ankle before extending that leg behind her, her back arched and her toes pointing toward the ceiling. With her free arm extended, she balanced on one leg, the entire movement smooth and improbably graceful.

"If you're curious, this is called Natarajasana," she said. "Isn't that a beautiful word?"

"I guess so."

After holding the pose for a minute, she repeated the position with the other leg.

"Is that your cat?" she asked, nodding toward the foyer behind me.

Over my shoulder, I saw Paulie pause, taking in the new arrival, before slowly ambling toward her. When Paulie was close, I watched as the woman lowered her hand to allow Paulie to sniff while continuing to hold her pose. Satisfied, Paulie made a beeline for the woman's hoodie and lay down on top of it, looking content.

"That's Paulie," I said.

"I love her coloring," she said. "For what it's worth, guys who like cats get the automatic green flag. I mean, you've never heard of a serial killer owning a cat, right?"

"I can't say that I've ever thought about it."

"It's because they're more independent and harder to control than dogs. Serial killers are all about control."

"Is that so?"

"It's what all those true crime shows on TV say." She shrugged, lowering her leg to the floor. Exhaling, she stepped off the mat and started rolling it up.

I shifted awkwardly, deciding to ask the obvious.

"Sorry if I missed the memo, but can I ask what you're doing here?"

"Yoga," she said, squinting up to me as if to say, **Duh.**

"No. I mean what are you doing here, at the house?"

Tightening the strap around her yoga mat, she

stood up and approached me, giving me my first real look at her face. Up close, I was instantly struck by her eyes. They were light green, almost too large for her face and framed by dark, sweeping lashes. And although she wasn't conventionally beautiful, there was something mesmerizing about her features, the wide mouth with a slightly crooked incisor and strong nose giving her an appearance that demanded a second glance. It didn't hurt that her warm olive skin glowed as if lit from within.

As she settled her full attention on me, her expression shifted, her brows knitting together in concern.

"What's wrong?" she asked.

"Excuse me?"

"You seem upset. Are you okay?"

"I'm fine. But you still haven't answered . . ."

"You're not fine," she said, not letting me finish. "You look like you've been crying. What happened?"

Thinking it wasn't the time or place to go into it, I took a step backward and remained silent.

As though reading my mind, she smiled before sitting on the floor. She began putting on her socks and shoes before finally looking up with disarming earnestness. "Sometimes it's easier to talk about things with strangers than with someone you know. In the past, I've found myself confiding to random strangers in the oddest places. Coffee shops, the gym, even the grocery store."

As I processed her words, I couldn't help but

blink. My sister's imploring voice filled my head, her words echoing those of the woman before me . . . **stranger . . . coffee shop . . . gym . . . grocery store . . .**

I knew there was no way she could have overheard the video; the hallway had been empty, and the parlor was too far away. But the coincidence was too much to ignore, and surprising myself, I heard the words before I could stop them.

"I received a video this morning," I said, my voice cracking. "One I hadn't expected."

Her expression softened. "Who was it from?"

"My older sister. She passed away, but she'd made arrangements with her husband to send it to me after she died."

She hugged her arms to her chest, as though feeling my pain firsthand.

"I lost someone close to me, too, not so long ago, so I can imagine the shock you must have felt," she said, her voice quiet. "What's your sister's name?"

"Sylvia."

"Can you tell me about her?" she asked. She scooted toward the sofa and leaned against it, as if settling in for a long conversation. Something about her voice—inviting and instinctively sympathetic—made me feel strangely safe. I hesitated before seating myself in one of the armchairs opposite her.

I began to talk, and as I settled in, the words poured out of me without conscious thought or direction. I rambled on about my parents and my sister's heart condition, enough to paint a picture of my upbringing, but mainly about Sylvia and how much she meant to me. Fighting back tears, I recounted some of our last conversations and my subsequent breakdown, and I briefly described my recent stint in the hospital. In the end, I played for her the video Sylvia had sent, my hands shaking despite my best efforts to still them.

Through it all, the woman's gaze never strayed, and I knew that both my sister and the woman sitting before me had been right. It **was** easier to speak openly to a stranger. Or, I thought, maybe to **this** stranger. With Dr. Rollins, I'd often held back; I'd even lied in my last words to him. But with this mysterious, empathic woman, I'd left nothing out.

When I was finished, she leaned toward me.

"Thank you for sharing all that with me," she said. When I nodded, she went on. "It's so strange that your sister and I used almost the same words, don't you think?" she pressed. "I promise I wasn't eavesdropping."

"I know you weren't," I said.

"It's uncanny. Maybe even a little spooky."

"Yes," I admitted.

I watched as she sat up and began freeing her ponytail from its scrunchie. "I hate when these things get tangled in my hair."

"I wouldn't know," I said, pointing to my near buzz cut with a halfhearted smile. "Do you want coffee? I really need coffee."

"Tea is better for you," she chided with a smile.

"Then I take it you don't want any?"

She shook her head. As I rose, I saw the scrunchie fly from her fingers, skittering beneath the armoire.

"Wow!" She laughed. "That thing took off like it was launched from a slingshot."

I squatted in front of the armoire, spotting the scrunchie near the wall. It was going to be difficult to reach, but before I could get down on all fours, she waved me off. "Go make your coffee. I'll get it. I have skinnier arms."

At the threshold of the parlor I paused, turning to look at her over my shoulder. "Thanks for listening," I said. "I'm not sure what came over me."

"Thank you for trusting me," the woman responded.

In the kitchen, I located the coffee I'd purchased the day before and set about prepping the coffee maker. Then, remembering Paulie, I rinsed and refilled her water bowl before grabbing her food bowl.

"Is Paulie still out there?" I called out.

"She's curled up on my hoodie," she answered.

"My sister got her for me. Did I mention that?"

"No, but it makes sense, given how close the two of you were. It makes me wish I had a sister. Or a brother for that matter."

Turning on the faucet again, I gave Paulie's food bowl a good rinse.

"You don't have siblings?" I called out.

"It's just me," came her answer.

"You never did tell me what you're doing here," I reminded her. "I assume you're staying in one of the rooms upstairs?" I pulled down a can of cat food from the cupboard. "And I just realized I never got your name."

Just then I heard a knock at the door, and glancing out the kitchen window, I saw Louise standing on the porch.

"Would you mind answering the door? I'm getting Paulie's food ready."

I pulled the tab and scooped some food into the bowl. There was only silence. At the lack of response, I set Paulie's bowl on the floor.

"Hello?" I called.

I made my way back to the parlor and scanned the area twice, but the woman was nowhere to be seen. Nor were her belongings. No rolled-up yoga mat, no battered metal water bottle. Paulie, however, remained curled up on the hoodie before I realized the hoodie was gone, too.

Weird, I thought. When Louise knocked again, I hurried to the door and pulled it open. In her arms was a gift basket, including wine and an assortment of cheeses, salamis, and crackers.

"Good morning," she said, holding out the basket. "This came for you, but you were out yesterday evening, so I signed for it."

I peeked in the basket and saw a card from Oscar that read, **In case you get hungry.**

"Thank you," I said. "And I'm glad you came by. Why didn't you tell me that someone else would be staying in the house?"

She frowned slightly. "Because there is no one else staying here."

"There obviously is," I countered. "She was doing yoga when I came downstairs this morning."

"I'm sure Mr. Aldrich would have let me know if he'd booked another guest. I'm quite certain that you're alone here."

"I don't know what to tell you," I said. "We talked for over an hour. And I'm not angry, just a little surprised."

Her frown deepened. "I suppose I have to speak with him then."

"If you do, let him know that it's fine with me if she's staying here. This place has more than enough room for both of us."

After saying goodbye, I shut the door and brought the basket to the kitchen before returning to the parlor. Paulie was still lying where the hoodie had been. Strange; if Paulie had been roused, it was unlikely she'd have returned to the same spot. And why hadn't she run to the kitchen when she heard me filling her food bowl? Normally she was hyperalert to the sounds of food preparation. Near the armoire I got down on all fours, but the scrunchie was nowhere to be seen.

Thinking the stranger had returned to her room,

I went upstairs and knocked on each door, calling out a friendly hello each time. Cautiously I turned each of the bedroom doorknobs, only to find them all locked.

Assuming she was in the bathroom or shower, and afraid of intruding, I retrieved my computer and went back downstairs, where I poured myself a cup of coffee. By then, Paulie had made it to her bowl and was eating, and I settled at the dining room table with my cup, catching up on world events. Despite a self-imposed news blackout during my time at the hospital, little had changed. Republicans and Democrats were sniping at each other, tensions were simmering in the Middle East, and a Hollywood actress had just announced an impending divorce.

As I read, I found my mind wandering to the events of the morning, still unable to believe how much I'd told the woman about myself, but mostly dwelling on the memory of her eyes. Though it was surely my imagination, they seemed to change color as different emotions flickered across her face, darkening at the mention of something painful, glittering a bright emerald when she laughed, and fading to a dreamy aquamarine while she was contemplating something meaningful I'd admitted about myself.

I sighed, closing my laptop. There was no denying that I was looking forward to seeing . . .

Well . . . **her** again . . . whoever she was.

But for as long as I sat at the dining room table, she never did come back downstairs. With a trace of disappointment, I packed up my things and headed out to meet Oscar and his family.

CHAPTER 8

What time was it, she wondered, looking up from her book as if surfacing from a dream. She always lost track of time when she read. When she and Grandma Joyce had lived in the cottage, she'd crawl into bed with a book, and the next thing she knew, Grandma would be peeking into her room and demanding to know what she thought she was doing, staying up past midnight on a school night. Grandma would turn out the light and threaten to take away the books for good if she couldn't control herself, which even as a child she knew was an empty threat.

She glanced down at the illustrated copy of **A Christmas Carol** open on her lap. She blanked on why she had chosen this classic tale, given that it was almost summer, but when she saw the quote etched beneath the illustration of Scrooge and the phantom, she smiled:

Now,
you're just a stranger,
who knows,
all my secrets.

Ah yes . . . she'd chosen this title because of Tate. Adorable Tate, with his short hair and dimple in his chin and tailored clothes made to look as though they'd been bought off the rack like everyone else's. She'd heard him stagger down the stairs and into the parlor before staring at her gobsmacked through red, swollen eyes.

You didn't have to be a psychic to see the poor man was upset. And when he'd sat down and opened up to her, she could understand why. The facts of his lonely childhood were sad enough, but what really made her heart contract was the emptiness with which he had spoken of his parents. She and Grandma Joyce had had their conflicts—their personalities were like oil and water in many respects—but she'd never doubted her grandmother's love. Tate had loved and lost his sister, just like she'd loved and lost her grandma, but still, she knew it wasn't the same. Sylvia had meant everything to him, and by the time he'd described his visits with his sister as she lay dying, she'd had to fight the impulse to take his hands, he seemed so utterly bereft.

Of course, she hadn't done it, but when he'd shown her the video, she almost felt as though she had. Or rather, it felt like Sylvia was clasping both their hands, the three of them joined together in a circle of her making. Perhaps she'd been imagining it, but she also could have sworn there'd been a connection between her and Tate, like a spark between circuits. A smile crossed her lips, and glancing down at the book, she read the words she'd scribbled in the margin years ago:

Sharing a secret
whispers
in the dark dark
honesty and trust,
twin terrors, slowly evolving
(now glue)
without them
the world comes
apart.

She blushed, remembering her e. e. cummings phase, back when she was fifteen or sixteen. Although cummings would have been mortified by her teenage attempt at mimicry, these girlish sentiments nonetheless felt apt this morning. Tate's radical honesty and trust had affected her so deeply. He hadn't pretended to be someone he wasn't; he hadn't been afraid to reveal that he'd been in a psychiatric hospital or that he was still reconciling things about his past. He'd wept openly when speaking about Sylvia—how many men would do that in front of someone they'd just met?—and his hands were shaking as he played the video. He'd simply presented himself as he was. There was something courageous and beautiful in that, and she'd found herself returning to the memory of his open, vulnerable expression as his eyes searched her face.

She reminded herself not to get too carried away, even if this morning had been unexpectedly memorable. The last thing she needed was to develop **feelings** for a stranger. She was hardly in a state to get close to anyone.

She expelled an aggravated sigh. Her life was too much of a mess right now for her to even be thinking about interesting men, much less a guest who would soon be returning to New York City. She needed to focus on figuring out her own next steps, she reminded herself.

Closing her book with a resolute snap, she stood and crossed the parlor. Reaching on her tiptoes, she returned the book to the shelf where it belonged.

CHAPTER 9

As soon as I entered the diner, I spotted Oscar waving from a booth in the corner.

"Where are Lorena and the kids?" I asked, sliding in across from him.

"On their way to serious injury and possible death if you ask me."

"You're going to have to explain that."

"They went to a trampoline park in Plymouth this morning, along with the nanny," Oscar said. "Leo saw a billboard last week, and he's been pestering us to go. And Lorena, brave mother that she is, finally agreed. She says that it'll help get their energy out. They'll meet us at the site in an hour or two."

"Great," I said.

"If you say so. Have you ever seen one of those places?" When I shook my head, he went on. "It's basically a building the size of an airplane hangar, and it's filled with a jillion trampolines lined up next to each other, where kids can go nuts."

"That sounds fun," I said.

"It would be if the kids were supercoordinated, but mine aren't. Well, maybe Leo is, but the twins? They can fall over walking to the bathroom. I'm expecting Lorena to call from the emergency room any minute now." When I laughed, he leaned in. "Hey, did you happen to notice what those two guys over there are wearing?" He nodded at a booth to the left of us.

I turned and spotted a couple young men sporting jerseys that Oscar's company—or former company, since he'd cashed out—had designed.

"Feels good to see people wearing your stuff, huh?"

"It does, but it's still kind of hard to believe, you know?" he said. "Growing up, I knew nothing about fashion. I swear I only ever wore my brothers' hand-me-downs. But now I see guys wearing my gear wherever I go, I live in a mansion in a fancy suburb of Boston, and I've commissioned you to build us a summer house. Had someone told me when I was young how my life was going to turn out, I never would have believed it."

"You were always the smartest guy in the room," I said. "You wouldn't have received a full ride to Exeter and NYU if you weren't. Weren't you voted Most Likely to Succeed our senior year?"

"That's just because of my side hustle running

midnight poker tournaments. It's a good thing the headmaster never found out."

I agreed with a snort. "By the way, thanks for the basket of goodies."

"Lorena's idea," he said, "but you're welcome."

He scanned the area, catching the eye of a waitress taking orders at a nearby table.

"Don't even bother looking," he said, tapping the large plastic menus on the table. "This place is famous for its lobster Benedict and smoked bacon."

"If I eat at all, I usually stick to a little toast with peanut butter and honey for breakfast."

"Boring."

"Maybe, but the sun is shining and the weather's perfect, so I think I can forgo the breakfast of champions."

He raised an eyebrow. "Somcone's in a good mood this morning."

My mind conjured up images of the woman I'd met earlier and I couldn't suppress a smile. "Yeah . . . I think I am."

"I'm glad to hear that," he said. "And the place I rented for you is okay?"

I nodded. "How'd you even find it? When I looked, there was nothing available."

"I visited the property last year," he answered. "I thought about trying to buy it, but it's been tied up in litigation, and I didn't want to wait. It would have been nice, though. It's almost twenty acres with ocean frontage."

"Expensive."

"Everything is expensive on the Cape these days. And, not that you asked, but I had to pull some serious strings to even allow you to stay there. Luckily the trustee who was appointed to manage the property sits on a local conservation board with me."

"Aldrich?"

"That's the one. I still think you would have been better off in Chatham, closer to where we're staying. Too much isolation isn't good for you."

"I'm doing all right," I assured him.

His eyes held mine as he debated whether to believe me, but he finally let it pass. "Well, if you get lonely out there, remember that we're only a car ride away."

"I will," I said, images of . . . **her** arising again. "In fact," I added, trying to sound casual, "you'll probably be happy to know I met someone this morning."

Oscar lifted an eyebrow in surprise.

"By someone, I assume you mean a woman?"

"I guess she's staying at the house, too."

"Really?" he asked. "I thought I rented the whole place."

"It's okay. I don't mind."

He gave a knowing grin. "Let me guess. She's beautiful, right? Like every other woman you've ever dated? And as soon as she heard your last name or saw your black American Express card, she was really into you, right?"

"This was different," I said. "And yeah, she is pretty, but we just talked."

"And by talking, you mean . . ."

"Words and sentences," I answered.

"Wow," he said, pursing his lips. "What's her name?"

"I don't know."

"How can you not know?"

"It didn't come up."

"Where's she from? Is she here in town for the festival?"

"I don't know that either."

"Then what the hell did the two of you talk about?"

"Just . . . stuff," I said, not wanting to get into it.

"Well, good for you," he said, when he realized I'd say nothing more. "I thought I noticed an extra bounce in your step this morning."

"I was walking normally."

He shrugged. "If you say so."

• • •

After watching Oscar polish off the lobster Benedict and a side of bacon while I nibbled on my toast, I followed him out, noting that the overcast sky had mostly cleared, leaving only patches of white floating in a cerulean sky. He'd parked in the opposite direction, so after agreeing to meet him at the site, I retraced my route back to my car.

As I took in the amiable surroundings, I found

myself marveling at the way the morning had turned out. If not for the encounter with the woman, I probably would have watched Sylvia's video over and over, my mood growing blacker with every viewing.

And yet, I hadn't. Even more surprising, I didn't feel compelled to watch it again. Somehow, it had slipped from my mind to the point that I had failed even to mention it to Oscar. In fact, I hadn't really thought about it since I'd shown it to . . .

Who was she? And how had I neglected to get her name?

I felt sure that I'd never met anyone quite like her before. Those luminous eyes projected an ageless wisdom, as if the nature of my grief were already intimately familiar to her. As if she already **knew** how I felt, even before I found the words to describe it. And yet never once did I feel judged. Only with Sylvia could I ever recall feeling that someone was so unquestioningly on my side, and it was startling to experience that with someone I'd just met.

Then again, it was possible that I'd simply projected what I wanted to see. I wasn't exactly the picture of equanimity and clear-sightedness these days. But I couldn't deny there was something beguiling about her and that I was very much looking forward to seeing her again.

• • •

At the site, I began to walk Oscar through the information and images I'd put together the night before, expecting I'd have to go over all of it a second time with Lorena. Luckily, she arrived only a few minutes later, and the three of us huddled in front of my laptop while the kids played on the swings and the slide. If trampolining all morning was supposed to have worn them out, it obviously hadn't.

I asked questions, listening to the two of them answer and sometimes disagree. In some ways, being an architect was a bit like being a marriage counselor, and I'd learned to tread carefully. I nodded, asked further questions, and suggested compromises. Through it all, I took pages of notes and set aside various attachments. By the two-hour mark, I sensed them growing fatigued and suggested we call it a day.

I combined the visuals that had caught their interest into a single folder and promised to email it to them as soon as I was back at the house. I recommended that they review them and start winnowing down the options, and I reminded them that it would be up to all of us to keep the project moving forward in a timely manner.

When I returned to the house I found Reece outside, working on a pipe near the broken fountain. I didn't see any other cars parked in front, but as I unlocked the front door, I felt a hopeful twinge of anticipation that I'd see the woman I'd met earlier. A quick circuit through the downstairs made it clear she wasn't around.

Disappointed, I pulled out the computer and notebook from my backpack and took a seat at the dining room table. While I could have worked at the desk in my room, it was equally quiet downstairs, and I spent the next hour transcribing my handwritten notes. I was halfway through when I heard a knock at the door. On the porch were Louise and Reece. I stepped aside to let them in.

"I called Mr. Aldrich after our conversation this morning," Louise said, "and he confirmed that he hasn't spoken with anyone else about the possibility of staying here."

Her words were baffling considering what had happened. "So it's just me?"

She nodded. "Just to be sure, I went upstairs to check the other rooms while you were out. There's no evidence that anyone is staying, or even spent time, in any of those rooms. The doors are locked, the furniture is still covered, and the beds aren't even made up."

"Then what was that woman doing here this morning?" I asked, bewildered.

Reece cleared his throat. "After Louise told me about her conversation with you, I explored the grounds," he said. "I found a group of people camping at the edge of the property. There were eight of them. They'd set up tents, a portable grill, even strung a clothesline between some trees. They said they were in town for the music festival. It's not the first time it's happened. The festival attracts a lot of young people, and some of them may have heard that the house has been empty for a while."

"You think she was one of them?"

"Though they denied it, I think it's probable. Since it rained last night, I'm guessing one of the young ladies was simply scouting out someplace dry and didn't realize the house was occupied." He looked uncomfortable.

"How did she get in? If the door locks automatically?"

"Maybe the door wasn't closed all the way?"

I tried to remember whether I'd checked the night before; I remembered turning out the lamps, but as for the door, my mind was a blank. "I guess I could have accidentally left it cracked open after I got home from the store."

"It might be a good idea to engage the dead bolt as well before you retire to your room in the evening," Louise suggested, "to prevent anyone from entering the house again. Just to be on the safe side."

"I'll do that," I said.

They took my comment as their cue to leave, and it wasn't until I was closing the door behind them that I realized something.

The woman had left when Louise had come to the front door, which meant there was no way she could have slipped past Louise without her noticing.

• • •

After I finished the notes, the evening was a quiet one. Bored, I found myself researching the history of Heatherington. One click led to the next as I went down an online rabbit hole and learned quite a bit, although I suspected that I'd soon forget most of it.

When I began to yawn, I dead-bolted the front door, made sure the windows were latched, and confirmed that the hallway bathroom door was shut. I locked my bedroom door as well, wondering about the illegal campers while secretly hoping I'd catch sight of the mysterious woman somewhere in town over the next few days. I decided I might ask her to join me for coffee or tea if I did see her.

Paulie had followed me to the room again and curled up on the pillows on the bed. I went through my nightly routine before climbing in next to her. I scratched her cheeks and whispered, "Even if she wasn't supposed to be here, you liked her, too, didn't you? Next time, make sure to get her name, okay?"

After turning out the lights, I fell asleep quickly, only to awaken a few hours later. The time on my phone read half past two in the morning. I listened, hearing nothing that would have interrupted my slumber. It wasn't until I rolled over and closed my eyes again that I heard . . . **something . . .** the sound so faint I could barely make it out. I focused, gradually discerning a rhythm to the noise; it was coming from **inside** the house.

Curious, I pushed back the covers and crawled out of bed. After opening the bedroom door, I heard the sound more clearly, though the hallway was empty.

It took me a moment to realize the bathroom door was open, but just a crack.

My heart began to hammer in my chest. I specifically remembered making sure the door was closed on the way to my bedroom. Then again, I reminded myself, it was an old house. The latch might be worn or stripped, and it was possible the door opened on its own if it was balanced incorrectly.

But the noise . . .

It was growing steadily louder. Gradually, I began to make out what it was: the sound of someone crying in the hallway bathroom.

My first thought was to retreat to my bedroom and call Reece and Louise. Or the police. But all at once, the sobs gave way to a piercing scream, like someone being hurt. Instinct took over, and I rushed toward the door. Yanking it open, I was confronted with absolute darkness . . .

Just like the dream . . .

But as the screams continued, my eyes adjusted to the darkness, and I was able to make out a shadowy figure near the bathtub, dark hair cascading down her back. I startled at the sight and scrabbled at the wall, my fingers seeking the light switch. As soon as I turned on the light, the scream stopped, like a needle being lifted from an old-fashioned vinyl record.

No one was there at all.

In disbelief, I stepped into the bathroom, my eyes

darting from one corner to another, seeing no one. I pulled the shower curtain aside but again . . . empty.

I knew that I hadn't imagined that scream, and remembering what Reece had told me about the old house, I turned on the bathroom faucet. The pipes squealed, and though I tried my best to believe they might have been the origin of the sound, I knew they weren't.

Eventually I made my way back to my room, but I couldn't sleep. Yesterday, I'd heard someone humming in the kitchen, and just now I'd heard screaming in the bathroom, and I lay in bed, afraid my hallucinations were getting worse. They weren't just visual anomalies anymore; now they were auditory as well, and for the first time, I felt a kind of terror that there might be something really wrong with me.

In the morning, bleary-eyed and on edge, I pulled on a pair of sweats, hoping that a long run would make me feel like myself again.

But I wasn't sure that anything could cure whatever it was that was ailing me.

CHAPTER 10

From the window, she watched as Tate stepped off the porch and began to perform a few gentle stretches in the grass. Noticing the distance between the tips of his fingers and the ground as he rcached toward his toes, she thought, hiding a smile, that a little yoga might do him some good. Tugging his New York Road Runners T-shirt over his narrow hips, he took a few quick steps before setting off at a brisk pace. A few lingering tendrils of mist curled around Tate's ankles as he disappeared down the drive, his figure growing smaller before fading away completely.

Turning away, she wandered to the bookshelves again, curious to see if Tate had borrowed anything. Which was fine, of course—that's why the books were there—but she liked to know, so she could keep track of them. That was also the reason for the small whiteboard with the erasable marker in the tray. Guests were supposed to note the title of any book they removed from the parlor.

Sadly, fewer visitors browsed their little library now that a television had been mounted to the wall. Grandma Joyce hadn't wanted a television at all, but too many guests had complained over the years about missing important sports broadcasts. Rather than installing one in every bedroom, however, Grandma Joyce had put one in the parlor to end all the rumbling.

Pulling **Charlotte's Web** from the shelf, she basked in the memory of discovering it as a child. Flipping randomly to a page, she read:

After all, what's a life anyway? We're born, we live a little while, we die.

So true, she thought with a wistful smile. It wasn't Shakespearean in its eloquence, but upon reflection, she decided it was a pretty good summation of things. In the margins, in her own childhood scrawl, she read the words

That's so sad!

Next to that, she'd added a frowny face. She couldn't remember how old she'd been when she first read the book. Six or seven, maybe, but E. B. White's words had clearly made an impression on her. Closing the book, she wondered how different her life would have been had she gone off to college, or perhaps culinary school, since she'd always loved to cook. Even Grandma had wanted her to continue her education, but back then she'd made excuses—that her grandma was getting older; that even with Louise and Reece around to help, there was too much work for them to manage. That she'd go back to school in a few years, once she knew what she really wanted to do with her life.

Looking back, she knew that really, she'd been afraid. Afraid that she wasn't smart enough. Afraid that she wouldn't make friends. Afraid of living in a bigger, busier place, despite her curiosity about exotic cities of the world. Afraid of becoming someone different, someone she didn't yet know and might not want to be.

She put the book back on the shelf, satisfied that all the books were in their proper places, though she straightened a volume of poetry that was slightly off-kilter. Few guests these days were readers; instead, they spent every free minute with their faces buried in their phones, making her ache for what they were missing. Even the most artfully constructed Instagram post couldn't compare with a Wallace Stevens poem or an essay on French cooking by M.F.K. Fisher.

She hoped Tate was a reader, although why it should matter was a good question. Despite reminding herself that it would be a good idea to maintain a professional distance, she admitted that she wouldn't mind talking to him again, possibly even over a glass of wine. She couldn't suppress a devilish grin at the thought of what her grandma would say to that idea. She could almost hear her succinct rejoinder:

You're not dumb so quit acting dumb.

Anyway, it was already clear that Tate had come to Heatherington for work, so he probably wouldn't be around much. It was for the best, and yet . . .

Behind her, she heard Paulie meow, and she glanced back over her shoulder, watching as the cat sauntered over to her food and water. When Paulie sniffed at her empty bowl and shot her a pointed look, she shook her head apologetically.

"I'd open a can for you, but I don't know how much to give you."

Taking a seat on the sofa, she tapped the cushion, beckoning to the cat. Paulie studied her before approaching, and a moment later, she leapt onto the far end of the sofa and curled into a ball.

"You already need to nap, Paulie? You just woke up."

Paulie yawned in response and began licking her paws. She turned to look out the window, wondering if she should make a trip into town. There was the Barefoot Contessa cookbook she'd ordered waiting for her at Bookends, the town's beloved independent bookstore, but picking it up would mean passing right by her shop, where invariably Nash would be, and she felt herself recoil. Had he really believed he could get away with it? That she, a child of her thrifty, meticulous grandma, wouldn't have questioned the $50,000 loan he had taken out using the business as collateral, or the amateurishly faked invoices that had started showing up in their books six months ago? Perhaps he thought that her other problems would distract her from any financial irregularities; she should have known something was amiss when he kept assuring her that he **had her back,** and that she should **focus on taking care of herself.** This from the guy who seemed to prefer volunteering elsewhere whenever he could, leaving most of the actual work in the store to her.

Her absence this past week—and the fact that she wasn't taking his calls—had probably tipped Nash off that she knew what he'd done. Because the money hadn't yet been returned, she suspected it was gone, lost in some Ponzi scheme, or frittered away on whatever vice had gripped him.

She let her head fall back on thc sofa cushion, wearied by these relentless worries and the white-hot rage that sometimes engulfed her. As much as Heatherington was home, these days she often felt that its walls were closing in on her. She told herself that she needed to set aside her fear of leaving—she needed to set aside all her fears, period—and simply take a chance. She thought again about the application form for Le Cordon Bleu culinary academy in Paris, the one she'd bookmarked on her computer. To leave Heatherington for good and study in Paris . . . that would be something, and she wondered what Tate would think.

Surprised by Tate's sudden intrusion into her thoughts, she tried and failed to banish his image. She realized that in his own way, he'd inspired her. If he could find a way to heal and start over despite all he'd lost, then perhaps she could, too.

Scolding herself for thinking about him, she rose from the sofa and made for the kitchen. What she needed was a distraction, she decided, pulling open the door to the cellar and descending the stairs. On the shelves in the far corner, she located the boxes of puzzles, some with hundreds of pieces, others with more than a thousand. Knowing that more pieces meant more distraction, she began sorting through her choices.

CHAPTER 11

The sun burned off the low-lying mist, revealing spectacular skies, but my morning run yielded little clarity about the events of the night before.

Back at the house from my run, I didn't bother to shower before finding my keys and driving into town. At the diner, I ordered toast and coffee, watching through the windows as the downtown slowly came to life and fretting over whether the auditory hallucinations—the humming in the kitchen and the sobbing last night in the bathroom—would start occurring more regularly.

Like the flickers . . .

Tired of worrying, I opened the phone and surfed a few news sites, clicking on whatever story happened to catch my eye while I had my breakfast. Somewhere around my third cup, I began to feel a little better. Maybe it was the caffeine or maybe it had to do with the murmurs of quiet conversation emanating from other tables, but I remembered Louise mentioning that the house made noises in the wind. I had no idea what might sound like humming or crying or a scream, but it was possible that I'd heard **something,** and because I'd just woken up each time, my mind could have turned the sound into something else.

It wasn't a perfect explanation, but it was better than the alternative, and I drove back to the house, feeling more prepared to face the day. As I mounted the porch, I spied Reece in the garden, stabbing at the ground with a hoe, like he was trying to kill a snake. To my mind, if he really wanted to make a difference in the garden, he should have been using hedge trimmers or pruning shears, but I supposed it wasn't my business.

Louise, meanwhile, was just outside the cottage, using an iron rod to beat a rug she'd draped over a clothesline strung between two trees. She must have sensed my presence because she glanced in my direction. I waved, and she returned the gesture.

Inside, Paulie dozed on the sofa. I emptied and washed her food and water bowls before opening a can of food. By the time I put them both on the floor, Paulie was waiting. I watched her start to eat before heading upstairs to my room.

• • •

After showering, I checked my laptop. Oscar and Lorena had sent responses to the material from the day before. We'd have a lot to discuss later, but in the meantime, I needed a quick nap; my lack of sleep the night before was catching up to me.

I woke up an hour later, refreshed and alert, and trotted down the stairs. I set my backpack on the dining room table and went into the kitchen, where I gulped down a tall glass of water. Then, shouldering my backpack, I left the house and engaged the dead bolt. As I approached my car, I heard Reece and Louise bickering near the cottage, both sounding frustrated.

"What do you mean postponed?" she demanded. "What happened?"

"I don't know," Reece answered. "I'm planning to call him later."

"Does he know how important this is?"

"I said I'll call him later, but he's just going to tell me there's nothing he can do!"

Tuning it out, I opened the passenger door and was taking a last glance at the house when I spied a woman with long dark hair move past one of the parlor windows. When she reappeared in front of the second window, recognition dawned on me.

In shock, I bolted back toward the house and bounded up the steps. The key was already in my hand, but when I entered, a quick survey revealed no one in the parlor. The kitchen, too, was empty.

In the dining room, however, a figure crouched beneath the table on all fours, angled away from me. On the table was a partially completed jigsaw puzzle, and even from where I was standing, I could tell it consisted of hundreds or even a thousand pieces, all of them facing up. The box sat on the table next to a sweating glass of ice water, and I suddenly felt dizzy, thinking **This is impossible.** I'd retrieved my backpack only a minute or two ago, and there'd been nothing else on the table.

"Oh hey, Tate. Good morning," she said, looking over her shoulder at me. Her gaze was friendly, even inviting, and I continued to take in the scene, terrified I was hallucinating. But I wasn't. The reality of her presence reverberated in my very bones.

"What are you doing here?" I choked out.

"Well, you can see I'm working on a puzzle," she answered, "but I dropped one of the pieces, and I'm having a devil of a time finding it. It's perfectly camouflaged."

I watched as she ran one hand slowly over the rug, trying to locate the piece by feel; as she had yesterday, she wore yoga pants, though white this time, with a navy New England Patriots sweatshirt.

"I've always loved puzzles," she mused, as though talking to herself. "But games are better for two people, don't you think? Especially the old-fashioned ones. There's something nostalgic about them."

"I guess," I said.

"How was your run this morning?"

"My run?"

She gave a quizzical smile. "That's what you were doing, right? I watched you take off down the drive."

She was here this morning? Before I went to breakfast?

"How did you get in the house?"

Her face clouded while her forehead wrinkled slightly. "That's an odd question."

"I locked the door last night."

"I do live here," she said with an awkward laugh. "But hey, since you're just standing there, do you have a second to help me look? Can you see it from where you're standing?"

Speechless and frantically searching for an explanation, I wondered if there was another entrance to the house, down in the cellar perhaps, something like a storm door. As for the puzzle, the only explanation was that she'd started it on a large piece of cardboard and slid it onto the table before filling a glass of water, adding ice cubes, and crawling under the table . . .

But how had she managed all that in the short time I'd been out of the house?

"Are you going to help me or not?" she asked.

Unnerved, I scanned the rug beneath the table and spotted something gray and irregularly shaped. As if no longer in control of my muscles, I found myself pointing at it.

"It's over here," I said, "next to the chair."

She rose in a single fluid movement, and I watched as she rounded the table, her eyes focused on where I was pointing, before she skipped over to pick it up.

"Thank you. I can't tell you how frustrating that was." Her face lit up with amusement, and I caught the faintest scent of licorice, triggering memories of my last conversation with Sylvia.

"Who are you?" I sputtered.

"Didn't I tell you yesterday?"

"No."

"Sorry about that!" she said with a sunny smile. "My name is Wren. Like the bird." Her expression softened. "How are you feeling today? After you left yesterday, I got to thinking that our conversation might have been a lot for you."

After I left? I was talking to you from the kitchen and YOU left . . .

"Uh . . . I'm okay," I said. "Better, I think."

"Good," she said. "I did my best to channel Ethel Lampier. Have you come across her in town yet?"

I could only shake my head.

"She's an old hippie with short gray hair, and she's frequently dressed in tie-dye. I think it reminds her of when she followed the Grateful Dead back in the 1970s. Anyway, she used to teach fourth grade at the elementary school—she even taught me—but after she retired and her husband died, she set up shop in the park downtown. She's probably there now, in fact. As soon as the weather begins to warm, she sits in a lawn chair with a handwritten sign offering ADVICE OR A FRIENDLY EAR, for ten dollars every fifteen minutes. She's kind of an institution in Heatherington, but like I said, I took one look at you and knew you needed a good listen. I've certainly been there myself," she added.

Impossible, I continued to think, feeling one or two or ten steps behind. **All of this is impossible.**

She nodded in the direction of the parlor. "There's a book on the second shelf from the top on the left called **Poems for Any Occasion,**" she added. "After we talked, I thought of a poem by Keats called **Endymion** that you might want to check out. You don't have to read the whole thing, but the first few lines remind me of your relationship with your sister."

Oblivious to my churning thoughts, she brightened, focusing on something behind me. "Is that Paulie? Are you finally up from your nap, sweet girl?" she called, moving past me and squatting with her hand outstretched. Over my shoulder, I saw Paulie meandering toward her.

"I didn't say anything yesterday because you were clearly upset, but usually, I don't allow pets," she said, letting Paulie sniff her hand. "Even though you should have cleared it with me first, I'm going to let it slide because Paulie obviously likes me."

"I don't think you're supposed to be here," I said, finally finding my voice.

She tilted her head. "Why would you say that?"

A small crease appeared on her forehead, her green eyes widening slightly. Just then I spotted Reece and Louise in the yard outside the window. Desperate to prove I hadn't been imagining things the day before, I raised a finger.

"Can you wait here for a minute? I'll be right back. Don't move, okay?"

I turned and strode to the door. Pulling it open, I called out to them, watching as they turned.

"She came back again, and she's here now!" I shouted. "Come quick!"

They hurried toward me, and when they reached the door, I swiftly led them to the dining room before coming to a sudden halt.

Wren was nowhere to be seen. Nor was the puzzle, the empty box, or the glass of ice water. Louise and Reece flanked me as I frantically eyed the latched windows, the door to the kitchen, and the area beneath the table.

"She was just here," I protested as I took a step forward, the word "impossible" echoing in my mind again. I searched for stray puzzle pieces on the carpet and splashes of water on the floor. "She was putting together a puzzle!"

When I whirled around to face them, Louise and Reece silently exchanged looks of concern.

"I know what I saw," I insisted. "There has to be another way into the house."

"There's no back door," Reece said. "I mentioned that it was unusual even when the house was originally constructed—"

"I meant the cellar," I interrupted, feeling flustered. "Through the storm door in the cellar."

"There is no storm door in the cellar," Reece countered.

"Then you tell me how she got in and out." When neither replied, I went on. "She said her name was Wren. She said it's her house and that she lives here. She told me Ethel Lampier was her teacher in fourth grade . . ."

I watched as Louise blanched and Reece took a step backward in shock.

"What's going on?" I asked. "Do you know her?"

"What did she look like?" Louise asked.

"Dark hair, beautiful green eyes, medium height, kind of pretty."

As I described her, Reece's face flashed with anger. He seemed to grow in size, his body practically vibrating.

"Why are you doing this?" he asked, the words coming out in almost a snarl. "Do you think it's funny?"

I met Reece's eyes, refusing to back down. "I'm not sure what you're talking about."

"Wren?" he demanded. "Dark hair with beautiful green eyes? That's what you said?"

"So?"

"You and I both know that's not possible."

"You're going to have to enlighten me."

He drew a breath, and I could see in his expression how upset he was. "Wren Tobin," he finally said, "died almost two years ago."

CHAPTER 12

At the site, I spotted Oscar and Lorena monitoring the kids in the play area, but I was still disoriented after the events of the morning. I'd barely been conscious of the drive over and, in retrospect, was amazed that I'd made it without incident.

I couldn't stop searching for an explanation, convinced there were only three choices. The first, that it was yet another hallucination, was too terrifying to consider. If I was seeing and hearing things with this kind of vivid detail, did that mean I was schizophrenic and had to check myself back in to the hospital? Still, because there'd been nothing insubstantial or feverish about the encounters, that possibility didn't feel right to me. The second option—that Wren was a ghost—was so preposterous that I couldn't entertain it; it went against everything I knew to be true and reliable about the world. Which left, of course, one final option: that a woman pretending to be Wren Tobin was sneaking into and out of the house.

Yet that raised even more questions, because it meant that Reece and Louise had to be involved. Louise, after all, had been at the front door when Wren disappeared yesterday morning, meaning Wren—or her impostor—couldn't have slipped past without her knowledge. But why then had Louise and Reece accused me of lying when I claimed to have seen her?

It struck me as a textbook case of gaslighting, but to what end? Were they trying to drive me out of the house, or were their motives more nefarious? Did they somehow know about my stint at the hospital and imagine I would be easy prey?

Most baffling of all, **How had the puzzle and glass of water appeared and disappeared?**

With a frustrated sigh, I climbed out of the car, unable to hide my agitation. Oscar must have noticed something amiss because he signaled to Lorena that he wanted to speak to me alone.

"What's going on?" he asked when he was close. "You look like you've seen a ghost."

I almost laughed as I set my backpack on the picnic table. "You wouldn't believe me if I told you."

"Try me," he said, clearly worried.

I glanced toward the edge of the bluff and caught sight of the blue water beyond; in the play area, the kids were swinging and sliding and chasing each other under Lorena's watchful eye. The normalcy of the day felt almost jarring, considering all that had happened.

"Do you remember the woman I mentioned yesterday?" When he nodded, I went on, relating everything that had happened at the house since I arrived. When I finished, I could see the concern in his expression.

"Do you think this might be something you should speak with your psychiatrist about?"

I shook my head. "She wasn't a hallucination," I insisted. "She was too real for that."

"Isn't that what hallucinations are? As opposed to fantasies?"

"Can we just focus on the third option?" I snapped in frustration.

"Despite the magic vanishing puzzle?"

"Humor me."

He didn't seem convinced but nodded anyway. "Fine," he said. "I think the real question, as you've pointed out, is why you're being targeted."

"You said yourself that I was the first guest to stay there in a while," I argued. "Maybe Reece and Louise are more upset than they let on about having to open the house again and they don't want me there."

"Playing the devil's advocate, how would hiring a woman to do yoga in the parlor or put together a puzzle get you to leave?"

"I think it's the fact that she disappears from the

dining room, or screams in the bathroom, that they want me to focus on."

"Then I should call the trustee and let him know what's going on."

"No," I said. "I don't want to get Wren into any trouble."

"You do know that's not her real name, right?"

"Of course."

I could feel him trying to read me.

"Wait a second," he said. "You **like** her, don't you?" he asked.

"No," I said, thinking, **Yeah, kind of,** before pushing the thought away. "I don't know her. And, yes, if the situation continues to spiral, you can speak with the trustee. For now, though, I think it's probably best to let it go."

In the distance I heard Lorena call for him. "Hold on," he said. "Be back in a second."

After he walked off, I heard my phone ding with a news alert, reminding me that I was holding a small computer in my hand. Curious about the real Wren Tobin, I googled her name and "Heatherington, MA." When the images loaded, I stared at the phone in shock. It was her. In one of the photos, she was even wearing the same white yoga pants and navy blue Patriots sweatshirt I'd seen less than an hour ago.

It was her.

No question about it.

• • •

"Obviously," I said, grappling with this new information, "it's just someone who looks an awful lot like her." When Oscar had returned to the table and seen me staring openmouthed at my phone, he'd gently wrested it from my hand and swiped through the various photos.

"You're certain you've never seen her before yesterday?" he asked.

"One hundred percent. And I never heard the name Wren until she told me."

"Maybe you passed her on the street somewhere?"

"I would have recognized her."

He considered that. "It can't be a hallucination then. Your mind couldn't conjure up someone who looks exactly like a real person you haven't yet seen."

"Which is why there must be another entrance to the house somewhere."

"What if there isn't?"

"What do you mean?"

"What if you're dealing with the second option?"

"That I'm seeing a ghost? C'mon. You sound like Sylvia now."

He raised his hands. "All I'm saying is that there's a lot out there that we still don't understand. And, just so you know, I'm not entirely closed to the idea that something happens to us after we die."

When I said nothing, he handed back the phone. "She is cute, though. Not my type, and she's not like the willowy blondes you've tended to favor in the past, but definitely cute."

"Who's cute?" Lorena said, walking up.

"You are, Buttercup," Oscar said.

She made a skeptical face but placed a gentle hand on his shoulder anyway. "Who were you really talking about? Are you seeing someone, Tate, and just happened to forget to mention it to me?"

"No," I answered.

"It's a long story," Oscar interjected smoothly.

"I like long stories," Lorena said, leaning in. "What's her name?"

Feeling caught, I looked at Oscar, who only shrugged. "Wren," I offered. "Like the bird."

"I like that name," Lorena said. "When can I meet her?"

As always, Oscar came to my rescue. "He's not quite sure it's going to work out."

Lorena gave an easy shrug. "Well, if that changes, let's all grab dinner together. And by 'let's all,' I mean just the four of us. I'd hate to scare her off for good with our little monsters. Are you two ready yet? We need to get going before the kids start falling apart."

"We're ready," I said, pulling out my laptop, and within a few minutes, we were deep in planning discussions again. As we went over the details, I found it impossible to stop thinking about Wren—or whoever she was. Her resemblance to the deceased Wren Tobin was startling, and I wondered where Reece and Louise had found her.

Still, the mystery of how she, the puzzle, and the full glass of ice water had vanished so quickly continued to plague me, like a bruise I couldn't stop touching.

• • •

Oscar and I made tentative plans to meet for lunch the following day while Lorena and the kids were at the beach.

After leaving the site, I continued to obsess over the mystery of Wren and devised a plan to put my theories to the test. After swinging by the grocery store to pick up items for dinner, I stopped again at a nearby drugstore, where I purchased a roll of clear tape, a spool of brown thread, and a small pair of scissors.

I pulled up the long drive and peered at the cottage, relieved to see that Louise and Reece seemed to be out; their truck was absent.

Once I was out of the car, I made a careful circuit around the exterior of the house, noting that the main floor was elevated approximately four feet, typical of homes constructed early in the last century. Pausing beneath each window, I searched for ladder imprints or footprints, finding none. Nor did I see any sign of hidden entrances, and as an architect, I knew I would have spotted them. After locating the crawl space, I fetched the flashlight from the pantry and explored the space thoroughly; I found no trapdoors or footprints, only cobwebs. Likewise, the exterior of the cellar was encased in solid concrete, with no door in evidence.

Satisfied by my inspection, I brought my belongings inside before visiting the cellar and the rest of the main floor on the off chance I was wrong. A meticulous search of every wall and cabinet left me even more certain I hadn't missed anything, which meant, of course, Wren—or whoever—had left by a more obvious route. While I was calling for Reece and Louise, she must have scooped the puzzle pieces into the box and tossed everything, along with the glass of water, out the dining room window before exiting through the same window.

It struck me as an elaborate setup and escape, and it didn't explain how the windows had all been latched in the aftermath, but it was possible I'd missed one. Nor did it shed light on who she was, or even whether Reece and Louise were actually involved with her appearance.

And I wondered again whether I was losing my mind, and what that might mean for the rest of my life.

• • •

I was standing at the kitchen window prepping a simple dinner when Reece and Louise returned. There were bags of groceries in the back of their truck, but instead of getting out right away, they were having a heated conversation, judging by Louise's gesticulations.

Finally, the two of them stepped out of the truck. Reece hefted the grocery bags and headed inside;

Louise, however, lingered, and turned to stare at the house.

Strangely, I could have sworn she looked frightened.

• • •

After dinner, I unpacked the items I'd purchased from the drugstore. My low-tech plan was simple: I tore off a strip of tape and applied it to one of the kitchen windows. Then, using the scissors, I cut the tape nearly all the way through, leaving only a shred intact. I tested it, making sure that if the window opened, the tape would be broken, leaving evidence behind. I repeated the process on every window and door on the main floor. Then I propped the dining room chairs beneath the knobs of the cellar, pantry, and front doors.

On my way upstairs, I cut a length of brown thread, securing it with tape on either side of the first step at about knee height, so Paulie wouldn't disturb it. I confirmed that even a gentle touch was enough to make the thread fall. I repeated this at three more locations on the stairs, thinking that once I turned out the lights, the thread would be nearly invisible.

I taped every spare bedroom door on the upper floor, the hallway bathroom door, and the windows in my room, but left my bedroom door open. It took some time to unwind after all of that, but I eventually fell asleep with my phone at the ready.

• • •

Again, I woke in the middle of the night. I listened hard, hearing nothing, but turned on the flashlight on my phone. Starting the video recorder as well, I crept from the bed. At my doorway, I shined the flashlight into the darkened hallway, relieved to see that all the doors were still closed.

Suddenly—straining credulity—I heard the latch click on the bathroom door and aimed the light and camera toward it. I heard the squeaking hinges and the sign tapping against the wood as the door swung fully open; then, I heard the unmistakable sound of water splashing into the sink echoing in the hall as the pipes began to squeal.

Fighting a rising tide of fear, I approached the open door, keeping my phone raised. Strangely, the glow from the flashlight diminished with every step, as though black gauze was slowly being layered over the light; by the time I reached the bathroom, there was barely enough light to see the water gushing out of the faucet into the sink. I began panning the room and jumped at the sight of a figure silhouetted in shadow in the corner.

It was then that I heard what sounded like a rhythmic whisper.

I strained to confirm what I was seeing and hearing. In the dim light, I was finally able to make out the figure of a woman wrapped in a towel with her back toward me, her hunched shoulders heaving as though she was hyperventilating.

"Wren?" I asked. "Is that you?"

The rhythmic whispers coincided with every heave of her shoulders and rush of her breath. Though she didn't seem to hear me, they began to grow louder, and I could finally understand the words.

"Help . . . me . . . help . . . me . . . help . . . me . . . help me . . ."

"Are you okay?" I asked.

She slowly spun around to face me, her long hair obscuring her features; in the next instant, however, the movement too fast to register, she was kneeling in the bathtub, with her back to the faucet.

After slowly bending forward at the waist, she whipped her body backward, the back of her head smashing into the faucet with a sharp, sickening crunch. Like a horrific scene on repeat, it happened over and over, one crunch after another in blinding succession, the sound like a pumpkin exploding on asphalt after being dropped from the roof.

Horrified, I lunged for the switch, turning on the lights, and all at once, she was gone. The sounds ceased, without even an echo remaining. No Wren, no slamming head, no water gushing from the faucet.

With a shaking hand, I aimed the camera at the sink, filming while it drained.

• • •

Freaked-out—I could hear my inner voice screaming, **What the hell!**—I stopped the video and steadied myself enough to take three photos of the sink before staggering back to my room with shaking hands. I tossed on my dirty clothes and turned on every light in the room. Frantically, I checked every window and confirmed that none had been opened. Next, I hurried down the now quiet hallway, terrified by the idea of another appearance, but all was quiet. At the far end, I turned on the lights, and then, one by one, examined the doors that led to the other rooms, finding no broken tape.

Descending the stairs, I clutched the rail as I stepped over the threads, all of which remained undisturbed.

I checked the windows and doors on the main floor next, already knowing that I'd find them all unopened. With a lurching feeling of dread, I sat down at the dining room table. I opened the photos app on my phone, and there, at the bottom, was the video I had taken, along with the three photos. The video was thirty-two seconds long.

Terrified to see what had or hadn't been captured on film, I opened the photos first. Using my fingers to expand each image, I saw drops of water in the sink and felt myself exhale, unaware I'd even been holding my breath. It was the same in the next two photos: the faucet **had** been turned on.

But had I done it myself? With my stomach in knots, I wondered whether I'd sleepwalked or entered some sort of fugue state and didn't remember my own actions; I wondered, too, whether that was better or worse than hallucinations.

Uncertain, I started the video, immediately feeling a keen sense of déjà vu as the scene unfolded.

The recording began in the bedroom, then moved into the hallway, illuminated only by the light on my phone. I turned up the volume, and a few beats later, I heard the latch click and the tapping of the sign as the bathroom door slowly opened. I heard the faucet turn along with squealing pipes. The camera shook slightly as I approached, and again—just as I remembered—the light grew dimmer. Finally, in the bathroom, I saw water rushing into the sink. The camera panned, coming to a stop in front of the bathtub. Over the next few seconds, I heard my own voice questioning someone.

There was, however, no figure wrapped in a towel, nor could I hear the rhythmic, whispered pleas for help.

I felt a surge of disappointment, but when the camera panned to the bathtub, I jumped in my seat at the sound of a sickening crunch immediately followed by more, exactly as I remembered. Then the light turned on and the bathroom was empty. There was a final shaky pan of the camera, the video zooming in on water slowly draining from the sink.

When it ended, I sat back in my seat, my mind racing.

No one had entered the house, and it hadn't been a hallucination.

Yet it couldn't be a ghost because ghosts didn't exist.

Except, of course, maybe they did.

• • •

I stayed up the rest of the night, repeatedly reviewing the video. I downloaded it to my computer and then, just to be sure, emailed the video and the photos to both my business and personal email accounts. I couldn't make sense of why the video had captured the sounds but not what I'd seen, but the whole idea of **making sense** was obviously moot.

I spent a few hours on the internet, reading accounts of other people's encounters with spirits, concluding that most of them were either outright fables, hoaxes, or frauds, or were easily explained by natural phenomena. There were a handful of testimonies by what appeared to be honest, relatively normal people, but they mostly mentioned fleeting images, nothing even close to what I'd experienced.

When dawn broke, flooding the house with pale light, I found myself parsing each encounter with Wren, unable to shake the feeling that she'd come to me for a reason.

Help me . . . help me . . .

Desperate to speak with someone about it, I texted Oscar, asking him to meet me in two hours at the site and promising to pick up food and coffee on the way.

Luckily Oscar was an early riser and responded with a thumbs-up emoji within seconds. I planned to examine the hallway bathroom sink and the door before I met up with Oscar when I suddenly remembered what Wren had said to me the day before. Moving to the parlor, I searched the bookshelves for the book she'd referenced regarding my relationship with my sister and quickly found **Endymion.** The first few lines were highlighted.

A thing of beauty is a joy forever:
Its loveliness increases; it will never
Pass into nothingness

The words made my throat tighten. In the margin an adult's handwriting spelled out the words **You meant the world to me, and I'll never forget our times together.**

I closed my eyes as a wave of bittersweet longing washed over me, amazed that Wren had known just the words to help ease my loss.

CHAPTER 13

Oscar was already seated at the picnic table when I showed up with breakfast burritos and coffee.

"What's going on?" he asked as I slid his meal toward him. "Your text sounded odd."

"Let's eat first," I said.

He squinted at me but eventually contented himself with devouring his food while I picked at mine. We chatted about Lorena and the kids until he stuffed the burrito foil back into the bag.

"You're up," he said.

Bracing myself—I knew I'd sound insane—I recounted the events of the past twenty-four hours. When I was finished, I handed him my phone. I watched him turn the phone sideways to better scrutinize the photos and video, then visibly startle at the sound of Wren's head smashing into the metal faucet. When it was over, he looked at me.

"I didn't see her."

"I know," I said.

"A skeptic would say that someone could have rigged something that remotely opens a door or turns the faucet on and off. Hell, a Hollywood special effects guy could probably do those things in his sleep."

I nodded, already having anticipated Oscar's response. "Before I came here, I took apart the faucet with tools I keep in the car," I said. "I also inspected the doorknob and the latching mechanism. There was nothing out of the ordinary, and I can tell you the latch isn't stripped. And nothing explains those sickening sounds on the video."

"In other words, you're telling me it's a ghost," he said, his words measured.

"Yesterday, you were the one who told me not to discount the possibility."

"I was referring to those weird visual flutters. A creepy woman in the bathroom or a lady doing yoga in the parlor is a little different. Gimme a minute, okay? I need to think."

He rose from the table, carrying his coffee cup as he wandered toward the bluff. After lingering there for a few minutes, he turned and headed back my way. When he sat, he puffed his cheeks in and out.

"This," he said, "is a lot."

"I know."

He sighed before interlacing his fingers. "If you're right about all this, it also explains Reece and Louise. They clearly weren't gaslighting you."

"So you believe me?"

"I'm edging toward it," he said. "But let's tackle this like a real-world problem, not just some logic-defying supernatural mystery, okay? Now that something unexpected has happened, what do you do?" He fixed me with a serious expression. "To me, there's only one sensible course of action: if I were you, I'd head straight back to the house, pack my bag, and leave. That's what most people would do if they were staying in a haunted house."

"I'm not sure I want to do that," I answered, shifting uncomfortably on the bench.

"Yeah," he said with a rueful smile. "I figured that, or we'd be having a different discussion this morning. Because, let me guess, you want to help her, right?"

I remembered my last conversation with my sister. "I think Sylvia would want me to. She said she always wanted to help the ones who were in pain but didn't know how."

"Which begs the obvious question: How do you help a ghost? What are you supposed to do?"

"I'm hoping Wren can tell me."

"Which one? The daytime one or the nighttime one?"

"Maybe both," I said. "I feel like they represent different versions of her."

"How does that work?"

I'd been pondering that most of the night. "If my sister was right, the daytime version of Wren is closer to the person she used to be—her entire soul, so to speak—and the nighttime version is the thing she's becoming . . . like, what's left of her soul when all the goodness and humanity have leached away."

I squinted at Oscar, thinking again how crazy all of this sounded.

"And unless you can help her, the friendly one will eventually fade away completely, and the crazy, scary one will be all that's left?"

"I feel like that's what my sister believed."

"How long do you have? Or I guess I should say, how long does she have?"

"Your guess is as good as mine. Again, I'm hoping she'll be able to tell me."

"That's a lot of guessing and hoping," he said, drumming his fingers on the table. "We should start at the beginning. What do you know about her so far?"

"Just what I've told you," I answered. I went over everything again, including my suspicion that Daytime Wren didn't seem to realize she was a ghost, and didn't seem to be aware of her traumatized nighttime self either. "That's it. I know it's not much."

"Can she go outside or is she stuck in the house? Can you touch her or will your hand pass through her like through a hologram? Can she move objects in the real world?"

"I don't know. And I'm not sure those are the important questions anyway."

"What are you going to do?"

"I think," I said, following my instincts, "the first step is to earn her trust."

• • •

As usual, it was difficult to find a parking spot downtown, and we ended up on the same cross street I'd parked on previously, Oscar pulling in behind me.

"On the way over," Oscar remarked as we strolled in the direction of Pleasant Street, "I was thinking about that Sherlock Holmes quote, the one that says that if you eliminate the impossible, whatever remains, no matter how improbable, must be the truth. Have you heard that?" When I nodded, he went on. "The problem with this situation is that all the possibilities are impossible. It's just that one of them seems less impossible than the others, even if impossible is supposed to be a static term."

"That's a fair way to sum it up."

"I'm still not sure I understand what we're trying to do right now."

"She said games are better for two people," I offered. "If she shows up again, I figure we can play while we get to know each other. And in time, she might trust me enough to reveal how I can help her."

"Why don't you just tell her that she's a ghost and ask her?"

"I don't know what that would do to her," I said, glancing over at him. "It could add even more trauma and the daytime version might vanish completely."

Oscar walked a few steps in silence. "Okay," he

said. "Then why a game? Why don't you do something else she enjoys? Like yoga?"

"Because," I answered with a shrug, "if I tried to do her kind of yoga, I'd be in too much pain to even think."

"Now that," Oscar said, "I definitely believe."

• • •

The store was called Bird's Toys and Games, the name in gold stenciling on the front door, and was located a few doors down from the diner. The front section was piled high with videogames and electronic consoles, everything from Final Fantasy to EA Sports College to the Legend of Zelda, and, of course, Call of Duty. But the back half of the store was jammed with classic toys and games in a way that reminded me of neighborhood toy stores in the New York City of my youth. There was a single set of wide shelves running down the middle, shelving on the walls that reached almost to the ceiling, several tables of varying heights and sizes, and a handful of mismatched chairs. Stacks of stuffed animals, puzzles, cards, magic kits, and games covered every surface and shelf, with little apparent rhyme or reason. More haphazard piles sprouted from the floor, making the store feel like a hoarder's living room, but I liked it. It was the kind of place a kid would find exciting because every visit felt like a hunt for hidden treasure.

As I watched Oscar disappear down one side of

the center aisle, I wished again that my sister was around. She would have loved this place, but more than that, I wanted to ask her if she had any ideas about what I should do, or if she'd ever seen two versions of the same entity. Mainly, I wondered whether she'd ever felt drawn to any of them in the same way that I was drawn to Wren.

Because that was the thing . . .

I couldn't stop thinking about her. The more I'd come to accept the reality that she was a ghost, the more I felt as though not only did Wren need my help, but also I'd somehow beckoned her to help me. Aiding Wren in moving on before it was too late struck me as the most meaningful thing a person could ever do. I had no doubt that Sylvia would have found something romantic in the idea of two wounded souls finding, and somehow saving, each other.

"I don't even know what I'm supposed to be looking for," Oscar called from the back of the store, interrupting my thoughts. "If you're not sure she can move things in the real world, how are you supposed to play a game?"

"Just keep looking," I said. "You'll know it when you see it."

I left him to it, pondering other questions as I wandered down the other side of the aisle. What was Wren's story? Who was she? I wondered about her childhood and the friends she'd had; I wondered if she was a homebody or liked to spend her weekends going to bars and clubs in Boston. I wondered who she'd called when she had a rough day, or even what she liked and disliked. Did she prefer movies or concerts? Tacos or pizza? Deserts or rainforests? There was so much I didn't know, including whether I would ever see her again, an idea I didn't want to contemplate.

"Good morning," I heard a voice say behind me. "Can I help you two find something?"

I glanced over my shoulder and saw a sandy-haired man a few years younger than me, sauntering in my direction.

"Maybe," I said, turning around. "I assume you work here?"

"Actually, I own the place," he said. "I know it probably strikes you as a bit disorganized, but believe it or not, I have a pretty good idea of how to find anything and everything." He gestured expansively at the chaos surrounding us. "I can't tell you how many people post videos about the store after they visit, which is a godsend as far as advertising goes."

There was something slightly glib and overconfident about him, although maybe I was being unfair. He was a fast talker, and being more reserved myself, I tended to be a little suspicious of voluble salespeople.

"I'm not sure what I'm looking for exactly."

By then, Oscar had returned to my side. "Do you have any games with pieces you don't have to move or dice you don't have to roll?" he asked.

"Like card games?" The man's eyes lit up. "We have some deluxe editions, really cool, edgy ones for adults—"

"Not cards," Oscar said.

The man brought a finger to his chin in what felt like an exaggerated show of concentration. "That's tough. Most board games have dice or pieces." He scanned the shelves and piles surrounding us. Then his face brightened. "I know! What about a classic like Charades?"

I considered the idea, and when I glanced at Oscar, he shrugged as if to ask, **Why not?**

"Let's do it," I said.

The owner extracted a box from the bottom of a precarious tower before leading us to the register to ring up the purchase. He put the game in a plain brown paper bag and handed it to me then pulled out a business card. He flipped it over and scribbled something as he said, "This is my cell number if you're ever looking for something specific. And the next time you come in, you'll be entitled to the 'regulars' discount!"

I tucked the card into my wallet as Oscar and I left the store.

"Do you know how crazy this is?" Oscar said. "You just bought a game to play with a ghost."

"I know."

"Lorena still thinks Wren is real."

"I know that, too."

"We probably shouldn't tell her about this."

I walked a few steps without saying anything. "Why are you going along with all this?"

Oscar stopped walking and turned to face me. "Because I remember the way you talked about Wren after you first met her."

"And?"

"You were happy," he said, reaching out to squeeze my shoulder, "and I haven't seen you like that in a long, long time."

• • •

Oscar insisted on following me back to the house, and after we arrived, he gazed at it.

"This place looks a lot more haunted than it did the last time I saw it."

"Can you tell me anything about the litigation? Or the house?"

"It's about money," he said with a shrug. "I guess the trust wasn't completely clear as to who's supposed to receive the property, and now, even the town and the conservation land trust are claiming partial ownership. There are a bunch of litigants and lawyers involved, so I backed off. As for the house, all I know is that it was once a bed-and-breakfast, but the real value is in the land. Whoever gets it will likely tear the house down and either subdivide the property or offer a rare estate-size lot for a new build."

I nodded, leading Oscar into the house and watching as he inspected the parlor before stopping in front of one of the windows. I set the package on the gaming table. Oscar unlatched a window and pulled it open, examining the torn strip of tape left behind.

When I raised an eyebrow, he shrugged. "Just making sure."

In the dining room he checked the windows, too, both of us eventually realizing that they'd been painted shut and couldn't be opened at all. On the stairwell, the threads were no longer attached, and I guessed that Louise had come by while I was out to change the towels and sheets.

Upstairs, after pointing out the hallway bath, I went to my room and discovered that I'd been correct about the sheets and towels. The sight of my dirty laundry reminded me that I should probably find a cleaner where I could drop them off. By the time I rejoined Oscar, he was turning the faucet on and off in the bathroom and listening to the sounds of the pipes.

"It definitely doesn't sound like that smashing noise."

"No, it doesn't."

"It's creepy in here, though."

"It's just a bathroom."

"No," he disagreed. "When it comes to Nighttime Wren, I would guess that this is her prison."

"Why would you say that?"

"It's just a feeling," he said. "But I'd be willing to bet that this was where she died."

CHAPTER 14

Troubled by Oscar's hunch, after he left I searched online for Wren's obituary. No cause of death was listed, but I dug a little deeper and—piecing together details from a few social media pages—I discovered that Oscar had been right.

Wren Tobin, age twenty-nine, had slipped and fallen in the hallway bathroom two years ago, drowning in the tub.

• • •

The knowledge of how she died left me strangely bereft. It made her seem even more tragic somehow, and I thought again about that last conversation with my sister. Had Wren remained in the house because of some undisclosed trauma or some unresolved issue? It struck me that dying young was traumatic no matter the circumstance, but there was still too much I didn't know.

After consuming a hastily concocted lunch in the dining room and needing to do something that would keep my mind from dwelling on the unanswerable, I dug out my sketchbook and pencils from my backpack. I enjoyed putting pencil to paper in the early stages of the design process, and drawing usually had a soothing effect on me, dating back to my prep school days.

Until Oscar and Lorena finalized their decisions, there was no reason to create the entire front elevation, but because they were favoring shingle-style homes, I figured I could sketch parts of what I'd begun to imagine, including the porch, both floors, and part of the roofline. Those types of homes shared certain characteristics. I started with the front door and let my instincts take over after that, allowing ideas to surface in an organic, intuitive way. Still, whenever I paused, my thoughts immediately drifted back to Wren, and eventually, as though I'd somehow summoned her, I heard a voice calling from the parlor.

"Is this a photo of your sister?"

The pencil froze in my hand, and I smiled, thinking, **She came back.** I rose and felt an inexplicable pang of self-consciousness. Quickly, I straightened my shirt and ran a hand through my hair before moving to the parlor, where I found Wren staring at the photo I'd placed on the mantel.

She was wearing a white sundress, sandals, and a faded denim jacket stenciled with the name **Monkey Tears** above a pair of embroidered guitars. I assumed it was the name of a band, though I'd never heard of them.

"Yes, that's Sylvia."

"I thought so. I can see the resemblance. She has a pretty smile."

She turned then, her olive, sun-kissed skin complementing her windblown hair as if she'd just come from a walk on the beach. She wasn't wearing any makeup or nail polish, and her dark lashes naturally accentuated her unusual eyes.

"What?" she asked. "Do I have crumbs on my face or something in my hair?"

The mirth in her tone was enough to break the spell, and I laughed. "Nope. No crumbs, nothing stuck in your hair. I just wasn't sure I'd see you today."

"Why wouldn't you see me?"

"Sometimes I get lost in my work," I improvised.

"Is that what you were doing in the dining room?"

"I was making a drawing for a friend. I'm an architect."

Her eyes were almost hazel in this light. "I don't think I've ever had an architect stay here before."

"That's surprising," I joked. "Architects usually only patronize the finest establishments."

"I'm honored," she said with a smirk. "But I must say, I think you're a little strange."

"Why?"

I watched as she pushed a wisp of hair from her eyes before motioning to the photo. "I'm still trying to figure out why you put a photo of your sister on the mantel. It's a little unusual to put it out here in the common area instead of your room, isn't it?"

"I'm sorry about that. I'd be happy to bring it upstairs."

"You don't have to. I kind of feel like I know her now, and I doubt any of the other guests will care."

Just then, Paulie jumped down from the chair and padded toward Wren.

"Hi, Paulie," Wren said, lowering herself and holding out her hand. Again, Paulie sniffed it, but Wren didn't attempt to touch her. I wondered if part of her, perhaps the part that wanted to keep the truth of her situation hidden even from herself, knew it wouldn't be possible.

"She must have missed you," I said. "When my friend Oscar was here earlier, she didn't stir at all."

"Your friend was here?"

"Just for a little while."

"When?"

"A couple hours ago, maybe? A little less?"

"Huh," she said, wrinkling her forehead. "That's weird. I wonder why I didn't hear him. Or you, for that matter."

I could sense her growing confusion and she seemed to shimmer slightly, before becoming almost translucent. Startled by this new phenomenon, I tried to backtrack. "Now that I think about it, it might have been before that," I said. "I wasn't really watching the time."

Paulie turned away from her hand, and Wren stood, seemingly still uneasy. "I guess that must be it. But still . . ."

When she trailed off, I cleared my throat and changed the subject. "I'm glad to see you, though. I wanted to thank you again for letting me keep Paulie here."

It took a moment before she responded. "I've always loved animals," she finally said, regaining her usual form. "When I was little, I wanted to be a veterinarian. And I probably would have been, except I hated science and math. Oh, and I tend to faint at the sight of blood."

"That would have made it tough."

"My high school guidance counselor told me the same thing," she said with a crooked grin.

"If you're not a vet, what do you do now? Aside from renting rooms to architects, I mean?"

"This and that," she answered. "I could tell you, of course, but I read somewhere that women should cultivate an air of mystery."

"Why?"

"I don't know. And I'm not even sure if it's true. But I am curious about your work. Will you show me your drawing?"

"Of course," I said.

As she edged past me, I caught a distinct floral scent—jasmine, maybe, or gardenia. I was mesmerized by the sway of her figure as she moved ahead of me to the dining room. She was now drinking from a glass of ice water that had appeared in her hand.

I shook my head, thinking, **Wow. Wow, wow, wow.**

Was that how it worked? I wondered. Had she imagined she was thirsty and then unconsciously conjured a glass of water? Or did she think now that she'd had it all along? I didn't know, but it raised further questions about her level of awareness about all sorts of things. Did she believe that she'd come downstairs from her room and was about to leave, for instance, or that she'd just arrived back home after being somewhere else?

I watched as she sipped her water and leaned over the table before glancing up at me. "This is stunning," she said. "You're an artist."

"I've been drawing for a while," I said, trying to silence the commentary in my head and follow her lead for now. "It's been my hobby since I was a teenager."

"I wish I could draw, but I can't remember the last time I even tried. It was probably back when I was in third grade."

"If you'd like to try again, I have plenty of paper and pencils." I gestured at the supplies littering the table.

At my words, her expression began to shift again, as

though the idea was troubling to her. "Maybe later," she said. "But I might like to watch you draw."

Because you know, somehow, that you can't?

"Anytime," I said, instead.

"And is this what you've been doing since your friend left?"

"Pretty much."

"You should try to get outside. It's a beautiful day."

"I was outside earlier," I said. "I went to the site with Oscar. He's building a summer house."

"Where's the site?"

"Off Old Mill Road," I answered. "There's a dirt road leading to a bluff that overlooks the ocean."

"You're kidding," she said, her surprise evident. "I know that spot."

"Seriously?"

"When I was in high school, my friends and I used to go there all the time. We'd listen to music and party and fantasize about our glorious futures once we escaped this little backwater. We were trespassing, of course, but it never stopped us."

I smiled. "Your parents never found out?"

"My grandma did," she said. "My mom died in a car accident when I was little, so my Grandma Joyce raised me."

"And your dad?"

"Great question," she answered with a shrug, "and I never did find out the answer. My grandma didn't talk about him much except to say 'good riddance,' so I'm guessing he wasn't in the picture for long."

"Can I ask what happened to your grandma?"

"She died of Covid three years ago, right after it started."

In my mind, I reconstructed the time line, wondering if it was still 2023 for her, the year of her own death.

"I'm sorry."

"Me, too," she said. "You would have liked her. She had this crusty exterior, but inside, she was as softhearted as they come, and I miss her like crazy. I think that's why I feel like I know a little about what you were going through after you lost your sister."

When I said nothing, she tipped her head toward the parlor.

"Do you want to go sit down? Or am I interrupting your work?"

"We can sit," I answered. "I was thinking about taking the rest of the day off anyway. Just let me get a glass of water first."

"If you're taking the day off, you should pour yourself a glass of wine."

Thinking that a glass of wine might be just what I needed, I found the glasses and opened the wine from the gift basket. When I returned from the kitchen, she was no longer wearing a sundress and a denim jacket. Instead, she was sitting on the sofa in black stretch pants and a red crop top, the other outfit nowhere to be seen. As she'd done the other day, she had one leg tucked up beneath her and was staring out the window. Her fingernails and toenails were painted red, matching her shirt. And in what I supposed might be regarded as a faux biblical miracle, her glass of ice water was now a glass of white wine.

I tried to disguise my amazement as I took a seat in the overstuffed chair opposite her.

"I love to sit here in the afternoons with a glass of wine," she said, not looking at me. "There's usually an hour or so when I have the place to myself, and the light in here is beautiful."

"Definitely beautiful," I said, studying her striking profile. She gave me a sidelong stare then, a coquettish tilt to her head.

"Why does this almost feel like a date?"

"I think it might be the wine."

"But it's not a date, right? Believe me, the last thing I need right now is a date."

"Of course not." I shrugged. "But what's going on? Would you like to talk about it?"

She twirled her glass, seeming to debate whether to say more before raising a hand to massage the back of her neck. "Let's just say that right now my life is complicated to the point that I feel almost paralyzed."

"That sounds overwhelming," I said. I took a sip of wine, watching as she did the same. "But I know so little about you that it's hard for me to know how to help."

"What would you like to know?"

Everything, I thought. But wanting to downplay my interest, I went with something easy.

"What's Heatherington like?"

She leaned back and sighed. "You've seen it. Most of the year, it's a quaint little town off the beaten path, where everyone knows each other's business. But then comes the festival and the warm weather, and the summer tourists start arriving, and for a few months, the whole place feels like it's not really our town anymore. By the same token, businesses here, like this place, depend on those tourist dollars to get everyone through the winter months, so we smile and do our best to make everybody feel welcome."

"Was it a good place to grow up?"

"For the most part, yes. But I think a lot of people tend to have a love-hate relationship with their hometowns."

"Which one is it now?"

"I don't hate it, but . . ." She paused, wiping the condensation off her wineglass. "I've been fantasizing a lot about what it would be like to make a fresh start somewhere else."

I felt a stab of sorrow, knowing it would never happen.

"Where would you go?" I asked.

"Paris or Rome," she said, her voice almost dreamy. "Or maybe Barcelona. Buenos Aires. But what do I know? I've never been anywhere."

"You're not a traveler?"

"No," she said. "Not like your sister, anyway. After you told me about her adventures, I'll admit I was a little jealous."

I smiled. "Have you always lived on the property here?"

"Not always," she said, "but for most of my life I have."

"Why open a bed-and-breakfast?"

"It was my grandma's idea," she answered with a shrug. "I guess my grandpa had a lot of life insurance, and after he died, the proceeds were placed into a trust for my grandma's benefit. Trust proceeds were used to buy the house and land because my grandma wanted space. Then she turned it into a bed-and-breakfast to help with the expenses, so the remainder of the trust wouldn't be depleted. As you can probably imagine, the weather here means the house takes a beating, so there's always something that needs repairs. If you ask me, she would have been better off moving to a condo in Boston and investing the rest, but she wasn't a city person. She loved working with her hands. Our garden was a marvel while she was alive, and for a long time she did most of the repairs herself, until she fell off a ladder and broke her hip. Which is why I suppose it was a good thing Reece and Louise showed up when they did."

"What's their story?"

"My grandma's younger brother, Tommy, was a troubled soul. He was in and out of prison most of his adult life until he died in a failed armed robbery attempt. Reece was his son, and he obviously didn't have much when it came to father figures. But Reece was family. In fact, aside from me, Reece was the only family she had left, and I think my grandma felt sorry for him. I was only six or seven when he showed up in search of a job. Grandma always told me that the sins of the father shouldn't be borne by the son. She was good that way, and it worked out well. Reece and Louise do most of the heavy lifting around here, and I couldn't run this place without them."

"And what about you?"

"What about me?"

"What do you like to do in your spare time? When you're not working or doing yoga or putting together puzzles?"

"I ride my bike. Take walks on the beach. Read poetry. Watch thunderstorms. Find shapes in the clouds. How about you?"

"Nothing that romantic."

"You did tell me that you worked a lot."

"My sister thought so."

She smiled. "I think I would have liked your sister."

"You two would have gotten along well," I said. Then, "Oh, by the way, I read that poem you mentioned."

"**Endymion?** By Keats?" Her face was animated.

I nodded, recalling the lines again. "It was perfect," I said.

"I thought you might think so. As bad as I was in math and science, I like to think I made up for it in English. I considered going to college and majoring in it, but that never quite worked out. I still love reading, though. Especially poems."

"I read what you wrote in the margin. That was you, right? After your grandma passed?"

"It was a hard time," she conceded. "It was a different hard than it is now, but in the end, hard is hard. And now it's my turn to ask you a question."

"Go ahead?"

"What's that?"

She pointed to the package I'd left on the gaming table.

"I bought you something."

"You did?" Her eyes widened, glittering with anticipation. "What is it?"

I got up and retrieved the package, offering it to her.

"Would you like to open it?"

She withdrew slightly, and I mentally kicked myself again for the dissonance I'd created with my request.

"Would you do it for me?" she asked. "I don't want to spill my wine."

I pulled the box from the plain paper bag and

held it in front of her, allowing her to read the lid. I watched as a delighted smile spread across her face.

"Charades?"

"I thought it might be fun."

"I think," she said with a touch of wonder, "that my heart just did a little backflip."

• • •

I opened the box, but when I suggested going over the rules, she merely laughed.

"Not only do I know the rules, but I should probably warn you, I'm really good at this game. I once pulled Ulysses as a card, and my partner was able to figure it out within seconds."

"How on earth did you do that?"

She indicated one word, with three syllables. I watched as she pointed at me; when I said, "Me?" she shook her head and pointed to herself. When I said, "You," she nodded and then cupped her ear to indicate that it "sounds like." At that point, she puckered up and pretended to blow a kiss. When I said "liss," she pointed out the window and rolled her arm in a wave-like motion.

"'Sea' or 'seas,'" I said. "You-Liss-Seas. I get it. But now it's my turn to warn you: I'm going to be terrible at this. As in, I'll probably point at a lamp if my card says 'lamp.'"

She rolled her eyes before taking another sip of

wine, which made me realize that I needed to fortify myself with a refill. Unlike her, I couldn't refill my glass by concentration or magic alone.

When I returned, I set my glass on the table, then pulled out the timer and the cards.

"Would you like to go first?" I asked.

"Sure," she said. She set her glass on the table next to mine and reached for a bowl of potato chips that hadn't been there earlier.

"Does first mean that you're going to act it out or that you're going to guess?"

"I'll act, you guess," she said. "But my fingers are greasy," she said. "Would you mind showing me the card? And no peeking."

I nodded, realizing that she could move things she conjured up but not things in the real world. I reached for the card as she rose from the sofa, and I watched as she licked her fingers before moving to a clear spot in the room.

"Whenever you're ready," she declared, and I showed her the card. She thought for a second, then leaned forward, put one hand in front of the other, moved them both back and forward at the same time, and then raised them repetitively up and over her shoulder.

Flummoxed, I volunteered, "Lifting potato sacks?"

Her mouth fell open in shock before she shook her head.

"Vacuuming!" I called out. "Archaeology!"

Continuing to shake her head, she kept repeating

the motion before standing up and hugging her arms, as if she were shivering. Then she went back to the original motion again.

"Oh," I said, suddenly getting it. "Shoveling snow!"

She shook her head before sitting back down and staring at me in disbelief.

"Really? Lifting potato sacks?"

"You looked like you were straining."

"Archaeology?"

"I thought you were digging."

She burst into peals of laughter, the sound effervescent. "You really **are** bad at this," she said with affection.

"Do you want to stop playing?"

"Not a chance."

• • •

We played for hours, talking, drinking wine, and convulsing in hysterics at my incompetence. While honestly trying my best, I found myself blurting out phrases that had never been uttered by anyone, anywhere. Blue matador. Radar dog. Balloon pasta. Hungry funerals. Still, I'll admit that I also pushed the envelope a little because I loved hearing the sound of her laugh. It was infectious and, I suspected, cathartic for both of us.

When it was my turn to act out the clues, I wasn't much better. Halfway through the game, my card showed Fred Astaire, and I pointed to her fingernails indicating that it rhymed with the color; as the sand continued to drain from the timer, I began pointing at the stairs, which she called steps, until throwing up her hands in frustration. When I revealed the card, she tilted her head, her nose wrinkling in puzzlement.

"Why didn't you just start dancing? I would have gotten it."

"I don't know how to dance."

"How can you not know? You just move your body."

"I'd probably look like an archaeologist lifting potato sacks."

She giggled. "One day, I'll teach you."

"One day," I said, "I might take you up on that."

• • •

Between rounds, I asked questions. She told me more about her grandma and shared a few adventures from her childhood. I learned she preferred pizza to tacos, rainforests to deserts, and that she would rather go to concerts than movies. She also described some of the townspeople, a few of whom seemed to be genuine characters.

After her second glass of wine, she revealed her dream of studying at Le Cordon Bleu in Paris and then traveling the world, working in the kitchens of restaurants she read about in **Gourmet** and the Michelin Guide. "I know it's ridiculous," she said, suddenly self-conscious, "especially for a small-town girl who never even went to college."

My heart ached again. Really, how could I encourage her, knowing that her chance to follow her dreams had ended for good?

For my part, I talked more about my upbringing in New York and my time at Exeter; I also explained what I found so satisfying about my work as an architect, especially the balance between art and engineering. And I told her about my love for Oscar and Lorena, trying to capture their gift for making life seem easy and joyful despite the chaos.

What most surprised me was how easily the conversation flowed, our give-and-take as natural as if we'd known each other for years. Now and then, she would pause as if trying to decide whether to confide even more secrets. But I tried not to press. Instead, I'd change the subject or offer up a ludicrous response to whatever she was acting out, just to hear her laugh again.

There was something undeniably charismatic about her, a quality I knew must have drawn all kinds of people into her orbit. As the afternoon wore on, our shadows lengthening in the waning light, I forgot about my purported mission to help her. Truth be told, I forgot that she was a ghost at all. All I knew was that I didn't want the day to end.

As I poured the last of the wine into my glass, she raised an eyebrow.

"You're lucky you don't have to drive."

"I am lucky," I said. "This has been the best afternoon I've had in as long as I can remember."

"Because you're playing hooky? Or getting killed in Charades?"

"I think it has more to do with the company," I said. "Another round?"

"I admire your ability to overlook your lack of ability in this game, but absolutely."

I smiled and was reaching for another card when the sunlight slanting through the windows suddenly dimmed. The sun had dropped below the horizon, and when I turned back to the sofa, Wren was gone, with no evidence she'd been there at all.

CHAPTER 15

After cleaning up and returning the Charades box to the gaming table, I fed Paulie and refreshed her water bowl. I thought about trying to work, but since I'd finished most of a bottle of wine, I figured some fresh air was an even better idea.

I roamed the property, replaying the afternoon as dusk settled in. I'd been on countless dates, and while this might not technically have been a date for all sorts of reasons, it was close enough, and I couldn't remember another one quite like it. If there'd been any downside at all, I realized, it was that I was no closer to finding out what I could do to help her.

By the time I returned to the house, stars had begun to speckle the sky. I sat with Paulie on the sofa, and the photo of my sister on the mantel caught my eye. I found myself wishing again I could talk to her. Then, remembering, I pulled the phone from my pocket and texted Mike, checking on how he was doing and asking if he would send the second video. Minutes later, my phone dinged.

> I'm doing all right, but sometimes I get flattened by grief out of nowhere. I found a support group which has helped, and my family has been great. Still some days are harder than others. How are you? What are you up to?

I responded, letting him know that I'd been commissioned to design a house on the Cape and promising to keep in better touch. After he forwarded the video, I hit play and again saw my sister, looking the same as she had in the first video. She must have recorded them back-to-back.

> Hi Tate,
>
> I don't know how you felt about my first video and whether you did what I asked, but this one should be easier—no homework this time. I'm going to tell you a story instead, the story of how I knew Mike was The One for me.
>
> On our first date, we'd chatted in Jess and Molly's coffee shop in the East Village; the next time we met, he'd taken me to lunch. I could tell he was a nice guy, but he was also painfully shy. The poor man could barely meet my eyes, and as an unrepentant extrovert, I wasn't sure I could ever be compatible with someone so introverted,

so the jury was still out on him. Later, he would tell me that I intimidated him. Can you believe that? Me? Of course, it had more to do with our family money, not so much me. We laugh about it now, but still.

For our third date, he met me outside my loft, and we took a cab uptown to the school where he worked. It was Saturday so no one else was around, and he brought me to his classroom. Ten or twelve chairs were scattered around the room, as well as a drum set and a bunch of wind and string instruments. In the corner was a battered old piano, nowhere near as fancy as the grand piano in our living room at home. But he'd laid a single rose on one of the chairs, and after asking me to sit down, he went to the piano and rolled up his sleeves. Then he began to serenade me with songs by Billy Joel and Elton John. When he sang and played, I could see he was no longer nervous or shy. His beautiful spirit and confidence shone through, and that's when I knew there was more to him than I'd ever dreamed, something that transcended mere extroversion or introversion.

If you're curious, he still plays and sings for me, and it's one of the joys that fill my cup. Along with ordinary pleasures, like making dinner together or snuggling while bingeing a TV show, or taking the dogs to play in the dog run in Tompkins Square Park. That's what love really is, Tate. It's the simple, tender moments reserved just for the two of you. There's beauty in that kind of everyday commitment. I know you've never been able to envision something like that for yourself, but I also know your heart, just as I further know you will find love one day. There's someone out there who has the key to unlocking all your defenses, and when you find her, it will change your life forever.

If the first video had left me reeling, this one made me smile through my tears. I remembered the story of their third date because she'd recounted it to me before, but this time it resonated even more deeply.

I watched the video a second time, promising myself that I'd call Mike when I got back to the city and meet up with him for a walk and a meal. I'd been too wrapped up in my own grief to realize that his suffering must have been even greater than mine. After all, he had already won life's greatest prize, only to lose it.

• • •

I was still feeling the effects of losing so much sleep during previous nights, but I didn't want to miss Nighttime Wren if she materialized. Despite being a light sleeper, I was worried that my exhaustion might prevent any sounds from awakening me. Perhaps it was overkill, but I decided to carry the bench at the foot of the bed into the hallway, placing it near the stairs. I returned to the room to fetch a pillow and blanket along with my phone. Setting the phone on the floor, I made sure the hallway bathroom door was open before turning out the hallway lights. The bench was too narrow and the padding too thin to be called comfortable, but when I lay down and closed my eyes, sleep overtook me right away.

• • •

It was Paulie who woke me. I was dreaming when I hazily felt her jump onto my chest; a moment later, she nuzzled at my cheek. My eyes fluttered open, the images of the dream I'd been having dispersing like the tail of a comet. I glanced around, the world slowly coming back to me.

I heard a rumble in Paulie's throat, and reaching for my phone, I turned on the flashlight, clarity returning as I gently moved Paulie to the floor and sat up. I could make out the sound of water pouring from a faucet, along with the sound of somcone humming. I rose, hit the video record button, and slowly approached the bathroom door.

As before, the light dimmed with every step. I reminded myself to tread carefully, as this version of Wren was unpredictable. At the doorway, I shone the light into the darkened bathroom, and I saw her towel-wrapped figure near a tub half-filled with water, the faucet still running. Her back was to me, her arms slack at her sides.

"Wren?" I asked.

She didn't seem to hear me.

"Do you need help?"

She shuddered before suddenly turning to face me, her eyes terror-stricken. She thrust her hands up in a defensive position.

"What are you doing in here?" she shouted in panic. "Who are you?"

"It's me . . ."

"Get out!" she screamed, cutting me off, her voice becoming more panicked with every second. "Get out, get out, **get out**!"

Suddenly she arched her back, as if someone had pulled her hair from behind, and shrieked in agony. She stumbled backward, as though trying to keep her balance while being tugged, and I scrambled for the light switch. In my panic, I missed it, and all at once, Wren was only inches from me. Her skin was bloated and greenish gray, her cloudy eyes bulging as blood streamed onto her shoulders. I knew then that this was how she'd looked in death, and I fell back, stumbling across the hallway. I felt and heard the thump as the back of my head smashed into one of the bedroom door handles before I collapsed to the floor.

Starbursts clouded my vision even as I watched the bathroom door slam shut, forcefully enough to make the floorboards vibrate. Despite the pain, I made myself stand and rushed back to the bathroom, sure I would find it locked. But the door swung open easily, and hitting the light switch, I saw that Wren was gone. So, too, was any evidence of water in the tub.

When I gently touched the back of my head, my hand came away bloody.

CHAPTER 16

There was dried blood on the pillowcase when I woke in the morning. Though the wound had clotted, my head ached, and the spot was tender to the touch. I took some ibuprofen and, in the shower, gently washed the blood from my hair. After getting dressed, I moved the bench, blanket, and pillow in the hallway back to where they belonged and added the pillowcase to my pile of dirty clothes. After dropping the laundry bag near the entrance to the kitchen, I started the coffee maker and reminded myself to stop at the laundromat in town on my way to see Oscar and Lorena later this morning.

I made a peanut butter and honey sandwich for breakfast, then filled a plastic baggie with ice from the freezer, holding it to my head while I ate and gulped down coffee.

"I thought I told you that tea is better for you than coffee."

I jumped, spitting out a mouthful of coffee before turning to see Wren leaning against the counter, holding a mug of tea, looking sunny and rested. She was wearing a flowered yellow sundress and a pair of sandals.

"I didn't hear you come in."

"That's because I'm stealthy," she said with a wink. "It used to drive my grandma crazy. I'm sorry for startling you, though."

"It's okay," I said, wiping the coffee up with a paper napkin.

"Is your hangover that bad?" She sounded amused.

"No," I answered, shifting the bag of ice on my head. "I stumbled last night and hit my head."

"Yet another hazard of drinking too much," she teased.

"Just so you know, I dumped the last glass in the sink."

"I'm not judging."

"It kind of sounded like you were judging."

"Maybe a little." She smirked. "Can I see your head?"

"Sure."

She pushed off the counter, and for a moment I was able to see through her, as if she were a faded, threadbare version of herself. But almost before I registered the change, she was back to normal.

I removed the baggie as she approached. She bent over my head and winced. "Ouch! That looks like it hurts. I think you might need stitches."

"It stopped bleeding, so I think I'll be all right." Remembering her limitations, I pulled out the chair next to me, angling it away from the table so she could sit. "Would you like to join me?"

She debated for a moment before edging around me and taking a seat.

"I guess I have a little time," she said.

"Busy day ahead?"

She cupped the mug of tea and hesitated, as if weighing how much to tell me. "There's someone in town I need to talk to, but I'm not sure whether I'm ready to do it today."

I studied her, wondering again if she could leave the house or if she simply imagined she still could. "Friend or foe?" I asked, skirting the issue.

"Friend," she said before letting out a sigh. "Or he was at one time. He's my partner at my business downtown and . . ." She hesitated. "Can we not talk about it right now? It'll just upset me."

"Of course. It's way too early for serious conversation anyway."

She smiled. "What's on tap for you today?"

"I'm bringing Oscar and Lorena to meet with a few general contractors," I said.

"Are you going to show them your drawing?" she asked.

"I'm not sure yet," I said. "I don't know if the house will even look anything like that in the end."

"Then why would you go to the trouble?"

"It helps me come up with ideas," I explained.

"I looked at it again this morning," she said. "While you were bumping around upstairs. You know what I think it needs?"

"What's that?"

"Window boxes," she said, "beneath the windows on the upper floor. To make it feel more like a home, you know, not just this huge, impersonal house."

My mind drifted to the drawing, and I imagined how it might look if I followed her suggestion. "Maybe," I said. "I'll think about it."

She set her mug on the table. "What were you doing upstairs? You were making a racket in the hallway."

I was moving furniture back to my room after a night experiencing a real-life horror movie.

"Cleaning up," I said. "I have to drop my laundry off this morning."

"Is that what's in there?" she asked, gesturing at the bag. When I nodded, she made a quizzical face before going on. "Why don't you use the washing machine in the cellar?"

"I've always sent my laundry out."

Maybe it was the way I said it, but after a beat, her eyes widened with delighted shock. "You don't know how to do laundry, do you?"

"I've never had to do it."

"Of course you haven't," she said, her delight still evident. "It's just that I've never met an adult who didn't know how to do laundry before."

"You don't have to look so pleased about it."

"I'll show you."

"You don't have to," I protested.

"Do it for me. I'd hate to think that you lack basic life skills."

"Will it take long?"

She gave an exasperated sigh. "Go get your clothes," she said.

I picked up the laundry bag and trailed Wren to the cellar door. When I reached the bottom of the steps, I glanced over my shoulder and saw her descending, filing away the knowledge that her movement wasn't limited to the house's main floor. I brought the bag to the counter.

"I'm not going to do it for you," she said. "This way you'll remember."

She had me separate my clothes into lights and darks. Then, pointing to the machine, she walked me through the steps. I adjusted the load size, temperature, and time, and added the pile of darks. She suggested I read the box to determine how much detergent I needed, and I dutifully followed the instructions.

"Now what?"

"Now you close the lid and turn it on. Easy, right?"

"I'll still have to dry and fold."

"Poor you," she teased.

We chatted in the kitchen for another hour while I downed two more cups of coffee. Her mug of tea hovered at half-full, no matter how much she drank. When it was getting close to the time I had to leave, I rinsed the coffeepot and hand-washed my cup and plate. We returned to the cellar, and she showed me how to work the dryer but recommended that I wash the other load when I returned home, so it wouldn't sit in the washer all day.

"It would have been more convenient just to drop it off," I observed.

"But then you wouldn't have started your day off by learning something new, and that's always a good thing."

The cellar's shadows played over her face, making her seem even more mysterious. "I'm afraid of what you're going to say when I tell you that I can't cook," I said.

"If you were that afraid, you wouldn't have mentioned it."

I went to my room to gather my belongings, half expecting her to be gone when I came back downstairs. But I found her in the parlor, staring out the window. She met my eyes before following me to the door.

Outside, the sky was cloudy at the horizon, and I saw no sign of Louise or Reece. I walked to the door and ventured onto the porch, wondering if she'd follow, but she remained just inside the threshold.

Because she can't leave the house?

"Thanks for the laundry lesson this morning," I said.

"Anytime." She surveyed the grounds before bringing her eyes back to me. "Will I see you later?"

"I hope so," I said, surprised by how much I meant it. "I'll be back this afternoon."

"I'll be here," she said.

"I'll pick up another game for us to play."

"I'd like that."

"Any preference?"

"You'll know it when you see it," she assured me. Then, softly: "I'm really glad you're here, Tate."

I felt a lump form in my throat. "I am, too."

• • •

I met Oscar and Lorena at their rented house in Chatham. They left the kids in the care of their nanny while the three of us carpooled in Oscar's SUV to the first meeting, though it meant putting one of the car seats into the rear compartment so I could fit. I had to sweep the seat first and saw piles of Cheerios and crackers hit the carpet, but at least the leather wasn't sticky.

"Welcome to my world," Oscar remarked as he watched me with amusement.

Since Lorena was with us, Oscar didn't ask about Wren, but I could see his burning curiosity whenever he glanced at me. I pretended not to notice, still trying to organize my own thoughts. On the plus side, carpooling allowed us to debrief after each meeting, and Oscar and Lorena said they preferred the second and third general contractors.

Upon our return to Chatham, Lorena joined the kids and the nanny in the front yard, where a game of croquet was under way. Oscar could barely wait to pull me aside.

"Did she show up yesterday?" he asked under his breath. When I nodded, he went on. "Let's meet for lunch tomorrow in Provincetown. We can walk on the beach, and there's this place that's famous for lobster rolls. It's supposed to storm all day Sunday, so let's take advantage of the good weather."

"What if I see her in the morning?"

"So?"

I like spending time with her.

"I'm not sure I should leave," I hedged.

He lifted an eyebrow. "I think you need a little distance. It'll do you some good."

I glanced toward Lorena, who was laughing at something one of the children had said, and was struck by the strange turns my life had recently taken, especially when compared to my friend's. I wondered, too, whether Wren would be upset if I was away all day, and it was that nagging concern—more than anything—that let me know Oscar was right. I was already losing myself to Wren, and for my own emotional health, I had to be careful.

• • •

On my way back home, I picked up a plate of salmon, rice, and vegetables from a local restaurant to reheat later for dinner. Heeding Oscar's subtle warning, I reminded myself again that it was one thing to help Wren but entirely another to fall for her.

And yet . . .

I couldn't deny that I was attracted to her. I wanted to believe that feeling was under control, but as I drew nearer to Heatherington, it grew stronger despite all the rational arguments I recited to myself. Remembering my earlier promise to her, I found a parking space halfway down the block from Bird's Toys and Games. Inside, I scanned the center aisle, thinking a word game might be just the thing given her love of books. I considered approaching the owner for another suggestion, but he was chatting with a customer near the register, so I also scrutinized various piles and shelves without luck. At the rear of the store, I had turned and gazed out the windows toward the street, watching passersby, when I noticed a flash of movement in my peripheral vision. When I closed my eyes and opened them again, the movement gave way to a steady pulsing.

The compulsion to look was almost irresistible, and I heard Wren's words from this morning.

You'll know it when you see it.

Following my instincts, I sidled toward the subtle but persistent blinking without looking directly at it. The flickering amplified, and I concentrated, trying to determine its exact location; I shuffled sideways again, still keeping the staccato bursts in sight. The pattern continued, but when I moved a third time, it vanished.

I turned, scoping out the shelves, taking in games and toys and stuffed animals before noting an object that seemed misplaced. It appeared to be a book bound between walnut covers, but when I pulled it from the shelf, I realized it was something else. There were hinges on the spine, and in raised calligraphy on the cover was the word "Boggle." I opened the hinged box and peeked inside, admiring the classic wooden dice and glass-covered grid exposing the letters.

I faintly remembered playing an inexpensive plastic version of the game once or twice as a kid. I recalled that the goal was to assemble words using the displayed letters after shaking the container. If Wren could conjure a glass of water or magically change her clothes, I suspected she'd be able to find a way to create a pen and pad of paper as well. I wondered, too, whether she had somehow been responsible for the signals. It felt like her handiwork, and I thought again about the rules that governed her existence.

I brought the game to the register just as the other customer was leaving.

"Back again?" the owner asked, smiling. "How'd the Charades work out?"

"It was a good recommendation," I said, sliding the purchase toward him. His face registered surprise.

"I was wondering if this would ever sell," he mused.

"Why?"

"It costs a lot more than the regular game," he said. "It's a collector's edition; not too many of them were made. My former partner special-ordered it because she was passionate about Boggle. We don't carry too many expensive specialty items. I was surprised she didn't take it home for herself."

I felt the hairs rise on the back of my neck. "You had a partner?"

"We were partners until a couple of years ago," he said, scanning the item. The cost rang up on the register, to which he applied a 10 percent discount. "Because you're officially a regular," he declared, flashing his too-white teeth.

"Can I ask what happened to your partner?"

"Uh, yeah," he said. "Unfortunately, she passed away."

A chill ran through my body. "Wren?" I asked.

"Yes," he said, startled. "Did you know her?"

"A little."

"It was such a tragedy," he murmured in a voice a touch too pious for my liking.

"Yes," I agreed. "It was."

• • •

When I returned to the house, I immediately saw that I was alone on the main floor. Storing my dinner in the refrigerator, I left the game on the sofa and brought my belongings upstairs. By the time

I returned to the main floor, Wren was in the parlor, examining the game. She was dressed as she had been earlier, though she had added the jean jacket I'd seen the day before.

"Hey there," I said.

"I have this game in my store downtown," she commented with a trace of wonder. "I always felt it should be displayed like art, not hidden away in a closet somewhere." She turned toward me. "Did you get this at Bird's Toys and Games?"

I nodded. "I found it on the shelf in the back of the store. Would you like to play?"

"Not just yet," she demurred, the outline of her figure blurring a little around the edges, as if someone were smudging her boundaries in chalk. "I feel a little . . . out of sorts right now."

I kept my eyes on her face, willing her shape to stabilize. **Please don't disappear.**

"How about we relax, then? Since the house is quict?" I offcrcd.

To my relief, she solidified again, her limbs and the sweep of her dress regaining their usual weight and form.

"Would you mind?" she asked.

"Not at all."

She took a seat on the sofa while I sank into the armchair opposite her. I watched as she leaned forward, reaching for a half-filled glass of wine. "There's more wine in the refrigerator if you'd like a glass."

"I'm okay," I said, knowing that even if she could drink the wine she imagined was there, I would be unable to. "I had plenty yesterday."

She smiled. "How did your meetings go?"

"They went well," I said. "I think any of the three contractors will do an excellent job, but it'll be up to Oscar and Lorena. And they have good instincts when it comes to hiring the right people. Oscar's a bit of a genius that way."

"Did you tell them about the window boxes?"

"I didn't," I said. "But I will."

"You don't have to," she said with a laugh. "I don't even know why I'm telling you what to do with the house. You're the expert."

"I don't always get everything right." I shrugged.

"I like that you're willing to admit it. A lot of men can't."

I glanced toward the window, noting that there was still a little time until dusk. "So, you own a toy and game store, huh?"

"Once the vet thing didn't work out, I had to do something. Maybe because of my grandma, I felt like starting my own business was something I was supposed to do."

"When did you open?"

"Five years ago," she answered. "In the spring of 2018."

Doing the math, I confirmed that she did indeed think it was still 2023. "Why toys and games?"

"Aside from my love of games, you mean?" she

asked. "Vacationing families like to buy things for their kids, but because Heatherington is too small to support any of the big-box stores, the only place you could buy games or toys was the drugstore, which had an extremely limited selection." She tilted her head. "At the time, it seemed like a good idea."

I studied her. "I'm hearing a 'but' in there somewhere."

"Even though I love games, running a store wasn't my bucket-list dream," she said.

"You mean, like culinary school? Working at a fancy restaurant in Europe?"

She nodded. "Sometimes I wish I could go back to the younger version of me, so I could undo some of the wrong turns I made."

"I think everyone feels that way at times."

"It's different with me," she said, her voice pensive. "I don't know why, but I can't shake this feeling that it's too late for me to ever change anything."

Unable to think of a response that would be both compassionate and honest, I remained silent.

"Was Nash in the store?" she finally asked, coming back to me, an edge to her voice. "When you were there?"

"I didn't get his name, but he said he was the owner. He seemed friendly."

"That's Nash," she confirmed. "He's all about projecting the right image. He volunteers for the historical society, he's an officer in the Heatherington Downtown Association, he's a deacon at his church, and he drives a Prius so that other people know how much he cares about the environment."

"Those are good things."

"They are . . ." she said, hesitating. After a tense moment, she expelled a sigh. "I just found out he's been stealing from me, which is why I haven't gone into the store lately. I don't know what to say to him."

"Why do you have to say anything? Why don't you call the police?"

"I don't think they'd be able to charge him with anything," she said. "We're both authorized to access the line of credit we set up, so technically, he didn't do anything illegal. He faked some invoices, too, but that was minor compared to the 'business loan' he took out, using the store as collateral. I made copies of all the documents and have them in a file. But . . ." She ran an impatient hand through her hair. "It is a lot of money, but it's the betrayal that hurts the most. I've known him since high school, and I loved him like a brother."

"What are you going to do?" I asked.

"I'm going to show him the information I've collected, talk to him, and try to get him to return the money." She crossed her arms, bitterness clouding her face. "To think that he persuaded me to borrow money from my grandma to finance the opening of the store. Grandma Joyce was reluctant—she'd always had her doubts about Nash—but he convinced me. It's one of my biggest regrets."

Her voice was bleak as she went on. "If that doesn't

work, I guess I'll get my attorney to file suit and it'll probably get ugly. I've known his wife, Sheila, ever since I was in kindergarten, and she's still one of the nicest people I know. I'm sure that she's in the dark about all this. Which means she's an innocent victim, too, as are their kids. And when lawyers get involved, their lives are going to become a living hell."

"Sounds painful," I said.

"Yes," she agreed. She put down her wineglass before offering a half smile. "I probably shouldn't have told you any of that. I'd rather no one know anything about it just yet."

"I promise I'll keep it between the two of us," I said. "And I can understand why you didn't want to discuss it this morning."

"I have a question for you, though. Different subject."

"Go ahead."

She leaned toward me, elbows on her knees. "Were you right, or was your sister right, about the reason you've never fallen in love?"

I debated how best to answer. "For my sister, love came naturally. It was easy to find, and easy to keep alive. And who knows, if you're lucky enough to meet the right person like she did, maybe it is, but I think Sylvia felt I wasn't really open to the possibility that someone like that even existed for me." I tried to smile, but it felt more like a grimace. "Maybe my childhood ruined me forever."

Her expression was gentle. "I don't think you're ruined. I think it's more likely that you haven't met the right woman yet."

Unbidden, the thought arose that perhaps I had, and that I was sitting across from her now. "Possibly," I conceded.

"Do you think you'll know when you meet her, the right woman?" Her expression was unreadable, but I thought I detected a provocative note in her question.

"According to my sister, I should be on the lookout for tender moments," I said. Pulling my phone from my pocket, I queued up the video from the night before. I rose and took a seat beside her before hitting play. She watched in silence before giving me a sidelong look.

"No wonder she fell in love with Mike," she commented. "I'm almost in love with him, too. No one's ever treated me to a private concert."

"I admit it was the ultimate romantic gesture. But now it's your turn. Have you ever been in love?"

She screwed up her face as she weighed her response. "No," she answered. "But I was close once, and there was another time when I tried to convince myself that I was."

"Do you want to explain that?"

"I think I was close to being in love with Brian, my boyfriend back in high school. We were together during our sophomore and junior years. He was sensitive and smart and we got along well, but his family moved to Arizona right before our senior year. I knew the move was coming for a long time, so I held back, you know? I wouldn't let myself fall in love because I was afraid of being hurt more than I already would be, and after he left, there was no chance for the two of us. He's married and lives in California now."

"And the time when you tried to convince yourself that you were in love?"

She looked away for a beat before raising her eyes to meet mine. "I'm married," she confessed. "Or more accurately, I'm separated and doing my best to finalize the divorce, even though he's fighting it. I never should have said yes to him in the first place."

I absorbed this news in silence, trying to figure out how she had managed to avoid mentioning it during our prior conversations.

"Why did you?" I finally asked.

She hesitated, then leaned toward me, her hands clasped in her lap. "Do you know the kids' game musical chairs?" she asked. "They play music and when the music stops, you're supposed to sit down, but they take away a chair every time the music starts again? That's kind of how I think about it now. I'd dated a few different men in my early twenties, and the music kept playing, but after my grandma died, it was like the music stopped for good, and Griffin happened to be the one sitting in the chair. I was afraid to be alone, so when he asked, I said yes. We hadn't even been going out that long."

"Do you want to talk about him?"

"Not right now," she said. "Griffin is a subject best avoided at the present time."

"Then how about some Boggle?" I suggested, hoping that the activity would restore her spirits.

When she nodded, I set the game on the coffee table.

"I'm going to get my notepad and a pen from upstairs," I said. "Do you need some paper?"

"No," she said. "I'll scrounge up what I need from the kitchen drawer."

By the time I returned, she was ready. I took a seat in the chair, relieved to see a sly grin playing on her lips.

"I have to warn you, I'm pretty good at this game."

"How did I know you were going to say that?"

• • •

We played while the sun drifted toward the horizon. As the afternoon wore on, she faded out once or twice, her color draining away first, leaving a grayish translucent shape whose edges dissolved. My stomach would twist in anticipation that she might not return, but then she'd snap back into focus, our conversation resuming where we had left off. At one point I touched on my earlier bout with depression, admitting that there were times when I'd considered suicide, and told her more about my stay in the hospital; as her eyes held mine, I marveled again at how comfortable I felt sharing such intimate details.

There were a few uncanny exchanges where she seemed to know what I was thinking even before I did, and I found myself wishing that we had met years earlier. I wanted to believe that our connection would have been as instantaneous and powerful as it felt now, but part of me doubted it. I was a different man back then, after all; barricaded behind my brittle façade, I never would have given her a chance.

Nor did I think she would have been drawn to my former self. Instead, I was gradually coming to believe that it was our shared understanding of loss, and our hard roads back, that had brought us together. There was something melancholy in her expression as she broke eye contact to stare out the window once more. My gaze followed hers, admiring the painted sky of sunset before I realized what I was seeing.

I sighed in disappointment, knowing she'd be gone when I looked back.

• • •

That night, I repeated my routine from the previous night, though I set the bench closer to the hallway bathroom door. I'm not sure what awakened me later, for I heard nothing at all in the bathroom, but I readied the flashlight on my phone and began recording.

Near the door, I steeled myself before entering and reminded myself that this version could be both terrifying and unpredictable. Again, the light grew dimmer, but this time, Wren was on her knees in front of the tub. She was facing me though her head was bent, her hair hiding her face like a curtain. I cautiously edged toward her.

"Wren?" I said, my voice barely above a whisper. "What are you doing?"

After an extended beat, her body shivered, and I watched as she slowly raised her head. I recoiled as I recognized her death mask, the mottled skin and cloudy eyes. Dark blood trickled down her shoulders. I braced myself, but she made no sudden movement toward me. Instead, as she stared, her jaw opened and shifted from side to side, as though she was trying to remember how to speak.

"I wanted to take a bath," she whispered, not to me but rather, **through** me.

"What happened?"

She cocked her head, holding it at an unnatural angle. Behind her, the faucet turned and the pipes squealed as water began filling the tub.

"I couldn't get away," she said, her voice eerily flat.

"How can I help you?"

"I couldn't get away," she repeated, louder this time.

"What do you need me to do?" I pressed.

Instantly, she was no longer kneeling but standing before me, only inches from my face. In shock, I reared back, losing my balance. I hit the floor on my back and watched as she leaned over me and stared with what seemed like curiosity. She tilted her head one way, then the other, tendrils of her long hair snaking toward my face. I heard an unnatural clicking in her throat before her mouth opened, her jaw dropping lower and lower, elongating her face into something from a nightmare, her words finally emerging as a screech.

"I couldn't get away!"

In terror, I squeezed my eyes shut, waiting for the pain to come, but there was nothing. All at once, her scream died away, and water stopped flowing into the tub. Not even an echo of sound remained.

When I opened my eyes, she was gone.

CHAPTER 17

In the morning, I folded the clothes I'd washed the day before and started another load of laundry before eating breakfast at the dining room table. I expected Wren to arrive at any minute, but she didn't. Restless, I sat on the sofa in the parlor with Paulie and reviewed the video from the night before. As in the previous recording, there was no sign of Wren, only the sound of my own voice; but last night, I'd had the sense that she recognized me. I wondered what, if anything, that signified. Meanwhile, I couldn't stop worrying about Daytime Wren, who was fading away more frequently, rapidly being subsumed by the nighttime version.

How much time did she have left?

There was no way to answer the question, so I wandered out onto the porch, noting the overcast sky and stiff breeze. Oscar had mentioned that a storm was headed our way, and a quick check of my weather app confirmed that it would rain this evening.

Still hoping to catch a glimpse of her, I made another circuit of the house, even visiting the cellar, where I moved the laundry from the washer to the dryer. With no sign of Wren and hours to kill until I was supposed to meet Oscar, I returned to the dining room table, idly examining the drawing of the house I had made. Recalling Wren's suggestion, I considered adding window boxes beneath the windows on the upper floor. Smiling, I thought, **Why not?** The worst that could happen was Oscar and Louise wouldn't like it.

After I'd sketched in the first box, I had to admit that Wren had been right. They would make the house feel warmer and more welcoming, so I started drawing a second one.

• • •

By the time I got to Provincetown, the breeze had kicked up to a steady wind. The temperature had begun to drop as well, and gray clouds were gathering in the sky, but Commercial Street was still crowded with pedestrians. Quick peeks in the windows of restaurants I passed indicated that most were doing a brisk business.

Unlike Heatherington, Provincetown was right on the water. It was the most visited location on Cape Cod and generally overrun in the summer, thanks to its historic lighthouses, beautiful beaches, and lively nightlife. While it obviously boasted more activities and places to shop than Heatherington, I understood why Oscar and Lorena had chosen the location that they had. They wanted to live somewhere quiet while remaining close enough to P-town to enjoy what it had to offer.

Oscar had pinned his location, making it easy for me to find him in the parking lot at Herring Cove Beach. Due to the overcast weather, the lot was mostly empty, and I spotted him right away. Like me, he was wearing a light jacket, but he'd added a scarf, beanie, and gloves.

"It's not that cold out here," I said, eyeing him with amusement.

"It's cold enough."

"We could go straight to lunch if you'd rather. I wouldn't want you to catch a chill."

"Ha, ha," he said, making a face. "Anyway, I can't. I promised Lorena that I'd take regular walks while she's back in Newton. She thinks I don't get enough exercise."

"Do you ever exercise?"

"What's the point? People get in shape, which means they have to exercise even harder, which means they get in even better shape, and on and on and on. It's a vicious cycle if you ask me."

"Some doctors actually claim that exercise will help you live longer," I said with a straight face.

"And doctors used to promote cigarettes on television. I've seen the ads on YouTube."

"Still have a comeback for everything, don't you?"

"I've always considered it one of my better qualities," he said with a raffish grin. He pulled his beanie lower. "You ready?"

On the sand, my senses were flooded with the scent of the ocean and the bracing feel of the wind. The water was the color of iron, merging with the slowly darkening clouds at the horizon, lending an austere beauty to the afternoon. In the distance, a couple was strolling near the water's edge, while another visitor walked his dog. A small group of families were flying kites, but for the most part, we had this stretch of sand to ourselves.

"How's it going, my friend? Anything weird to report?"

As we trekked along the waterline, dodging the incoming surf, I caught him up.

"You know how crazy all of this sounds, don't you?" he panted when I was finished.

"I do," I said.

He trudged a few steps in silence.

"But you're pretty sure she's blinking in and out more often when she's with you? Like a brownout?"

"I haven't kept an exact count, but it seems that way."

"I'd wager that the increasing frequency isn't a good sign."

"I know."

He turned to watch the churning waves, clearly thinking. "You said that Daytime Wren thinks it's 2023?"

When I nodded, he walked in a circle, idly kicking at a tangle of seaweed as he ruminated.

"What if Nighttime Wren thinks it's 2023, too?"

"Okay," I said, wondering where he was going with it.

"And what if she's reliving a memory, kind of like Daytime Wren does when she talks about other guests staying at the house?"

"Okay," I said again. "What would that mean?"

"I have absolutely no idea," he admitted, and despite my worries, I couldn't help but laugh.

"Thanks," I said.

"Don't mention it."

• • •

We walked for another hour as the temperature continued to drop. Despite our brisk pace, by the time we returned to the cars, the tips of my ears were pink, and I had buried my hands deep in my jacket pockets to keep them warm. Oscar enjoyed giving me grief for having ridiculed his extra gear.

Because parking was just as difficult in Provincetown as it was in Heatherington, Oscar rode with me to the restaurant. Fortunately for us, a portion of the lunch crowd had cleared out by then, and we were able to get a table without waiting. We promptly ordered Caesar salads, lobster rolls, and a mountain of fries, and planned to split a platter of clams casino and mussels as appetizers.

"Don't tell Lorena what we ordered," Oscar mumbled when the waitress walked off. "Just say I had a salad and soup."

"It'll be our secret."

Later, as we dug into our meal, I kept thoughts about Wren to myself. Instead, we talked a little about Lorena and the kids, but mainly about the house. He said that both he and Lorena were closing in on several definite design features, and using a napkin and a borrowed pen, I sketched out a few basic options I'd been mulling to create the number of bedrooms they wanted—including the addition of a guesthouse on the property—while still allowing for plenty of common space where family and guests could hang out together. Oscar mentioned that they were leaning toward the second contractor, and I nodded, unsurprised by their quick decision.

When we finished, we took a leisurely stroll up one side of Commercial Street and back down the other, shaking our heads at some of the tackier items in the tourist shops. But with the sky growing even more pregnant with heavy clouds, the crowds began to thin, and we finally made our way to my car.

I drove us back to the beach parking lot. As we drew near Oscar's Escalade, I noted a rusty pickup nearby with an elderly golden retriever in the truck bed. An older man sat in a lawn chair on the sandy shoulder abutting the parking area, which puzzled me as the beach wasn't even visible from the lot, obscured as it was by a large dune. The dog raised his nose with every gust of wind, whining as he paced frantically from one end of the truck bed to the other. Bundled up in a peacoat with a wool cap pulled low over his forehead, the old man paid the dog no mind as he drank steaming coffee out of a red thermos cup. Only then did I realize that he'd sunk a fishing pole into the earth, as though he were shore fishing. On the end of the line was a feather, which was tossing in the breeze.

"What do you think he's doing?" Oscar asked me under his breath.

"I couldn't begin to guess."

Before I could stop him, Oscar approached the man, halting at a respectful distance. "Hi there," he started. "I hate to disturb you, but my friend and I were wondering what you were doing with the fishing rod."

The old man scrutinized both of us, taking his time to answer as he unscrewed the thermos and poured more coffee into his cup.

"Just checking the wind so I know when the rain will start," he said and then grunted. His cheeks were ruddy and windburned, as if he'd spent a lifetime near the sea.

"And it works?" Oscar inquired, intrigued.

"Forecast says the rain will be coming at seven

or eight tonight. The feather there, with the way it's moving and twirling, says it'll arrive at four thirty-five." He squinted up at Oscar through rheumy eyes. "Gotta read the feather's message."

Oscar grinned at me, no doubt because the answer was as nutty as he'd expected.

"Is that why you're not near the water? Because it messes with the forecast?"

"No." He looked at us as if we were idiots. "It's because of Bingo."

"Who's Bingo?"

"The dog," he said, hooking a thumb over his shoulder at the truck. "You know who Bingo is."

"Why would I know Bingo?" Oscar asked.

"Because of the story."

"What story?"

"On the TV," the old man said.

"You mean the news?"

"That's it."

"I didn't see the story."

The old man looked up, baring his yellowed teeth. "If you don't know about Bingo, then why are you asking about him?"

It took Oscar a second to process the question, but it was clear he wasn't quite sure how to answer. "I'm sorry," he said. "We didn't mean to disturb you. We'll be on our way. Have a nice afternoon."

He had started to retreat in the direction of the Escalade when the old man's voice stopped him.

"I can tell you about Bingo if you want, because the news got it wrong. They turned it into something sweet and syrupy instead of telling the truth."

Oscar looked at me, and we both shrugged simultaneously.

"I'd love to hear your version," Oscar said.

"Bingo has been coming here every day, even in winter, for the last four years. If I don't bring him here, he finds his way to the beach on his own, and I have to drop everything I'm doing and come get him because otherwise people complain that he's not on a leash. I've been called to account by the police about that and even fined once. In winter, I stay in the cab, of course, but Bingo's always in the back so he can see Henry better."

"Who's Henry?"

"Henry's my neighbor, and Bingo used to be his dog. He used to sit out here in his car at night and drink, finishing off half a bottle of Jack Daniel's by himself." The old man shook his head. "Anyway, one night four years ago, I guess he was stumbling around with the bottle in hand—probably going to take a leak—and he fell. The bottle smashed on the asphalt, and he came down right on it. A shard of glass cut his femoral artery."

Oscar and I stared, unsure how to respond. The old man went on, clearly eager to tell his story. "Old Henry bled out right here in this parking lot, and Bingo was in the car the whole time, watching it happen. When the beach patrol found him the next morning, Bingo had near torn apart the interior. He was barking like crazy and hurling himself against the windows and doors."

"That's terrible," I said, eyeing the dog with sympathy.

"I took in Bingo as Henry didn't have any family. But Bingo keeps coming back here to this very spot." He grimaced. "The news stories were all about how Bingo keeps coming back because he's waiting for Henry to return, like that dog in Japan who waited for his owner at the train station." He turned in his lawn chair to look at the dog, who continued to whine and pace. "But he's agitated, see? Upset. Unsettled. I've had dogs all my life, and I tell you, Bingo isn't waiting for Henry's return." He fixed us with a look of utter conviction.

"He keeps coming back to this spot because he senses Henry's presence in this parking lot," he said. "Because Henry can't let go."

• • •

Oscar and I were quiet as we parted ways, each disturbed by the sight of Bingo pacing in the truck bed, and the old coot's story. I knew we were both thinking of Wren and wondering again what it was that kept her tethered here.

Once again, I wished Sylvia were around to help me understand this strange and improbable world, whose existence I had scoffed at until a few days ago. Perhaps she could have explained whether my interactions with Wren were responsible for the increased speed at which she seemed to be slipping away, or whether it would be happening this quickly regardless.

As I was pulling up the drive, the first drops of rain began to hit the windshield. Glancing at the digital clock on the dash, I somehow wasn't surprised to see that the time was 4:35 P.M.

• • •

I jogged from the car to the porch, entering the house just as it started to rain in earnest. The storm made the parlor dimmer than usual, but a quick glance revealed no sign of Wren there, or in the kitchen or dining room.

It was only when I circled back to the parlor that I noticed the wood stacked on the fireplace grate, more logs on the rack, and a bag of kindling, indicating that Louise and Reece had been inside. On the mantel, I found a lighter and a brief note saying that if I intended to use the fireplace, I should remember to open the damper. It added that if I needed help getting the fire lit, I could call them, and Reece would be able to assist.

Though I'd never started an actual fire—when I was growing up, our fireplaces had always been tended by the housekeeping staff—I assumed I could figure it out. I could almost hear Wren telling me that it was something an adult should know how to do, like laundry.

Feeling a chill, I went up to my room and dug a Patagonia fleece out of a drawer. I was plucking at the fabric to adjust it when I heard a familiar voice from my bedroom doorway.

"If you're going to change your clothes, you really should consider closing the door. Some of the other guests might not be as easygoing as I am," Wren drawled, a provocative lilt to her voice.

She can come upstairs, I immediately thought, unsure why I had been thinking of this floor solely as Nighttime Wren's domain. When I turned to face her, I was struck again by how attractive she was. She was dressed in jeans and a black turtleneck sweater, her eyes outlined in smoky gray, and a dark lipstick accentuating her wide mouth, all of it coming together perfectly.

"You're right," I said. "I wasn't thinking."

"Do you mind if I come in? I want to show you something."

"Please," I said.

She hesitated, the outline of her body growing fuzzy and indistinct for a moment as she stood on the threshold. Then suddenly she relaxed, gaining density as she moved to the window.

"Come here," she said as she crooked a finger.

I approached, standing close but not quite close enough to touch her.

"Do you see the bench out there?" She pointed, squinting slightly. "The one by the bluff?"

"I saw it when Reece showed me the property."

"Do you know why it's there?"

"Because of the view?"

"That's what most people think," she said. "And some guests have sat out there, but that's not why my grandma put it there. She put it there for me. That was my punishment bench. I spent a lot of time there when I was in high school. It was her version of a time-out."

"It seems better than standing in a corner."

"You'd think so, right? But if you ever take a seat on it, you'll notice it's situated in a spot where you can't see the beach or even the waves. All you see is water and sky and nothing else. You know how boring that is? The monotony is unbearable."

"I think my sister had a coffee mug that said we should try to find beauty in everything."

Wren laughed. "Of course she did, but even your sister would have struggled to spend an hour out there. You feel like you're the last person on earth." She leaned toward me, almost as if she were going to nudge me with her shoulder, but stopped short. "It was rough punishment for a teenage girl who hated to be alone."

"It obviously worked," I said. "You seem okay to me."

"Just **okay**?" She glared at me in mock outrage. "Is that what you think of me?"

I opened my mouth to respond, but no words came out.

"Just kidding." She giggled, her image fading again

as she sashayed to the door. I laughed, trying to pretend I hadn't noticed.

"Want to join me downstairs? I don't think any of the guests have returned yet, so we have the parlor to ourselves."

I nodded and followed her down. I was about to ask whether she was going to get a glass of wine when she picked up a mug from the gaming table, the string from a tea bag hanging over the lip. She took a sip before sitting down on the sofa. Paulie immediately crossed the room and hopped up next to her.

The sky beyond the window flashed, followed by the distant sound of thunder.

"Looks like we're in for a real storm," she observed. "Makes me happy, because I love a good thunderstorm, but it's strange. It was supposed to be sunny and hot all weekend."

Perhaps, two years ago, I thought, **it had been.**

"I'm pretty sure the rest of the week is supposed to be warm."

"Just in time for the festival," she said. "My soon-to-be ex, Griffin, will be thrilled," she said. "Did I mention he's in charge of the whole thing?"

"You didn't," I answered. "Can I ask what the deal is with the masks?"

"Most of the bands who will be performing are local bands from the Northeast—and I don't mean big cities like New York or Boston or Philly. For some reason Griffin thought it would be good marketing to lean into their mostly unknown status on the theory that people would focus on the music instead of the lack of so-called brand names. The festival's slogan is 'All About the Music'—as in, **not** about the names. Hence the idea of having them all perform in masks." She snorted. "In reality, the crowds really get into the masks, and the performers just push them up on their heads."

"Why doesn't he bring in any well-known bands?"

She shrugged. "Heatherington isn't big enough to interest bands with even a modicum of fame. The only reason he can line up the bands he does is because it's not yet summer, and the performers treat it as a rehearsal for the festivals and shows they're really gunning for. And then there's Griffin, who's part of the problem."

I watched while she rose from her seat and started toward the kitchen, no doubt wanting to dispose of her tea bag, but she disappeared entirely within a few steps. I suppressed a twinge of nervousness until she reappeared in the parlor.

"Griffin's father owns a car dealership in Provincetown," she continued, oblivious to my anxiety. She took a seat again, going on. "His two older brothers work there, but Griffin always wanted to do his own thing. The dealership is the largest sponsor of the festival, and Griffin still gets a check from his dad every month, like an allowance. He has visions of taking this festival and turning it into an East Coast version of Coachella or managing one or more of the bands that happen to make it big or becoming a music producer. He has plenty of dreams," she said. "Unfortunately, most of them are fueled by alcohol and drugs."

"Was he ever violent?" I asked, frowning.

"He never hurt me," she said, "but in the end, he scared me. When he got drunk or high, he would become angry and unpredictable. Anything could set him off—the way I was dressed, the wrong food in the refrigerator, the way a waiter spoke to him." Her voice dropped so low I had to lean forward to hear her. "There were holes at our house where he'd punched through the drywall. And a lot of mismatched glasses and plates because when he worked himself up into a rage, he liked to throw things."

"It sounds awful," I said.

She shrank into herself, as though rebuking herself for her mistake. "I know you're probably wondering how I could have married someone so messed up, but when we dated, he kept the worst of it hidden from me. He was charismatic and fun, always ready to have a good time, and he had a way of making me laugh whenever I needed a boost. Obviously, living with him was a revelation."

"When did you know that you had to leave him?"

"I suspected he was an addict within three months, so I brought it up to my friend Dax. I've known Dax for years, and he works as a substance abuse counselor here in town, so I asked him whether he thought Griffin could change, or if he thought rehab would help if I could persuade Griffin to go. When Griffin found out that I was sharing details about our marriage with Dax—right around the six-month mark—he went berserk and threatened to kill us both. We were at the farmers market of all places when he found out, and Griffin became totally unhinged. That was when I knew, for my own safety and sanity, that I had to get away. Besides, I couldn't wait any longer because of the property here."

"What do you mean?" I asked, puzzled.

"Do you remember when I said the house and property were held in trust?" When I nodded, she went on. "The trust terminates three years after my grandma passed away, which is in another month or so. I'm the sole beneficiary, and even though we're separated, Griffin is dragging out the divorce proceedings in the hope of claiming joint ownership." Her mouth tightened, and her hands clenched around her mug. "He honestly believes he's entitled to half of it, just like he thinks he's entitled to money from the dealership, even though he doesn't do any work for them. My grandma will roll over in her grave if that happens."

"Can he claim ownership? Even if it's an inheritance?"

"My attorney is confident, but I'm more in the scared-but-hopeful category," she said. "The problem is that I borrowed money using the trust as collateral to purchase furniture for his house, and now Griffin is claiming that the trust was part of the marital pot all along."

"I'm sorry."

"Me, too," she said. She took a long, slow breath as though trying to calm herself. "Anyway, after that incident at the farmers market, I moved back here. I let him keep the furniture and never even went back to pick up my clothes."

"Did you ever get them back?"

"Oh, sure," she said. "Griffin eventually brought them to the edge of the property and dumped them. Unfortunately, they were covered in paint. He said he accidentally spilled a can on them, which is why you see me these days in the same few outfits. Pretty much everything else I owned was ruined."

I was quiet for a long time, thinking about what she'd said concerning Nash and Griffin, unsure how to comfort someone who had been through so much. "It sounds like you've had a really hard year," I said, wishing I could offer more.

"Yeah," she said with a wan smile. "I would have been better off in the psychiatric hospital with you. And I haven't even told you about Dax yet."

"I'm almost afraid to ask."

"And I'm too tired to tell you about it now. Between the three of them, I think that's why I've felt so scattered lately." She held her eyes closed for a moment. "I feel bad about burdening you with all of this."

"I'm glad you did. It makes me feel like I know the real you."

"Warts and all."

"I like your warts."

She smiled, but there was sadness in it. "Don't let Griffin hear you say that," she said. "According to him, I'm the devil."

"I'm not worried about Griffin."

"No," she said. "I didn't think you would be."

The parlor grew dimmer as the storm intensified. Rain began to sheet against the windows. As if on cue, her figure took on a translucent quality, gray shafts of light passing through her as she gazed out the window. I swallowed, trying to ignore my persistent worry.

"Do you want to try Charades again? Or Boggle?" I suggested.

"No," she said. "Maybe tomorrow. I feel like I need to hunker down tonight and figure some things out. Would that be all right?"

"Of course," I said.

"What are your plans for tonight?"

"I'll probably run into town and pick up dinner, something for tomorrow, too."

"You weren't kidding when you said you didn't cook, were you?"

"No."

"What if I show you how to make something tomorrow?" Her expression brightened. "On cold or rainy days, I used to make beef bourguignon over mashed potatoes and eat it with crusty bread. It makes the house smell heavenly. I can give you a list of ingredients to buy."

"Is it hard to make?" I asked doubtfully.

"Not if I'm there telling you what to do."

"Will it take long?"

"It takes a while to cook, so the flavors come together."

I pictured myself standing beside her while we cooked, basking in the sound of her laughter while a storm raged outside. I imagined drinking wine in front of the fireplace, feeling the warmth of the flames slowly fill the room. "I can't think of a more idyllic way to spend an afternoon," I said, and she smiled.

"I'm glad," she answered, holding my gaze. "Because I can't either."

CHAPTER 18

Sleep was all but impossible that night, even though Nighttime Wren didn't appear. I finally dozed off not long before dawn, and I was startled awake midmorning to the sound of thunder, a long, low rumble that reverberated through the house. At sundown yesterday I had watched Wren begin her ascent of the stairs, her shape fading in the deepening shadows until she vanished completely.

Trying to shake off a distinct pang of loss, I'd gone to the butcher shop and the grocery store to procure the ingredients she'd had me write down. As I'd walked the aisles and loaded the cart, I wondered where she went when she vanished, and if, in that netherworld, she daydreamed about me in the same way I did about her. I wondered if that place resembled a dream or a memory of a favorite place, or if she simply faded into a dark, empty void, from which her alter ego, Nighttime Wren, eventually emerged.

I reflected on the crises she'd been grappling with in the last months of her life and wondered if she'd had a confidant, someone unequivocally on her side. She'd mentioned friends that had moved away and people who had disappointed her, but she hadn't talked about finding solace or understanding from anyone. Though she might have simply omitted it, for some reason I got the feeling there'd been no one she could really turn to. I'd had the benefit of a psychiatrist and numerous social workers, as well as patients who were working through their own crises alongside me, but how had Wren managed? Had she cried in solitude, or tossed and turned all night, or taken long walks, wishing for someone to talk to? I was pained by all she'd endured and wondered whether her loneliness had somehow complicated her passing.

She was wonderful in so many ways. I adored her wide, unguarded smile and the way she ribbed me while also poking fun at herself; I loved the way her eyes glittered with competitive energy when we played games. I was falling for her, which made no sense, since she was no longer of this world. I knew there was no hope for a future between us, but in the short time I'd come to know her, it felt as though she'd already become part of me, and it was already hard to imagine my life without her.

I showered and dressed before gathering my phone

and computer and heading downstairs to start coffee. Because the heavy clouds made the house darker than usual, I switched on the lights in the parlor, as well as the dining room and kitchen. I fed and watered Paulie, and bringing my toast to the dining room table, I opened my laptop and started reviewing emails.

I immediately noticed that Oscar and Lorena had emailed me back. Clicking through the images they'd starred and reading through their directions made me think I had enough to begin the initial schematic designs, or even limited 3D renderings. After that we would progress to the design development phase, where Oscar and Lorena would decide on materials, finishes, and a thousand other practical and aesthetic details, and HVAC, plumbing, and electrical plans would come together. I knew they'd love the renderings, which I would create with specialized digital software that would show with incredible realism what their future home would look like.

But I couldn't bring myself to embark on the work. Instead, my thoughts drifted once more to Wren. The house seemed too quiet and empty without her. It was clear there was nothing but heartbreak ahead for me, but the truth was, I didn't care. I wanted to spend as much time together as we could, no matter what the future held.

And just like before, as though I had summoned her, I suddenly heard her in the parlor talking to

Paulie. Her voice was playful and affectionate, and it brought an instant smile to my face.

• • •

I found Wren on the sofa, bending over Paulie. She'd paired baggy faded jeans with a wide-necked green sweater, and when she glanced toward me, her eyes were the vibrant color of new spring leaves.

"Hey there," she said. "I'm sorry I slept so late. I think I was exhausted."

"It's all good."

"How did you sleep?"

"So-so," I admitted. "But I feel good now that I've had coffee."

"I wonder how you'd sleep if you gave up coffee for good."

"I'm not sure that's a life worth living."

She laughed before nodding toward the window. "I can't believe the storm didn't wake me. It's really coming down out there."

Following her gaze, I saw that the view was entirely opaque, as though the house was immersed in a cloud. In the dense shroud beyond the glass, I saw lightning flash and a few seconds later heard the low rumble of thunder. At the sound, Wren shimmered and blinked out briefly before reappearing.

"I kind of like it," I said, trying not to dwell on her increasing pattern of disappearances. "It gave me an excuse to skip my run this morning."

"Speaking of the storm, where is everyone? Why's it so quiet down here?"

"I don't know." I shrugged, playing along. "No one was here when I came down, but then again, I haven't been up that long. I'm guessing they're out doing whatever they came to Heatherington to do."

"Who would want to go out in weather like this?"

"Tourists," I answered.

"Festival people." She snorted. "They can be relentless for sure. Over the years, we've repeatedly had out-of-towners try to camp illegally on the property."

Wren's image faded out again for a few seconds. When she returned, she didn't seem to notice that any time had elapsed, although the green of her sweater had become a dusty gray. She ran a partially translucent hand through her hair, whose normal luster was now a bit muted.

"I heard," I said, trying to keep my voice even. "Reece mentioned it."

She nodded, surveying the room before noticing the fireplace. A slight frown crossed her face. "I'm surprised that Reece hasn't gotten the fire going yet. He usually does that whenever it rains. It's kind of chilly, don't you think?"

"Would you like me to get it going?" I offered.

She peered up at me with a skeptical air. "Do you even know how to start a fire?"

"There's wood and a lighter. How hard can it be?"

"It might be easier with some old newspapers, don't you think? Crumpled up beneath the grate?"

"Of course," I said, wishing that part had been in the note, too.

My discomfiture must have been obvious because she giggled. "There's a pile in the cellar we keep for just this purpose," she said. "In the back corner."

As I turned in the direction of the kitchen, I noticed Wren vanish and reappear out of the corner of my eye, her figure transmitting unsteadily, like an old TV broadcast. **Don't stare,** I told myself. **Act normal.** But when I returned with a small stack of newspapers, Wren was nowhere to be found.

• • •

I spent the next twenty minutes pacing from the parlor to the kitchen to the dining room, pausing in each of them, willing her to appear and growing ever more worried that she wouldn't. Or even worse, couldn't.

"Where'd you go?" I finally heard her say.

I sighed with relief as I left the dining room and spotted her where I'd last left her. On the coffee table in front of her sat a small plate of fruit.

"Just refilling Paulie's water bowl," I lied. I crossed the room and squatted down in front of the fireplace before beginning to tear pages of the newspaper in half. I crumpled them into balls and slid them beneath the grate, but because I wasn't sure how many to use, I opted for a lot. Just in case. When I glanced at Wren, she stifled a laugh.

"You're doing great," she said with an encouraging

wave. "And though I'm sure you don't need me to tell you, since you're obviously a pro at this, you might want to add some kindling beneath the logs."

"You're forgetting to remind me to open the damper."

"I was just about to say that."

When the kindling was in place and the damper open, I lit the newspaper, watching as it began to flame, hoping I'd done everything right. The fire grew, snapping as the kindling began to catch; a minute or two later, I was pleased to note that one of the logs had caught as well. I turned toward her, relieved she was still there and feeling undeniably proud of myself, despite how ludicrous it was. A man really should know how to light a fire.

Wren quietly clapped her hands, her eyes sparkling.

"Let me guess," she said. "First time?"

"Yes."

"Because your staff used to do it? Like the laundry?"

"Yes."

Amused, she reached for a grape. "Even though you've described it to me, I still have trouble imagining your childhood."

"I may not have known how to start a fire, but I can immediately spot the difference between demitasse, coffee, grapefruit, and dessert spoons."

"There's a grapefruit spoon?"

"It has a serrated tip, so you can more easily scoop out the segments of grapefruit."

"And I repeat: I find myself having trouble imagining your childhood."

I grinned before nodding toward her plate. "How's the fruit?"

"Fresh and delicious," she said. "Do you want some?"

"I had breakfast with Paulie."

Her gaze lingered affectionately on my cat. "Any chance you'd accidentally forget her when you leave? Because if you do, I promise I'll take good care of her."

"I appreciate that, but she's my little buddy," I said.

"A girl can try," she said. "And now, are you ready to learn how to cook a classic French meal? It takes a while, so we should probably get started soon if you want to eat by midafternoon."

"And if I'd rather have it for dinner?"

"Then we have plenty of time."

"Good. I'm feeling lazy," I said, flopping down next to her on the sofa. "Is it your recipe?"

"I'd love to take credit, but I can't," she said. "I adapted the one made famous by Julia Child, switching the meat to brisket and combining some steps so that I didn't have so many pans to clean. But the basics are all hers."

"How old were you when you made it the first time?"

"High school," she said. "I found the recipe online and I knew I had to try it. Of course, it took a bit of convincing when it came to my grandma. To her, French cooking meant snails and frog legs."

I smiled. "Did you cook a lot for the two of you?"

"I'd make something special once or twice a week. That was as much as I could manage, because as you probably noticed from the list I gave you, the more exotic ingredients can be tricky to obtain in Heatherington. Did you manage to get the beef broth from Let's Meat?"

"And the bacon and brisket," I confirmed. "He was just about to close when I arrived, so I got lucky."

"I'm glad," she said. "Homemade beef broth makes all the difference in this recipe, and he makes it every other day. It's way easier and less time-consuming than doing it yourself, and his broth is incredibly flavorful."

"I'll have to trust you."

At my prompting, she described some of the more ambitious recipes she'd attempted over the years, along with a few hilarious anecdotes about how they'd been received by her grandmother, who generally preferred her food as plain as possible. When Wren mimicked the faces her grandmother made while sampling her masterpieces, I found myself laughing harder than I could remember since I was a child. As the afternoon wore on, the conversation drifted, turning easily from poetry to the peculiarities of certain guests, to my dumber college pranks; we even compared notes on things we'd always wanted to learn but somehow never found the time to (she: playing the piano, using sign language, tap dancing; I: juggling, stone masonry, ancient Greek). Every now and then she would fade out, her figure becoming only half-visible; at other times she would disappear entirely for minutes, leaving me fretting until she returned. But for both our sakes, I tried to pretend that nothing unusual was happening. We merely picked up where we had left off, and by the end, I felt as though we could speak every day for the rest of our lives and never run out of things to say.

I added another log to the fire, and for a moment we both fell silent, watching and listening to the storm. Finally, she leaned toward me, her long lashes hooding her gaze.

"I think it's probably time to head to the kitchen."

"I hope I can pull it off."

"Are you ready for rule number one? When it comes to French cooking?"

"I can't wait to hear it."

"You're not allowed to start cooking until you've poured yourself a glass of wine."

• • •

In the kitchen, I opened a bottle and poured myself a glass of Pinot Noir; when I turned, Wren was holding a glass of white wine.

I raised my glass in a silent toast and took a sip, watching as she did the same. I set my glass aside. "Okay, boss, what do I do first?"

"You're supposed to call me 'Chef,' not 'boss.' But we're going to peel and chop, so you'll need the cutting board and the chef's knife."

She indicated where to find both, and after pulling the vegetables and herbs from the refrigerator, I got to work. There were quite a few items—an onion, a carrot, and garlic, among others—and while an expert probably could have done all of it in a few minutes, it took me closer to forty-five. I almost cut myself several times despite her unending stream of instructions on proper knife skills. Once that was done, the chopped materials neatly organized in separate ramekins and small bowls, she had me set out the other ingredients, as well as measuring cups and spoons.

As Wren instructed, I placed a Dutch oven on the stovetop and turned on the heat. I crisped the bacon, browned the cubes of brisket, and added the other ingredients including red wine; by the time I'd covered the fragrant mixture in the pot and eased it into the preheated oven, I felt like I'd accomplished quite a bit.

"What about the potatoes?" I asked.

"We'll keep those in the refrigerator for now. We'll peel, chop, boil, and mash them later. They're better right off the stove than if you have to reheat them."

"Is that it, then? For now?"

"Not quite," she said. She was leaning casually against the counter with one leg crossed in front of the other. "You need to clean up. Cutting board, knife, spoons, counters—all of it. A cluttered kitchen is the sign of a cluttered mind."

"Is that a real saying?"

"If it's not, it should be."

I put the spices away, washed and dried everything I'd used, and wiped down the countertops.

"Where to?" I asked when I'd finished and dried my hands on a dish towel. "Unless you want to stay in here."

She wrinkled her nose. "There's no place to sit comfortably in the kitchen. I was thinking about the porch, but it's too wet and cold outside."

"The parlor then?"

"It feels like we always talk in the parlor."

"We could try the dining room."

"That's even less inviting."

"I'm running out of suggestions."

"I know." She sighed. "I always wished the main floor was bigger and that we had a music room or a conservatory, someplace comfortable but with a different atmosphere."

"I could probably design something for you."

"I'm sure you could," she said. "But that'll be for the next owners if I decide to sell." She paused before her voice became more determined. "When I sell."

"You're selling?" I couldn't hide my surprise. "You didn't mention that."

"Officially, I hadn't even said those words to myself

until just now." She reached for her glass and stared into it before looking up at me again. For a moment the outline of her body shimmered and wavered but then stabilized again. I exhaled, relieved.

She went on. "I don't think I could stay in Heatherington even if I wanted to. For reasons we've talked about—and some we haven't—it's time for me to go, even if it scares me. I actually met with a real estate agent a couple of weeks ago to get an idea of the market and what she thought the property's value might be."

"And?"

"It's a lot," she said. "And that's a different kind of frightening."

"Why?"

"Because it means I have no more excuses," she admitted. "I'd have enough money to move away or go to culinary school or even camp out on a tropical beach for a year to figure out my next steps."

"I'm not sure I see the problem."

"You wouldn't," she said, studying her hands in her lap. "My world has always been tiny compared to yours. It's one thing to dream about living in Paris, but it's entirely another to do it. Even I know that dreams seldom match reality. All I can really say for sure is that everything will be different when I sell the property, and that's a little terrifying. Here, as hard as it's been lately, I know what to expect. But out there in the big, wide world? Everything will be unfamiliar, and I won't have this place to fall back on if it all goes sour."

Knowing what I did about her future, I felt a knot form in the pit of my stomach. "I'm not sure what to say," I murmured.

"There's not a lot you can say." She lifted her eyes to mine. "Unlike you, I'm not a brave person."

"I don't know about that. The unfamiliar is scary to me, too."

"I doubt you've been afraid of anything."

"Did I tell you that when Oscar came to my apartment and said he was finally bringing me to the hospital, I tried to escape?" When she shook her head, I went on. "He helped me pack up and got me into the car, but when we stopped for gas, I told him I needed to use the restroom inside. I went straight out the back door instead. I knew I needed help, but I was mortified by what people were going to think about me. I imagined friends and clients pointing and whispering that I had spent time in the nuthouse. That I couldn't handle my own life, or that I was messed up. That even my closest friend knew I had serious problems. I didn't want to be known, not only to others but to myself, as someone who was broken."

"Needing help doesn't mean you're broken."

"It's easy to say that now and I'm not embarrassed anymore. But back then? I'm still not sure how I summoned the courage to go through with it. Of course, Oscar wasn't about to let me get away. I hadn't even made it out of the parking lot before he pulled up next to me and asked where I was going. I told him I was going home."

"What did he say?"

"He asked me to give it a shot for a week, and if I still wanted to leave after that, he'd pick me up and we'd figure out another plan."

"He sounds like the best friend a man could ever have."

"He is."

"I'd like to meet him."

I wondered if she could. "One day," I said.

She pushed herself away from the counter and gave a languorous stretch, the neckline of her sweater slipping off one shoulder. "Why don't we go sit on the love seat by the bookshelves? It's close to the fire."

"Let me get a refill and I'll meet you there."

I poured another glass and followed her, mesmerized by her graceful movements, the long lines of her body. After spending so much time with her, I knew why Griffin had wanted to marry her not long after they started dating. I imagined that he hadn't been the only one who'd wanted her for himself; Wren, I suspected, had broken a lot of hearts.

She curled up on one side of the love seat while I added another log to the fire, adjusting it with the poker. Though I settled on the other side of the sofa, there wasn't much space between us. I could feel the heat radiating into the room, and up close, her eyes caught the movement of the flames, glowing with a mysterious depth.

"You did well in the kitchen."

I flashed my fingers. "I'm just glad they're all still here."

"Do you think you'll cook for yourself when you get back home?"

"I don't know," I said. "Probably not."

She tilted her head, a gleam in her eye. "Maybe when you taste your first creation, you'll change your mind."

"I might. But I'd only know how to make one thing."

"Sometimes, one thing is all you need to hold on to memories you never want to lose."

"Mm," I agreed, our eyes holding as we both took deep drafts of our wine.

Breaking the charged silence, I asked, "If you had a restaurant, what kind of food would you serve?"

"I go back and forth," she said. "I'd love to learn my craft under a legendary chef in the kind of fine dining establishment that critics revere, but ultimately, if I had my own place, I think I'd want to serve classic comfort food, made with only the best ingredients. But one step at a time, right?"

Feeling that now-familiar ache at the sight of her hopeful expression, I changed the subject. "Do you have a favorite restaurant around here?"

"Not really." She shrugged. "I've eaten pretty much everywhere on the Cape, but this area isn't really known for exciting cuisine. There are a few good places in Boston, but I don't get there very often. How about you? You're in New York, so you must have a hard time choosing just one."

"I have a lot of favorites," I agreed.

"I've never been to New York City," she said with a self-conscious laugh. "I've always wanted to go. The pictures make it seem so different than Boston."

"It is different," I said.

"Do you love living there?"

"It's home," I said, "and I can't imagine living anywhere else."

"I guess you'd be bored in a place like Heatherington, huh?"

I detected a trace of sadness in her tone, and I willed her to meet my gaze. "I've yet to be bored in Heatherington," I said, meaning it. "It's opened my mind to new possibilities."

She seemed to like that, and I watched as she ran the tip of her finger over the rim of her glass, making it hum. Then she stopped as though embarrassed. "Sorry," she said. "I do that when I'm nervous."

"Why are you nervous?"

"Thunderstorm. Wine. Roaring fire. The aroma from the kitchen. You and me sitting close. What you just said."

"If it makes you feel better, I promise to be a perfect gentleman."

"I know you will be," she murmured. "And I

appreciate that." She gathered herself before expelling a breath. "It's not you, Tate, but you should know that I'm not ready for a relationship."

"I figured that out the first time we drank wine together, when you made it clear we weren't on a date."

"I did say that, didn't I?" She hesitated, her expression conflicted. "Did I tell you about Dax?"

"You said he's a substance abuse counselor and you sought his advice about Griffin. There was a big blowup at the farmers market."

She twirled her wineglass. "He developed feelings for me," she confessed.

"That doesn't surprise me in the slightest."

"I wasn't digging for a compliment," she said. "But it's been doubly problematic because he's married, and his wife and I have a history. I still can't figure out what I did to make him think I'd be interested. Or maybe, deep down, I do know, but I was too dumb to see it at the time."

"What happened?"

"You can probably guess. Like I told you, I was talking to him about Griffin, and little by little, he began to mention problems with his wife, Tessa. When he finally suggested that we both leave our spouses and 'give our relationship a chance,' I told him he'd gotten the wrong idea. I stopped taking his calls and avoided him. But he kept showing up wherever I was, which I guess was when Tessa found out. Then one night, I found him on the porch looking in the windows. Reece had to run him off."

"Did you call the police?"

She nodded. "They told Dax that if he ever came onto the property again, he'd be arrested for trespassing." She stopped, her form disintegrating a little around the edges as she drew a deep, slow breath. When her natural color and shape coalesced again, she was hugging herself. "Anyway," she continued, "even thinking of going into town these days makes me nervous."

"What about a restraining order?"

"That's easier said than done, and it's complicated by the fact that his dad is a pretty well-known attorney here in town," she said. "Fear and the mere perception of being harassed isn't enough to get one. Judges need documented threats, and Dax only came to the house uninvited once. He's never touched or threatened me. It's just the opposite, in fact. He says he loves and cares for me. Even worse, I think his wife believes we had a physical relationship, and she hates me more than ever."

I let the silence stretch out for a beat. "Why are you telling me all this?"

She hung her head. "Because I want you to know the real, messed-up me."

"You're not messed up," I insisted.

She raised her face to mine, and for a long moment, neither of us said anything. Beyond the windows, the sky flashed again, and there was a loud crack of thunder. Rain blew sideways before dissipating into the mist.

"What are you thinking?" she asked, her voice hoarse.

I held her gaze, unable to look away.

"Wren . . ." I whispered, her name sounding like a promise.

"No, Tate . . . please," she said, stopping me. "Don't say anything. Just look at me and stay completely quiet for one minute, okay? Can you do that for me?"

I wanted to ask why, but when she brought her forefinger to her lips, I acquiesced. Instead of speaking, I sat in silence, watching the steady rise and fall of her chest as she breathed; I saw her adjust a strand of hair that had fallen in her eyes. Eventually she began to smile, raising an eyebrow as though daring me to break the silence first. Then she tapped her wineglass with her finger.

"All right," she said. "Now you can talk."

"What was that?"

"A game my friends and I used to play when we were kids, before any of us had even kissed a boy. When there was a boy one of us liked, we'd have the two of them stare at each other without saying anything. It was supposed to be like a movie moment. But back then, no one could last a minute. Someone would start laughing or they'd look away, and then you'd really know that the two were crushing on each other."

"What does it mean that I didn't look away?"

"It means you're an adult," she said. "And that you're ready for the next game."

"You want to play a game?"

"I do," she said. "It's kind of like this one, but it's the grown-up version." Her tongue darted between her teeth as she leaned toward me. "You have to promise that you won't break the rules."

"All right."

"I'm serious, Tate. I know how special these last few days have been. But I'm fragile right now and I think you are, too, so that makes it dangerous for both of us. Can you promise again not to break the rules?"

"I promise," I said.

She studied me before nodding. "Okay," she said. "We need to be standing, and you'll have to put down your glass."

I set my wine on the table and stood, watching as Wren did the same. She rounded the love seat, stopping in front of the fireplace, where I'd first stumbled on her doing yoga.

"Come here." She crooked her finger and I approached, feeling a little breathless.

"It's called the no-touching game," she said, moving until she was only inches away. "The object of the game is to get as close to each other as you can without touching. The first person who touches the other loses."

Slowly, she lifted her hand and brought it to my face, her fingers nearly touching my hair. She gradually followed the plane of my cheek and my jaw, almost like a caress, pausing her hand before lowering it back to her side.

"Your turn," she breathed.

I could see her pulse fluttering at the base of her throat as I lifted my hand and delicately traced the line of her collarbone, over her shoulder and down her arm, imagining the smoothness of her skin. It wasn't until I lowered my hand that I realized my heart was racing.

She went next, and with her eyes locked on mine, she framed my face with both hands before deliberately lowering them to my chest, where she hovered for a moment, then continued down my sides to my hips. Her fingers were so close they almost brushed the fabric of my shirt, and for an instant, I closed my eyes.

"I could almost feel your heartbeat that time," she murmured, the light from the fireplace dancing in her eyes. The logs sparked again, and I heard the snap; I could hear the ragged sound of my own breathing.

Carefully, I used a single finger to trace the air above each of her eyebrows and make ovals near her eyes. Her nose came next, then her jaw and finally her mouth. Her tongue darted out, moistening her lips.

"I want to draw you," I whispered when I was finished. "I want you to sit for me. Will you do that?"

She nodded. "Only if you raise your hand and spread your fingers."

When I did, she raised her hand to mine, mirroring it, our palms barely a hair's breadth apart. I could almost feel her palm grazing mine, the sensation sending shocks up my arms and continuing to linger as she slowly outlined each finger. In her eyes I saw an acknowledgment of her effect on me, and what I thought was a mirror of my own desire.

"You're beautiful, Wren," I whispered through the tightness in my throat. I moved even closer to her then, until our bodies were nearly touching. Our legs, our chests, our torsos almost joined as one, the distance between us so small that I could no longer tell where I ended, and she began.

She looked up at me, her lips slightly parted, her eyes promising so much more, and I knew I could no longer stop what was coming. Tilting my head, I moved my lips slowly toward hers and I hesitated, expecting her to stop me. But when she didn't, I leaned even closer, already imagining how it might feel . . .

But just as my lips touched hers, a loud crack split the air, and she vanished. In the same instant, the power in the house went out, casting the parlor into shadow. I lowered my head, berating myself for being so foolish but knowing I couldn't have stopped myself.

"I'm sorry," I whispered into the quiet room.

Closing my eyes, I tried to summon her once more. In my mind, I willed it, desperately trying to force an appearance. After a while I relented, and simply yearned for it, entreating the darkness for her return. But in the end, I remained alone, wishing more than anything that I could undo what I'd done.

CHAPTER 19

Disappointed in myself and even more worried about Wren, I fetched the bottle of Pinot Noir from the kitchen before returning to the spot where she had been sitting. I refilled my glass and took a long swallow before leaning back against the cushion, remembering her warning me not to touch her. She'd made me promise that I wouldn't, but I'd given in to my passion instead, and I wondered whether she was disappointed in me, too.

Paulie seemed to know I was upset, and she jumped up onto the loveseat. I scratched her cheeks and ran my hand over her back, feeling it arch beneath my touch. I set my glass back on the table. Uncertain how long the power would be out, I got up and added another log to the fire, replaying those charged final moments with Wren.

Outside, the storm was strengthening. As I brooded, time seemed to slip away, and I barely registered the strobe-like flashes of lightning and crashing peals of thunder. I'm not sure how long I'd been sitting there when I was startled by a sharp knock at the door. Pulling it open, I saw Louise and Reece, both in black slickers; in Reece's hand was a large, dented metal toolbox. Louise was holding a packet of table candles, along with a book of matches.

"We're sorry to disturb you," she began, "but we noticed that your power was out. Ours went out a little while ago."

"I'm not sure why," Reece explained, "but I'm guessing a lightning strike hit a little too close to the house."

No, I thought, **it was because I tried to kiss Wren.**

"Did you try resetting the main breaker?" he asked.

"I didn't," I admitted.

"There's a flashlight in the pantry, but I brought candles just in case you need them," Louise told me. "Why didn't you call or come get us?"

"I didn't think of it," I said. "But please, come in."

I held the door open while they removed their slickers, draping them over the porch railings. Once inside, Reece immediately headed for the kitchen, leaving Louise and me in the foyer. She set the candles on the side table along with the matches before her eyes took in the parlor, shifting from the games to the fire, and finally to the open bottle of wine and glass. Her nostrils flared as she registered the aroma drifting out of the kitchen and she looked at me with surprise.

"Are you cooking beef bourguignon?"

"I am," I answered.

"Wren used to make that."

I said nothing. When she realized a response would not be forthcoming, she moved away, pausing at the gaming table, where I'd left my purchases.

"She loved games, too."

Again, I remained silent, observing as she shifted from one foot to the other.

"Did you really see her?" she blurted out.

I wasn't sure I wanted to go into it with her, but because I'd already admitted that I had, I saw no point in denying it. "I did," I said.

"Doing yoga and putting together a puzzle?"

"Yes."

She nodded, pacing stiffly toward the sofa before turning back. I could see her assessing the half-empty bottle of Pinot Noir, wondering if I was a poor soul drinking alone in the middle of the day, or if I really hadn't been alone. She crossed her arms tight against her chest.

"You saw her today, too, didn't you?"

Though I didn't answer, I didn't have to. She already knew the answer, and a pained expression crossed her features. "I don't understand why this is happening. Neither Reece nor I have seen or heard anything, and we've probably spent more time in the house than anyone."

She walked to the window and watched the storm as she continued, her voice strangely distant. "I'm not sure if you know, but Wren died in the hallway bathroom upstairs. After the police concluded their investigation, there were issues with the trust, and in the end, Mr. Aldrich thought it best to close the bed-and-breakfast." She turned, her expression a mixture of curiosity and fear. "Do you think that's the reason you're seeing her? Because you're the first one to stay here since she died?"

I didn't know, so instead of answering, I asked: "What did the police say happened to Wren?"

"Accidental drowning." Though her delivery was flat, I had the sense she was reliving the painful event. "She'd been drinking that night. I'm not saying she was drunk, but the police concluded that it might have been enough to affect her balance. They said she fell and hit her head on the faucet. Her skull was fractured, and she was probably unconscious when she slipped under the water."

I flashed to the memory of Nighttime Wren repeatedly smashing the back of her head into the faucet, the image now making sense. Louise's voice was unsteady as she continued. "I was the one who found her, and I still have nightmares about it. The whole thing was devastating. I hadn't seen her that weekend, but I didn't think anything of it, and Reece didn't realize anything was wrong either. I didn't find her until Monday, when I came in to clean the rooms. She'd been in the water more than two days by then."

I couldn't help picturing Nighttime Wren and now understood her ghastly appearance.

"That must have been terrible."

"It was devastating." She sighed before turning toward me. "Can I ask what you and Wren talk about?"

"She wants me to help her."

Louise looked startled. "How?"

Before I could answer, our conversation was interrupted by a sparking noise and a sudden blaze of light from the lamps. Static hummed as the house came back to life, and a minute later Reece entered the parlor, toolbox in hand.

"One of the breakers is fried," he announced. "I've rigged it for now, but I don't know how long it'll last. I'll try to find the parts I need, but I might have to order them. The system is old, so they might not be in stock."

"And if the power goes out again?" I asked.

When he didn't answer, I heard Louise clear her throat. "Maybe," she said, "you should consider finding another place to stay."

It was the last thing I wanted to do, and realizing that I wasn't about to leave, she reluctantly lowered her gaze. They left without another word.

• • •

Once they were gone, the house was quiet, but I felt restless. I walked from the parlor to the dining room and then to the kitchen, waiting in each location for Wren to appear, but she never showed. To keep my mind occupied, I worked on the drawing of Oscar and Lorena's house, losing myself in whimsical details and adding textures and colors, pleased with the way it finally turned out.

Because the power had been off, I took a guess and added an extra half hour to the kitchen timer. I also watched a video on how to make mashed potatoes and followed the directions before finding the recipe by Julia Child that Wren had mentioned. I carefully worked through the remainder of the recipe and tossed the French bread in the oven right before the end.

The meal was savory and filling, the best I'd had in a long time. Perhaps a few cooking lessons would be worthwhile, I reflected as I cleaned up and put away the leftovers. When the kitchen was tidy, I meandered over to the bookshelves, pulling down a book of poetry at random. I flipped through the pages, stopping on a page with a highlighted stanza.

When all that we know, or feel, or see,
Shall pass like an unreal mystery.

When I read the title of the poem, I nearly dropped the book. It was "On Death" by Percy Bysshe Shelley.

I wondered if these words described Wren's confusion at everything that had happened—and was still happening—to her. Had she wanted me to find it, even led me to it? As I readied myself for bed, I longed to unravel the mystery of what Wren knew and what she didn't.

I wondered whether she would ever be able to tell me herself.

• • •

I spent the night in the hallway again. It didn't take long for me to fall asleep, but almost by habit, I awakened a few hours later. Holding my phone, I crept to the bathroom but found it empty. Just as I'd returned to my makeshift bed, however, I heard the squeak of a faucet and the groaning of pipes, followed by the sound of water splashing into the bathtub.

I steadied my breathing and got the phone ready; I again reminded myself to expect the unexpected. At the threshold, in the dim light of my phone I saw Wren seated in the bathtub, her head pressed against her knees. Her wet hair curtained her face, but I was able to see the deep wound in the back of her head, the blood gleaming thickly, like oil. Her skin looked like a monstrous, greenish casing.

She'd been in the water more than two days . . .

Only then did I realize she was crying. I crept into the bathroom, straining to make out what she was mumbling.

"I . . . couldn't . . . get . . . away . . ."

"What can I do to help you?" I asked.

The crying continued, but there was otherwise no response. Uncertain whether she was even aware of my presence, I tried another approach.

"My name is Tate."

She suddenly went silent, and I watched as she shuddered before slowly lifting her head.

"Who?" she croaked in a sandpapery whisper.

"I'm Tate," I said again. "And your name is Wren."

She was silent. After what felt like an eternity, she spoke, the sound barely audible. "Wren," she repeated.

"Yes."

"I . . . died," she said.

I swallowed. "Yes."

"In . . . the . . . bathtub."

"Yes. You slipped and hit your head."

She convulsed before going silent again, her body completely still. "No," she finally said.

Her response caught me off guard. "You didn't slip?"

Her breathing sped up as she began to rock back and forth, chanting under her breath as she gripped her knees close to her chest.

"Help me . . . help me . . . help me . . ."

"Wren!" I called out. "If you didn't slip, what happened to you?"

She went still for a long moment before I heard her voice again.

"Murdered."

Oh my God—

I flashed on our previous encounters in the bathroom; Wren's back suddenly arching backward as though being yanked by her hair; the way she'd stumbled as though pulled. The back of her head slamming into the faucet over and over, the action unnatural and terrifying . . . her screams, demanding to know who I was, demanding that I get out . . .

Like she'd been fighting someone . . .

"Who was it?" I asked. "Who did this to you? Was it Griffin? Or Nash?"

She convulsed again. "I don't know."

"Or maybe it was Dax?"

"I DON'T KNOW!" she cried.

She began to rise then; in the next instant, she was wrapped in a towel and standing before me, her face and skin nearly unrecognizable. She tilted her head to the left then the right; her mouth opened, then closed. Then, as though recalling my encounter with Daytime Wren that evening, she raised her hand to my face, her fingers close to my skin as she traced my jaw and my lips.

I tried hard not to flinch; her beautiful face was gruesome.

"Tate."

Her voice was that of her daytime self, the difference jarring and wrong in this version of her. Dizzy, I closed my eyes. When I opened them, Wren was standing farther away and she'd begun to cry again, her shoulders heaving. I watched as she banged her fist against her chest.

"I couldn't get away," she choked out.

"Wren!" I called to her.

She stared at me in terror.

"Who are you?" she demanded.

"I'm . . ."

I couldn't finish. Her arm shot out, her palm extended. Though she didn't touch me, I felt the force like a blow, and I tumbled backward out of the bathroom. As before, I landed on my back just as the bathroom door slammed shut.

Though I was certain she was gone, I scrambled to my feet and threw open the door, looking for her anyway. The room was empty.

CHAPTER 20

I spent the rest of the night downstairs in the parlor, knowing I'd never fall back asleep, and watched the sun rise in a partly cloudy sky. I'd already finished most of a pot of coffee, and my thoughts raced in ceaseless loops, switching direction without warning as I sat on the sofa. Snippets of my last conversations with Sylvia bled into memories of the hours I'd spent with Daytime Wren and flashes of my terrifying encounters with Nighttime Wren.

And I now knew that someone had murdered her.

My emotions whiplashed from grief to absolute fury that whoever had killed her had gotten away with it, and finally to uncertainty about what I could do to make things right. Unable to sit still, I stalked from room to room. I tried summoning her; when that didn't work, I called out for her, my voice echoing in the otherwise empty house, until I accepted that she wasn't going to appear. What I didn't know was whether it was because she didn't want to—had I scared her off with my attempted kiss?—or she couldn't, because she was no longer able to. The idea that I was out of time—that Daytime Wren had vanished for good—flooded me with panic. Though I reminded myself not to catastrophize—something I'd learned about at the hospital—I felt as anxious and lost as I had in the weeks following Sylvia's death.

Oscar's text, asking to meet for a late breakfast at the diner, was a welcome interruption. I hurried upstairs to shower, and on the way out, I slid the drawing of the house I'd finished into a manila envelope and tucked it under my arm.

I spotted Oscar in a booth near the front window. As soon as I sat down, a single glance told him everything he needed to know about my mental state.

"Tate—what's going on?" he asked, leaning across the table to touch my arm.

"I'm not in a good place," I said.

The waitress arrived before he could press for more details. He ordered the lobster Benedict as if on autopilot, and when she turned to me, I waved her off, asking only for water. She nodded and strode away.

Uncertain how to begin, I slid the envelope across the table. Curious, Oscar opened it and pulled out the drawing, studying it carefully before looking up at me.

"You drew this?" His expression was one of wonder.

"It's what I do, remember?" I said with a weak smile.

"Sometimes I forget that you're a genius," he mumbled, whipping out his phone. He snapped a series of photos, then sent them off with a whoosh. "I'm texting Lorena. She'll probably want to get it framed."

Outside the window a group of twentysomethings passed by wearing Halloween-style masks. Oscar set his phone aside and folded his hands in front of him. "Now, are you ready to tell me what happened?"

I nodded but wasn't sure where to begin. I could feel the weight of his scrutiny as the silence stretched out.

"I'm guessing you and Gigi had a fight?" he prompted.

"Gigi?"

"G.G.? Ghost Girlfriend?"

I cracked a smile despite myself. "Cute."

"And you're avoiding my question. Talk to me."

I took a sip of water, but it did nothing to soothe my stomach, and I pushed the glass away.

"Last night, I found out Wren didn't die in an accident," I said. "She was murdered."

Oscar's silence was notable for its measured quality, and it struck me that he was digesting this information with less skepticism than I'd anticipated.

"Catch me up," he said. "And don't leave anything out."

For the most part, I didn't. I walked him through the events of the past two days, telling him everything I knew and what I suspected. I left out only the part where I'd tried to kiss Wren, because I somehow wanted to keep that private. Even to me, my account sounded disjointed and somewhat incoherent, and separating the events as I recalled them from my theories and speculation left me exhausted. Oscar waited to see if I would add anything more. When I didn't, he finally raised an eyebrow.

"That game you played sounds mighty sexy," he commented. "Crackling fire, wine, thunderstorm . . ."

"It was," I admitted, squirming a bit under his probing gaze.

"I might have to try it with Lorena, although for sure I'm gonna lose. I can't keep my hands off her."

"As evidenced by the fact that you have five kids."

"Exactly," he said, smiling. "And **you** cooked a meal?"

"I did."

"Cooking, laundry . . . what's next? Making your own bed? I'm getting the feeling that this woman is helping you finally grow up."

Noting my wan expression, he turned serious once more.

"Let me make sure I have this straight," he said, before repeating all I'd told him. When I nodded, he went on. "You also believe the fact that she was murdered is the trauma that's keeping her from moving on? And you think you can help her by finding out who did it?"

"It makes sense, doesn't it?"

He drummed his fingers on the table. "This is kind

of like that dog Bingo's story we heard the other day, don't you think? Traumatic death? You and Bingo sensing the ghost? And according to the old coot, Bingo keeps coming back because he knows that his owner is in pain and the dog wants to help him but doesn't know how."

I nodded.

"Why now?" Oscar asked with a frown. "It's been almost two years, so why is she showing up now? Why not last year? Or next year? Or five years from now?"

"Maybe it's because I'm the first person to stay there since she died."

"Or maybe it's something about you."

"Because of my sister? Because she gave me her gift?"

"Maybe. Or maybe she sensed something in you that she needed."

All I could do was shrug. I'd asked myself the same questions the night before, without resolution. Oscar idly moved the salt and pepper shakers to the middle of the table, shifting them around like chess pieces as he spoke.

"I guess those questions don't really matter for now, compared to the big one. Even if you do suspect Griffin, Dax, or Nash in her murder since she was having trouble with all of them, how are you supposed to figure out which one it is? You're not a cop, you're not a private investigator, and I doubt the murderer will simply confess if you ask him point-blank."

"Maybe Wren will tell me something useful, something that will help me deduce the truth."

"And if she doesn't?"

"The only thing I can think to do is to confront them. Maybe one of them will admit to something if I scare them into thinking that I'm going to take my suspicions to the police, or that I'll wreck their reputation somehow. Rattle their cages, in other words."

"You want to tell a murderer that you're onto him?"

"They might reveal something or make a mistake."

"Or they could decide to take it personally and do something about it."

I rubbed my gritty eyes before fixing my friend with a determined look. "I have to do this, Oscar."

He seemed to study me, and though a flicker of worry crossed his face, he nodded. "Okay, buddy. Then I'm going to help you."

"You don't have to . . ."

He raised his hands to stop me. "You're my best friend. Besides, it's not every day that I get the chance to solve a supernatural mystery. I also know people in this town, people who might be able to help with the answers we need."

"Like who?"

"Aldrich, for starters, and Ray Dugan the chief of police." He pointed. "I also know that guy."

Across the room, a fit man with neatly trimmed

blond hair and a goatee was pulling out a chair at a table already occupied by a couple in their fifties. He wore a sports jacket and collared shirt, paired with what appeared to be an expensive pair of jeans. His shoes looked pricey, maybe even handmade. He smiled easily and extended a firm handshake to each of them over the table.

"Who's that?" I asked.

"That," Oscar said, "is Griffin."

"How do you know him?"

"I met him last year. He wanted me to become a sponsor of the festival."

"Why didn't you mention that you knew him?"

"Until now, it wasn't important, was it?"

Studying the man, I found it easy to see why Wren might have considered him attractive; he radiated confidence, and a certain slick charm. But I couldn't forget everything else she'd told me about him.

Griffin seemed to realize that Oscar and I were staring at him, and it took him only an instant to recognize Oscar. His face brightened, and after excusing himself from his companions, he rose from his seat. As he approached our table, he extended his hand toward Oscar, who, after a brief hesitation, shook it.

"Oscar my man," Griffin called out. "Great to see you again. How long have you been in town?"

"Just a week or so," Oscar replied with a faint smile.

"How's the family? Will they be here for the summer?"

"They're good. We're renting a place in Chatham near the beach," he said, adopting an easy bonhomie I knew well from his sales days. While the small talk continued, I studied Griffin, a little surprised. I'd pictured someone less personable, more of a slacker with a party-boy vibe, but upon reflection I realized that Wren would never have married someone like that.

Hearing my name, I snapped to attention and focused on the conversation again.

"This is Tate. He's the architect who's designing my house," Oscar said.

"Nice to meet you," Griffin said. "How are you enjoying our fair town? Are you finding any inspiration?"

"He doesn't need it," Oscar answered for me. "Check this out."

Oscar pulled the drawing from the envelope. "Wow," Griffin commented, though judging by his tone, his interest was feigned. He turned to Oscar again. "Are you coming to the festival this weekend? It kicks off Friday night."

"Thinking about it," Oscar hedged. "I'm not sure it's my kind of music."

"That's what you said last year," Griffin responded with a roguish smile. "I'll tell you what—I'll have a few passes held for you and the family. I'm pretty sure you'll be blown away. We have some amazing bands lined up."

Remembering what Wren had said, I suppressed a smile.

"Speaking of houses," Oscar said, changing the

subject, "Tate here is staying in a place I think you know pretty well."

"Oh yeah?" Griffin asked, turning back to me. "Where's that?"

"The former bed-and-breakfast on Fairview," Oscar answered.

Griffin blinked. "Seriously?"

"He's been there for a week."

Griffin bristled, and a charge coursed through the air. "I'll have to talk to my attorney about that."

"Why?" I asked, speaking for the first time.

"Because it's my house," he answered with a frown.

Oscar's gaze flicked to me before returning to Griffin.

"I was told that the place was owned by a trust," Oscar said.

"It is for now," Griffin huffed. "It's complicated, but essentially, I was married to the beneficiary of the trust when she passed away, so it's considered marital property."

"Wren?" Oscar asked.

Griffin couldn't hide his surprise. "How did you know?"

"I heard that the two of you were getting divorced," I interjected coolly.

He turned to me, a flash of anger—and something else?—surfacing before his expression went back to normal.

"I don't know where you heard that, but you're wrong."

Neither Oscar nor I said anything; instead, we waited.

"Not that it's any of your business," Griffin went on, raising his chin, "but we were crazy about each other." He gave an ingratiating smile. "Every marriage has its ups and downs, and we needed a little space to think clearly about what we both wanted, but just a week before she died, she begged me to give it another go. I agreed to call off the divorce proceedings."

We were interrupted by the waitress, who arrived with Oscar's food. Griffin moved aside to make room, and she put Oscar's plate in front of him. Griffin motioned to the meal, looking relieved.

"Let me get back to my friends so you can enjoy your breakfast, Oscar. I'll get you those passes—they'll be at VIP will call." Then to me, "Nice meeting you, Tate. Take care of my house, okay?"

I nodded without responding, but by then, he'd already turned away. On his way to his seat, he paused at another table, exchanging boisterous greetings and backslaps.

"Way to rattle his cage," Oscar said, raising a sardonic eyebrow. "I'm sure you've got him worried now."

"I wasn't ready to talk to him yet," I protested, still watching Griffin. He paused at another table for more glad-handing.

Oscar followed my gaze. "He doesn't really strike me as the out-of-control drug user Wren described to you, does he?"

"No," I admitted. "Honestly, he seems more like a politician."

"Yeah, he's a classic narcissist. I knew it within a minute of meeting him. On the surface, he's very charming, but he doesn't really care about anyone but himself." Swallowing a huge mouthful of eggs and lobster, Oscar pointed his fork at me. "That doesn't, however, mean he's a murderer."

I gave a reluctant nod.

"After I finish breakfast," he said, "we're going for a walk."

"Again?"

"We walked two days ago," he said. "You're supposed to do ten thousand steps every day. And since I'm going to be stuck in front of the computer all afternoon, you can keep me company. It'll do you some good, too."

Though I wasn't in the mood, I agreed, knowing that Oscar was right again.

• • •

The streets of Heatherington had been transformed. Gone were the families and moms pushing strollers; instead, the sidewalks teemed with older teenagers and people in their twenties, many of them wearing masks. Crowds gathered around street musicians on every corner. Most, if not all, of the restaurants, cafés, and bars in town had set up sidewalk stands serving beer, cheap cocktails, and fast food. The noise was cacophonous. Oscar flashed the envelope containing the drawing.

"I want to drop this off in my car, so it doesn't get ruined," he called out over the din. "Too many drunk kids who aren't watching where they're going."

"About your house," I began as we turned onto the side street where Oscar had parked. "I know I've been distracted since I've been here, but I promise I'm going to do a great job for you."

"What are you talking about? You're doing fine." Oscar waved a hand as if to diminish my concerns.

"I still haven't started the schematics or the renderings," I apologized.

"Don't worry about it," Oscar said. "Another few days won't make any difference in the long run. And anyway, Luca's had a fever, so our discussions about the house were minimal over the weekend. I feel like I should be apologizing to you."

"Never," I said.

We reached Oscar's car, where he placed the drawing on the passenger seat. Up the street in Liberty Park, a pair of older men were playing chess; not far from them, an elderly woman in a bright tie-dyed T-shirt sat in a lawn chair with a hand-painted sign next to her. Oscar closed the car door and turned to me as we started walking, his expression serious.

"I need to ask you a question," he said, "but I don't want you to get offended."

"Yeah?"

He drew a breath as though to steel himself. "How well do you really know her?"

"What do you mean?"

"I mean that, even with real people, you need to know them awhile before you can really get a sense of how dependable they are. And Wren isn't exactly a real person . . ."

He trailed off, as though still collecting his thoughts.

"Go on," I finally said, bracing myself for what I knew was coming.

"My point," he said, "is that Griffin's account in the restaurant was entirely different than Wren's, which means that one of them is lying. I know you'll say that Wren is telling the truth, but I'm just trying to point out that you've talked to Daytime Wren . . . what? Five or six times? And Nighttime Wren is downright scary. What if neither version of her has the best of intentions?"

"I know that's not the case."

"Do you?" He gave me a sidelong look.

We took a few steps before I finally answered. "One of those three murdered her," I said.

He merely stared at me, but I understood the point of his silence. Eventually, I heard him sigh.

"As we move forward," he said, "and yes, I'm still going to help you—I just want you to remember that everyone, including Wren, has their own agenda on this."

"I'll keep that in mind."

"On my end, I'll talk to Aldrich and the police chief. They might have some useful information."

"I appreciate your help."

"So what's the plan exactly? Whose day are we going to ruin tomorrow?"

I thought about it. "Nash," I said. "Might as well start there."

"Then look for that file Wren mentioned, the one with the copies she said she made. It'll help."

"And if I can't find it?"

"Then I guess we'll have to wing it. Do you want me to pick you up in the morning?"

"How about you text first?"

"In case Wren is there? Because you want to play strip poker or make a Denver omelet together?"

"I want to talk to her," I said. "She might have more information I'll be able to usc."

"Yeah," he said, clearly not believing me. "Right."

• • •

I was home right around lunchtime, but Wren was nowhere to be seen. I spent more than an hour looking for the file, searching every cabinet and drawer on the main level as well as the cellar without luck. Afterward, I wandered from room to room, waiting for her to appear, but when she didn't, I ruminated on Nash, Dax, and Griffin, wondering if any of them had enough reason to have murdered Wren.

Would you kill someone to stop a lawsuit? Or to

thwart a divorce that might deprive you of property worth millions, even if your case wasn't very strong?

At first glance, Griffin seemed to have a more compelling motive, but for Nash, losing his reputation might have been all that mattered. Dax's possible motivation, on the other hand, was less easily explained. Would he kill someone he supposedly loved because she rejected him?

I considered the possibility that Wren's death had resulted from an argument that escalated out of control. Had Dax surprised her at the house and made yet another attempt to convince her they were meant to be together? And had her additional rejection caused him to lash out?

Maybe. As I replayed my encounters with Nighttime Wren, I began to think they were memories that suggested a particular sequence of events. She'd decided to take a bath, during which an intruder had entered the bathroom. She'd screamed at him to leave, and sometime during the ensuing altercation her hair had been grabbed from behind—the image of her arching her back haunted me—and in the struggle, her head hit the faucet.

I was curious, too, about the extent of the investigation Louise had mentioned. Had forensics searched for fingerprints or DNA or hair fibers? Was it possible to find evidence on a body after it had been in the water more than two days? I hoped Oscar would be able to deliver some of those answers after speaking with the police chief.

As always, my thoughts circled back to Wren—I ached for her return with a pain that was almost physical. I berated myself again for trying to kiss her, wondering, again, where she had gone and whether she would ever return.

CHAPTER 21

Oscar texted first thing Tuesday morning to say that he'd be seeing Ray Dugan in a little while, so we made plans to meet afterward.

As I drank my coffee in the kitchen, I listened for any sign of Wren's return—she hadn't appeared in the hallway bathroom last night, or downstairs since I'd been awake. But there was nothing. Out of sorts, I had retreated to the parlor with a dog-eared volume of Mary Oliver poems that I'd pulled from the bookshelves when I saw Louise through the window, approaching the house. Tucked beneath one arm was a basket of cleaning supplies; in the other was a laundry bag. I let her in, and her gaze swept the room, as had become her habit.

"I haven't seen her lately," I said, answering her unspoken question.

She let out a breath as though relieved. "I'm sorry

for disturbing you," she said. "I was going to wait until you left before I came by, but Reece and I have an appointment this morning. Will my cleaning up bother you? I could always wait until the afternoon."

"It's fine," I said. "I'm finished in the bedroom."

"Would it be all right for me to vacuum the downstairs?"

"Yes, I'll be leaving soon anyway." Then, eager to gather as much information as I could before meeting Nash, I held up a finger. "But if you have time, I have a few questions."

She tensed slightly. "About Wren?"

"What was she like?" I asked. When she didn't respond, I added, "I don't think I can help her unless I know who she really was."

"She was family," Louise answered.

I waited. The silence stretched out, and then Louise's shoulders sagged as she lowered the basket to the floor.

"Everyone loved Wren," she finally said. "But she wasn't perfect."

"Please," I said, "I just want the truth."

"The **truth,**" she repeated, her expression almost thoughtful. "The truth is that Joyce doted on her. In the old days, people would have said Wren was spoiled. She was never an easy child, always quick to throw a tantrum when she didn't get what she wanted. I think that's the reason she didn't have a lot of friends growing up."

I tried to mask my surprise. "She didn't?"

"Maybe it would be more accurate to say that she couldn't keep friends. She'd have a friend for a year or two, and then they'd stop coming around. She'd replace them with someone else, and the pattern would repeat. I don't think that ever changed. As for her teen years, they were a heartache for Joyce. Wren didn't do well in school, she hung out with the wrong kinds of kids, and she got in trouble more than a few times—even got arrested once. Minor offenses—drinking, trespassing, and the like—but still." She shook her head. "Joyce used to tell me how much she was looking forward to Wren heading off to college so she'd finally have a break, but of course, Wren didn't leave."

"Why not?"

"Because she knew Joyce would always take care of her," Louise answered, as though it was obvious. "When Wren was growing up, Joyce bought her clothes and a car and paid her cellphone bill and gave her cash whenever she asked. Did you know that Wren even talked Joyce into lending her money to open a shop downtown? Joyce didn't want to, but Wren kept pushing and pushing until Joyce finally gave in."

"Really?"

Louise nodded. "It's probably not what you want to hear, but part of me thinks that the reason Joyce got so sick with Covid was because of the stress that Wren sometimes caused her."

She paused, seeming to realize how she sounded.

In the silence, I tried and failed to square this version with all that Wren had told me. I thought again about Oscar's question: **How well do you really know her?**

"You and Joyce were close, I take it."

"Very," Louise said. "She took care of us, and we took care of her. While she was alive, we never had to worry. And I apologize for what I said about Wren, but you asked for the truth."

"I appreciate it."

"I should probably get started so I can finish before my appointment," she said.

"I just have a few more questions, if you don't mind."

She looked at her watch and sighed. "Fine."

"Did you notice whether Wren was having problems with anyone in particular before she died?"

"Why would you ask about that?" Louise frowned. "Her death was an accident."

"I met Griffin yesterday," I said, ignoring her question. "They were married, right?"

"Barely, and it didn't last long. They were getting divorced."

"He told me that they'd decided to get back together, and the divorce had been put on hold."

"Not true," she scoffed.

"You sound sure about that."

"I am," she said. "I know for a fact that the divorce was ongoing. Not long before Wren died, Griffin dumped her clothes on the property after covering them in paint, which should give you an idea about the state of their relationship. They definitely weren't getting back together, no matter what Griffin says."

I took that in. "Did Wren ever mention any problems at the store?"

She raised her eyebrows, curious. "No," she said. "Why?"

"How about Dax?"

She hesitated. "Did Wren tell you about these people?"

Instead of answering, I said, "I heard Dax came to the property one night and that the police were called."

Louise let out a breath. "She told them that he was obsessed with her."

"Was he?"

"I don't know," she said. "Wren didn't really confide in me about her love life. Until that night, I'd assumed they were close. He was here at the house a lot after she separated from Griffin. I used to see them sitting on the porch in the evenings. And then one night he shows up and Wren calls Reece in a panic, claiming that Dax was peeking in the windows. I remember Reece sort of holding out the phone and looking at me with confusion while Wren was shouting on the other end, but I had no idea what was going on either." She made a skeptical face. "But yes, the police came out and Wren told them that Dax was stalking her. I don't know what happened after that, but he never came around again."

"Thank you," I said. "I guess that's it."

She lifted the basket and started toward the stairs before turning back to me.

"You said that Wren wants your help, but what do you think that means?"

I saw no reason to hide the truth. "I think she wants me to find out who was responsible for her death."

Her eyes widened as she digested the implication. "You think someone killed her?"

"I do."

"But the police already considered that possibility."

"Do you know if they spoke with Griffin? Or Dax?"

"I mentioned both of them to the police," she said before pausing. "Wait. Do you think one of them did it?"

"I'm just trying to figure out what really happened."

"It was an accident," she said, but it almost sounded like a plea.

"No," I said slowly. "She was murdered, and I'm going to find out who did it."

• • •

Twenty minutes later, I met Oscar at the bakery, where he ordered a donut and cup of coffee to go.

"Didn't you just have breakfast?"

"No," he said. "I met Dugan at the station, and I'm starved. By the way, Lorena—"

"I know," I interrupted. "Don't tell her about the donut, right?"

"I don't care about that," he said. "What I was going to say was that Lorena went nuts over your drawing. She responded, and I quote, 'I LOVE IT,' all caps, with a bunch of exclamation points. She kept gushing over the stained-glass window detail on the front door, the columns on the porch, the slate steps, and even the exterior color. But you know what she really loved?"

"I have no idea."

"The window boxes," he said. "She said they made it look like a real home."

"They were Wren's idea."

"What's the latest with her?" he asked, adding a copious pour of cream to his coffee.

"I haven't seen her since she told me what happened."

He took a bite of his donut and chewed as he talked. "And I'll say it again, like I did yesterday. I take it the two of you had an argument."

"Why would you say that?"

"Because she's avoiding you," he said matter-of-factly. "After a fight, it happens."

"We didn't argue."

"But you did something you shouldn't have, right?" When I didn't answer, he laughed before adding, "I'm teasing. I'm just trying to ease your worries about her disappearing. She'll show up again."

Glum, I shoved my hands in my pockets on the way out, hoping he was right. "I spoke to Louise this morning," I said and filled him in. His eyes reflected the same questions I'd had about the disparity between Wren's account and Louise's, but he made no comment. Instead, he asked, "I'm sure you're dying to know what Dugan had to say, right?"

"You never told me how you knew him."

"I made a financial donation to the police department right after I bought the property, enough to outfit the entire department with new protective vests. It's important to be a good citizen, and you never know when a little goodwill might come in handy. Like it did today, for instance. And, oh, he told me to tell you that he's going to call you."

"Why?"

"I had to explain my interest in all this, and it was impossible to leave you out of it."

"What did you say?"

"Mostly, I told him the truth. I said that you werc staying at the house, and a woman showed up who told you that Wren had been murdered and talked to you about suspects."

"And his response?"

"It sounded a little thin even to me, so I'm sure he feels the same way. I tried to make this 'mystery woman' sound credible, but I'll admit I was stretching." He made a wry face. "However, it was clear that he wasn't pleased about my inquiries. Obviously, he avoided most of the specifics about the investigation, but I did learn a couple of new things."

"Like?"

"For starters, I learned that Wren died on a Friday evening, the first night of the music festival. Her estimated time of death was hard to determine because she'd been in the water so long, but for reasons he didn't go into, they assume it happened sometime between nine and midnight." When he saw my expression, he raised a hand. "I know. It makes me wonder, too, whether there's some connection between what's been happening at the house with you and the fact that the symbolic anniversary of her death is coming up in a few days." He took a noisy slurp of his coffee before continuing. "Other than that, he pretty much confirmed Louise's comment about it being an accidental drowning. He also said that there was no evidence that anyone except Wren had been in the bathroom when she died and added that there was a gash in the back of her head that matched the blood and DNA on the faucet. According to the medical examiner, there was water in her lungs, confirming that the cause of death was drowning. And apparently, the police interviewed a lot of different people."

"Including Nash, Dax, and Griffin?"

"He didn't offer specifics of who exactly they spoke to, but obviously, there wasn't enough to press the issue or charge any of them."

I thought about that. "What about other DNA? Or fingerprints or hairs?"

"He said the forensics team did a full investigation, and he emphasized that they know what they're doing."

We were both quiet for a while before I ventured, "I'm hearing a 'but' in there somewhere."

Oscar finished off his donut and brushed the crumbs from his fingers. "If he's so certain it was an accident, why would he want to speak with you about the case?"

"Did you ask him?"

"I did," Oscar said, "which got him a little uptight. He began repeating himself, so I asked him something else I've been wondering about, something even you haven't mentioned to me."

"What's that?"

"Wouldn't she have been facing the faucet when she slipped and fell? People **always** face the faucet when they're getting in the tub, since that's the way they'd lie down in it. So how did she hit the **back** of her head?"

Oscar was right: I hadn't considered that. "How did Dugan respond?"

"He said the assumption was that she turned around while she was getting in or out."

I recalled Wren's appearance in the bathroom. "Maybe she was reaching for a towel? Because I've seen her wearing a towel."

"I suggested the same thing, and after hemming and hawing, he admitted that the only towels in the bathroom were folded and on the shelves. I'm guessing both those things bothered Dugan, too, but without any other leads, what else could he do? I have the sense that he's smart and plenty good at his job. Before he came to Heatherington, he was a detective in Boston. He finished his twenty and moved to Heatherington as chief."

"If he still had concerns, why close the case?"

"I asked him that, too."

"And?"

Oscar looked at me. "According to the original medical examiner's report, Wren's death was labeled suspicious, not accidental, meaning whoever examined her had the same questions I did. The same ones Dugan still has. Which also means, technically, even if the investigation is stalled for lack of evidence, I'm guessing it's still open."

• • •

After Oscar had drained the last of his coffee, we set off for Bird's Toys and Games. The sidewalks were even more crowded than the day before. Between my lack of sleep and the masks, not to mention Wren, my time in Heatherington was feeling increasingly surreal.

"When do you think Dugan will want to talk to me?"

"He didn't say, but the police department will

have their hands full with the festival, so I'm guessing next week at the earliest."

"What should I say to him when he calls?"

"Tell him the truth."

I stared at Oscar as if he'd grown a second head.

"I'm serious," he insisted. "You already told Reece and Louise you saw and spoke with Wren, and he might ask them about your 'mystery woman,' too. A lie would get you in trouble."

"But you lied to him."

"Barely," he answered. "But do me a favor when you do talk to him . . . Tell him that you were too embarrassed to tell me the truth about the ghost because you didn't want me—'the client'—to think you were crazy."

"He's going to think I'm crazy if I say that."

"Which means he's not going to waste a lot of time on you, so your life will be minimally inconvenienced."

"But I want him to keep digging."

"Then let's talk to our suspects and see if we can give him a real reason to take another look at what happened. Did you find that file Wren mentioned?"

"I didn't."

"Well, I guess we'll be flying by the seat of our pants," he said. "Do you know what you're going to say to Nash?"

"I'm going to ask him about Wren, and then slowly ratchet up the pressure." We stopped in front of the store. "Use your instincts, and feel free to join in whenever."

"I can do that," he said, rubbing his hands together. "This will be fun."

"I'm not sure that's the word I'd use."

"Especially if he's the bad guy."

I exhaled. "Yeah," I agreed. "Especially if he's the bad guy."

• • •

Inside, the store was bustling. A few teens were browsing the videogames at the front and several kids were looking at card games in the back, so Oscar and I made the silent decision to wait until the store was quieter before approaching Nash.

He recognized us, however, and though he was assisting the teens, his eyes immediately lit up; no doubt he was excited about the chance to recommend another expensive, hard-to-sell item. "Welcome back," he called out in a jovial voice. "Let me know if there's anything I can help you find!"

We pretended to browse until, after about fifteen minutes, the kids and teens approached the register with their purchases. A few moments later, the front door swung closed. Nash came out from behind the counter and hurried to greet us. He was already smiling.

"Back again, huh? I was thinking about the special Boggle set you bought," he said, "and I realized I forgot to show you an amazing luxury edition of Scrabble. You're not going to believe the quality. I think they only made about a hundred of them—"

"I'm not looking to buy a game today," I interrupted. "I came by to speak with you about your partner."

"Jonah?"

Oscar and I glanced at each other.

"You have a partner named Jonah?"

"Yeah, he bought in about eighteen months ago," Nash said, his smile wilting slightly. "He doesn't spend a lot of time here, though. He also owns the drugstore if you're looking for him."

I wondered whether Jonah knew about Nash's previous financial improprieties and somehow doubted it.

"Actually," I said, "I was hoping to speak with you about your former partner, Wren."

"Tate here is a good friend of hers," Oscar added. "Or was."

I could feel Nash's eyes swing from me to Oscar and back again. "How did you know her again? You're not from here, right?"

"We spent a lot of time together," I said, avoiding his question. "She even taught me how to make beef bourguignon."

"Oh," he said, not bothering to hide his confusion. "I didn't get your names." When we introduced ourselves, he frowned. "I don't remember Wren ever mentioning you to me."

"Hmm," I said, faking surprise. "She talked quite a bit about you. But anyway, do you have a few minutes?"

"Of course," he said politely. "Until a customer comes in, I'm all yours. What's up?"

I cleared my throat. "We were wondering whether you knew if Wren was having problems with anyone in the weeks before she died."

"What kind of problems?" Nash's expression clouded.

"Anything that comes to mind."

He stared blankly around the store, as if casting back in his memory. "Just with her ex, Griffin," he said after a moment, bringing his hands together. "But can I ask why it matters?"

"I'm not sure Wren's death was an accident. The medical examiner considered it suspicious."

Nash blanched. "You're kidding."

"Unfortunately not," I said. "I was also curious if the police ever spoke with you about what happened."

"They did," he said. "An officer came by the store, and we talked for a bit, but I didn't have much to say, since I only saw her once that week. Are they looking into her death again?"

"Between you and me," Oscar interjected, "I think there's a chance the case is about to become a lot more active."

"Oh . . . wow," he said. I could practically see his mind beginning to turn over, concern etched on his features. "I can't believe this."

"I feel like I owe it to her to find out what happened," I continued. "Can you think of anyone else she might have been having a problem with?"

He gave a nervous shake of his head. "People liked her, and the whole town was in shock when we found out what happened. But as for having problems with anyone, she didn't talk to me about those kinds of things," he said. "Our paths didn't really cross much in the store in the last year or so. Generally, either she was here, or I was here, and when we were both here, we'd talk about the business. I'm guessing her friend Dax might know more about it, though. She mentioned to me once that they'd been talking. He's a counselor over at the Mercy Center."

"Do you remember where you were the night she died?" I asked, switching tacks.

"I was at the festival like everyone else in town," he said.

"Can anyone verify your presence there between nine and midnight?"

His eyes swiveled from me to Oscar and back again. "Wait," he said, his voice beginning to rise. "Do you think I had something to do with what happened to her?"

"We're just asking you a few questions."

"I don't think I should be speaking with you about this." A steady flush was climbing up his neck.

"Because you don't have an alibi?"

"Alibi?" he gasped, his eyes widening. "Why would I need an alibi?"

I glanced at Oscar, noting his imperceptible nod.

"We know about the business line of credit you

accessed, the fake invoices, and the fact that Wren knew you'd been stealing from her."

Nash staggered backward. "I don't have any idea what you're talking about," he spit out. "And I don't know where you're getting your information . . ."

"Wren kept a file, and the bank has records," Oscar said, "so let's not bother playing games."

"We also know," I jumped in, "that Wren was planning to file a civil lawsuit to get the money back and that the last thing you wanted was for that information to become public. Small towns being what they are, the revelation would have ruined you. I'm sure the police are going to be very interested in this information."

"Are you threatening me?"

"We just want to know whether anyone can verify you were at the festival between nine and midnight."

With his fists clenched at his sides, Nash's entire body seemed to tremble. "This is ridiculous!" he shouted. "I would never have harmed Wren, and I'm not going to answer any more of your questions! I'm done talking to you!"

"Fine," I said calmly. "But you might want to think hard about that alibi of yours before we come back."

"And I'm guessing Jonah will want to scrutinize the books to see if you've been stealing from him, too," Oscar added.

"Not to mention that your wife is certainly going to want to know what you did with all that money."

Nash was vibrating with rage. "GET OUT!" he screamed. "I WANT YOU OUT OF HERE!"

"We'll be back," I repeated before Oscar and I left the store. As we started toward our cars, Oscar finally glanced over at me.

"I hope you never want to rattle my cage," he remarked with a grin.

"You think it worked?"

"I'm sure he's in free fall right now," Oscar replied. "Who's next?"

I pondered the situation as I unlocked my car, realizing that I needed more time to figure out our line of attack with Griffin, because I had a feeling he'd try to control the confrontation more than Nash had. "Probably Dax," I said, "but I don't know how to make contact with him, other than calling on him at the Mercy Center."

"I have an idea," Oscar said. "Let me make some calls this afternoon, and I'll tell you. On your end, keep looking for anything that might be useful. And like you said, maybe Wren will give us something we can use."

"I'm not sure she's going to be there."

He looked over at me before climbing into his own car. "One day, you're really going to have to tell me what you did wrong, because I'm dying to know."

I stuffed my hands into my pockets, remaining stubbornly mute.

CHAPTER 22

Once home, I finished the remaining beef bourguignon while doing a deep internet dive on Nash, Griffin, and Dax at the dining room table.

Of the three, information about Griffin was easiest to find, though little of it was helpful. The scores of links and articles about him mostly related to the festival. My search did turn up an arrest for drunk driving, though not how the case eventually turned out. For Dax, I found links to the Mercy Center and LinkedIn, which noted his education, training, and professional background; going further back, I also found a flurry of posts on various social media sites congratulating him on his marriage to Tessa four years earlier. Nash, on the other hand, was quoted in a few articles, which referred to him as the vice president of the Heatherington Downtown Association. I also found a photo of him and Wren cutting a large red ribbon in front of the toy store in an article from seven years earlier.

"What are you working on?" I heard Wren call from the kitchen. Although the sound made me jump, I felt an immediate sense of deep relief.

"Nothing important," I said, closing my laptop and turning toward her. She was wearing another sundress, this one cream colored with a pattern of small roses, and her hair hung in waves that suggested she'd used a curling iron. She was holding what looked like a glass of iced tea, and as she stood under the arched entry to the dining room, I thought I'd never seen anyone more beautiful. "How are you?"

"I'm not sure," she answered with a tentative smile. "Did you ever have one of those days where everything you were doing felt wrong somehow? Like you weren't where you were supposed to be? Or that you should be doing something else?"

"That pretty much describes every hour I spent in the hospital."

A smile flashed across her face, but it vanished as quickly as it had come. Her eyes were dark green today, like emeralds in the shade.

"I feel like I'm in a fog," she mused. "Like none of this is real, and if I blink, I might suddenly be somewhere else, or doing something else. I know how weird that sounds, but I can't seem to shake it."

I swallowed but tried to keep my expression steady. "Is there anything I can do to help?"

"Do you have time to sit with me?"

"Of course," I said. I rose and followed her into the parlor, conscious of how much I'd missed her. She took a seat on the sofa, but sensing her confusion, I decided to give her space. I had just sat down in the chair across from her when she blinked out of sight. Holding my breath, I counted to five before she flickered into sight again.

"I'm sorry," she said, running her fingers through her locks. "I don't know what's wrong with me."

"It's all right," I said, trying to project calm. "I'm just happy to see you again."

When she lifted her eyes to mine, her expression was serious. "I'm sorry for running out on you the other day," she said. "You caught me off guard, and I guess I got a little freaked-out."

"I'm the one who should apologize," I said. "I shouldn't have broken the rules."

She nodded, as though nervous. "What were you doing this morning? I didn't see you around."

"I met with Oscar," I said.

"At the site?"

"No. We were in town."

"I was there, too."

"You were?"

"I finally worked up the courage to speak to Nash."

I almost flinched. "How did it go?"

"About the way I thought it would. First, he tried to deny it, and then when I showed him what I'd found, he said the money was for store expenses.

Then finally, he said I wouldn't be able to do anything about it, since as co-owner, he had the authority to take out the loan."

"Did you ever find out what he did with the money?"

"Our discussion didn't get that far. I finally told him that unless he returned the money, I'd pursue legal action. That's when he got really angry, and I started to get nervous, so I left. I could still hear him shouting when I was on the sidewalk."

"What do you think he's going to do?"

"I have no idea," she said. "It was the first time I'd ever seen him out of control like that. It was . . ."

I finished for her. "Scary."

She nodded. "After that, I needed to walk so I could clear my head."

"I probably would have needed a sedative," I joked, wishing I could take her hand.

She cracked a smile. "I'm glad you're here," she said. "I was hoping you would be. I really needed to see a friendly face."

"I'm sure you know plenty of friendly faces around town," I said.

"There used to be more." She shrugged. "But after my grandma died, I kind of withdrew. I just couldn't bring myself to respond to people's calls and texts."

"I definitely know how that can happen," I assured her, thinking of my own slide into depression and isolation in the aftermath of Sylvia's death.

"After that, I threw myself into work, trying to

ensure that the toy store—and this place—survived the pandemic. And then, when Griffin came along, we mostly hung out with his friends, so one by one my friends drifted away. And now, it's just hard, you know?"

"I'm sorry, Wren. You didn't deserve to suffer alone."

Her eyes grew a bit brighter. "You're really good at knowing exactly what to say, did you know that?"

"I had a lot of practice at the hospital," I said.

"Maybe I should stay at a psychiatric hospital."

"I recommend it highly," I said with a smile.

For the first time, she laughed, though the sound rang a little hollow. "See what I mean? If I'd said that to almost anyone else, they would have immediately jumped to the conclusion that something was deeply wrong with me."

"Former patients tend to be kinder about such things."

"It's not just that," she said. "Being with you feels so effortless, and I can't tell you how much I've enjoyed our conversations over the last few days. I almost forgot what it was like."

"Talking to people?"

"Not just talking," she said wistfully, "but being genuine and authentic and real. Whenever I shared something with Griffin that was bothering me, he'd either make it about himself or use it against me later. He always had a way of twisting my words to mean something I didn't. By the end, I felt like I couldn't talk to him at all."

"So you started talking to Dax."

"And look how that turned out," she said with a disappointed laugh. "I should have known better. Do you remember when I told you about Brian?"

"The one in high school who moved away?"

She nodded, hesitating. "Before we became an item, Brian was seeing Tessa. They'd gone to the homecoming dance and a few parties together, but according to Brian, it wasn't serious. Tessa obviously didn't see it that way. Long story short, Brian and I started going out, and Tessa told everyone at the school that I'd sabotaged them. Fast-forward to not that long ago, and Tessa shows up at the store and begins screaming at me, accusing me of trying to steal her husband."

"And then he showed up here."

"That wasn't even the end of it. But you know what I realized? After that whole thing with the police? That in some ways, Dax was exactly like Griffin. They both used things I told them to manipulate me."

"That's terrible," I said, saddened by the unhappiness that had engulfed her.

"Have you ever done that? Exploited someone's trust to get what you wanted from them?"

"I don't think so," I said slowly. "But in all fairness, I'm sure neither Griffin nor Dax would have characterized their actions that way. People are often blind to their motives, especially when pursuing their own goals."

Everyone has their own agenda.

"They knew," she said, adamant.

Looking out the window, she collected herself. After a moment, she turned back to me, changing the subject. "How did your dinner turn out?"

"It was delicious."

"I'm sorry I didn't stick around to join you."

"It just meant more leftovers for me," I said. "I had some for lunch, in fact."

"I know," she said. "I can still smell it. Will you ever make it again?"

"I might," I said. "But it would be more fun if you were there with me."

Her gaze dropped, a flush rising under her golden skin. When she looked up, her eyes gleamed. "How long are you going to stay in Heatherington? I can't remember if you already told me."

"I'm here for another two or three weeks at least. And I'll be back and forth, of course, until the house is completed."

"You don't just draw the plans?"

"Sometimes. But in this case, I'll oversee the project from beginning to end."

"How long will that take?"

"For a house that size? Two years minimum, more likely three."

Her gaze was sultry as she spoke. "If you keep coming here, you'll have to be careful or we might end up becoming even better friends."

"I think we're pretty close now, don't you?" I answered, refusing to look away.

"I do," she said, her voice husky. "It makes me wonder why you took so long to finally show up."

Beyond the glass, the trees and leaves seemed to have gone still. I could feel the beating of my heart as I watched her deliberately raise her glass to her lips.

Had it been possible, I would have risen then and pulled her into my arms, pressing her body against my own. I longed to rewind the clock and change what had happened to her, to kiss her and confess how much she'd come to mean to me.

But I couldn't. Instead, I felt the words clamor inside me, the words that always came so easily to Sylvia, but that I had never been able to summon. I knew in that moment that I could never go back to living the way I once had. Wren had changed me, and my desire for her, sharpened by the knowledge that our time together was limited, struck me to the core. I wanted to tell her everything; I yearned to reveal the truth and find a way to be together. But I held back, fearing that I might drive her away for good. Instead, I heard myself ask, "Are you in the mood for a game?"

At my words, her face underwent a subtle shift. Was it disappointment I saw? When she shook her head, I realized I might have been imagining it.

"I'm too scattered to concentrate on a game. I just want to sit for a while."

"Would you mind if I made a sketch of you?"

"I wondered if you were serious about that."

"I was. And I am."

"You can draw people, too?"

"That's how I started."

She glanced at me from beneath lowered lashes. "You're not going to ask me to take off my clothes, are you?"

I laughed. "No. It will be a portrait, so the focus will be on your face. But if you're too warm or uncomfortable in your clothes, of course . . ." I waggled my eyebrows, and she smirked.

"What do I need to do?" she asked.

"Nothing," I said. "I'll get my sketchbook and pencils."

"Do I have to sit still and be silent?"

"You can move, and we can visit the whole time," I said. What I didn't tell her was that I could probably sketch her from memory.

"Okay," she said. "But while you're getting your things, I'm going to get a glass of wine."

• • •

I went upstairs to fetch my supplies, and by the time I returned, her glass was in her hand as she sat on the sofa. I pulled out a soft pencil and opened my sketchbook.

"This feels weird," she said, moistening her lips. "I've never had anyone draw me before."

"I hope not," I said. "That would make this way less special."

"What do I do?"

"We'll just sit and chat, but don't be offended if I'm not always looking at you."

"Will you show me what you're doing? Or are you one of those artists who insist on waiting until the end?"

"I'll show you whenever you'd like."

"How do you start? If you're drawing someone?"

"I don't know what other people do, but I always start with the eyes."

"Because they're the mirror to the soul?" she quipped.

"Because unless you get them perfect, the drawing won't be any good at all."

With pencil in hand, I focused intently, noting the striking bone structure and honeyed skin tone of her face, as well as the dense sweeps of her lashes. I started with a faint line, almost imperceptible, feeling myself settle into a removed yet comfortable zone. "Talk to me about your friends growing up," I prompted.

"Why?"

"Talking will help you feel less self-conscious," I promised.

I'm not sure whether she believed me, but she played along. While I continued to sketch, she began to describe her childhood friends, some of whom she still considered close, despite having drifted from them in recent years.

While reminiscing, she blinked out from time to time, sometimes in the middle of a story. Occasionally the color faded from her form until she became translucent, then invisible. At other moments, the outline of her body, even the distinctness of her features, dissolved and became fuzzy. A few times, she disappeared entirely for minutes. When these episodes occurred, I ignored the sudden clenching of my stomach and continued to draw from memory, as if she were still in front of me. The moment she returned, she would pick up her conversation where she'd left off, clearly unaware of what was happening.

Perhaps Louise had been right: Wren **had** cycled through friends, but to hear Wren tell it, there'd always been an explanation. Some friends moved on as interests diverged and they all matured; later, many moved away from Heatherington. She'd lost touch with others for less clear-cut reasons, and she observed that people sometimes changed, with which I had to concur. How many friends from high school and college did I still speak to, after all?

What emerged was that Wren had indeed been lonely, just as she'd admitted to me. Nonetheless, I again heard Oscar's warning: **How well do you really know her?**

Not as well as I wished I did, but all I could do was trust my instincts and follow where they led.

CHAPTER 23

Like a battery nearing the end of its charge, Wren's image stuttered, then blinked out long before sundown. It was earlier than ever, and quelling my omnipresent fears, I worked on the drawing until the moon rose above the tree line. For dinner, I drove downtown and sat at the bar of an Italian restaurant, brooding on Wren over a bowl of spaghetti carbonara.

When I exited the restaurant, teenagers and young adults in masks were thronging the streets. A flashing electric sign warned against public drinking to little effect; the few older people in town hurried to their cars, as though afraid that anarchy could break out at any moment.

Back at the house, I stood before the parlor bookshelves, pulling one book down after the other, searching for highlighted passages. Eventually, I paused over a sermon by Henry Scott Holland from 1910:

Death is nothing at all.
It does not count.
I have only slipped away into the next room.
Nothing has happened.
Everything remains exactly as it was.
I am I, and you are you.

Despite the absence of comments in the margin, I imagined those lines were Wren's way of telling me good night. Paulie followed me up to the bedroom, where I fell into an exhausted sleep. I willed myself to awaken in case Wren should appear, but the night passed uneventfully.

• • •

In the morning, I texted Oscar without receiving a response. While downing my first cup of coffee, I put final touches on the drawing, tapering Wren's eyebrows and adding the faintest of lines to the corners of her eyes. I was biding time, waiting for Wren, but when she didn't appear I went for a long run, hoping to settle my thoughts. On my return, I slowed to a walk with the house in sight and put my hands on my hips. I was still catching my breath when I noticed a distinct flutter of light by the cottage.

Shading my eyes, I realized I'd been mistaken;

the flickering hovered beyond the cottage, above the smaller of the two sheds. Watching for Louise and Reece, I jogged to the shed and pulled open the door. Inside, sunlight streamed through a single, dirty window. When my eyes adjusted, I spotted a pile of broken gardening implements and a wheelbarrow with a missing wheel. Along the back wall, shelves overflowed with used cans of stain and paint, bundles of wire, dirty paintbrushes, and what looked like a partially disassembled radio. A plastic garbage bag half-filled with debris sat in the middle of the floor; a ratty recliner and a drawer with missing knobs occupied a corner. A woman's bicycle leaned against one wall, both tires low but not quite flat, with canvas baskets draped over the rear tire. Above it more shelves sagged under the weight of assorted knickknacks and dusty cardboard boxes. Judging by the dirt and decaying leaves on the floor, no one had visited the shed in a long time.

Certain that I'd been led here for a reason, I browsed the shelves, peeked into the garbage bag on the floor, and shined my phone's flashlight into corners. Most of the paint and stain cans were less than a third full and largely dried out. There was nothing tucked into the cushions of the recliner, and the baskets of the bicycle were empty. Unwilling to give up, I reached for the first cardboard box.

It was lighter than I expected; as I pulled the flaps open, I discovered a mothballed assortment of women's clothing, some of which I recognized. There were yoga pants and halters, a few sundresses, jeans, a green sweater, and a few tops; near the bottom I found a jean jacket stenciled with **Monkey Tears,** and the Patriots sweatshirt Wren had been wearing while hunting for the puzzle piece. At the bottom were a pair of black pumps, some sneakers, and two pairs of sandals.

The second box was heavier. When I opened the flaps, the first things I saw were framed photographs: Wren as a little girl wearing a fancy yellow dress; Wren laughing in delight on a swing; a school portrait from her gawky middle school years; and another photo taken at her high school graduation, standing with her arm around a gruff-looking older woman, whom I assumed was Joyce. Additional photographs showed a high-school-aged Wren with two girlfriends lying on towels at the beach, and another with different friends at a bar, all wearing party hats and holding martinis. There was a lovely formal portrait, not unlike the drawing I'd made, and another snapshot of Wren and Joyce, heads together and beaming.

Beneath the photos, I found a battered doll most likely dating back to Wren's early childhood, and an old-fashioned recipe box filled with handwritten recipe cards. At the very bottom I found two thick expandable folders. The first contained personal and financial information, including her birth certificate. The second was of particular interest: the comprehensive record of Nash's wrongdoing that Wren had mentioned, complete with copies of invoices, bank statements, and printouts of emails. A yellow legal pad in the box also yielded two handwritten pages listing dates and brief descriptions of Griffin's transgressions during the short period of their marriage as well as their separation, some of which she'd already told me about. I assumed it was something that her divorce lawyer had asked her to compile.

Setting aside what I needed, I was about to put the box back when I glimpsed a wadded-up ball of paper on the shelf. I replaced the box and reached for the paper ball, moving to flatten it beneath the window's dim light.

It was a letter written on thick, high-quality stationery, in tight cursive script.

Dear Wren,

I want to apologize for the other night. The police warned me not to approach you again, but you must know I wasn't the one who told Tessa about us. I would never betray you or the confidences you've shared with me. And while I wouldn't wish Tessa's abusive behavior on anyone, now you know firsthand what her tirades are really like.

I'm sure you're already regretting what you said to the police. I know you didn't mean any of it, and I forgive you. Emotions can occasionally get the better of anyone, but truth prevails. I've seen the way you look at me, and I can still feel your body's imprint as you clung to me on the porch. You'd been crying, but when we came together that night it was the first time that I truly understood how two people can complete each other. I realized then that we are meant to be together forever.

I understand why you've been avoiding me. We're both married and it's a small town. It would be embarrassing for you to admit that we've fallen in love. But can't you see that we're in the same boat, and that it's easier for two people to row than just one? We can't let anyone or anything interfere with our destiny.

These last weeks have been a kind of torture. I've watched you at the grocery store, pulled in next to you at the gas station, even followed you as you rode your bike around town. I've seen the loneliness in your expression. I recognize that despair; we are both empty vessels without each other.

Wren, I'll do anything to protect the sanctity of our love, go anywhere with you. I'd follow you into the afterlife if need be. But I'm certain we can find our own private paradise right here in this world—just tell me where and when. I promise I'll be there.

Love you eternally,
Dax

I read the letter again, recoiling at its sickening implications, but wondering why it had been discarded this way.

Had it been found among Wren's possessions and crumpled up and tossed aside when Louise and Reece stored her things? Or had that been Wren's doing?

I wasn't sure.

I gathered the letter and files and left the shed, feeling like the hunt for Wren's killer was gaining momentum, even if I still had no idea where it would lead.

• • •

After I showered and ate, I peeked through the kitchen window. Reece was refueling the riding mower when Louise approached, saying something to him. Her familiar anxious gaze drifted to the house, and I ducked back. When I looked again, she was gone, and Reece was motoring off on the mower to another part of the property.

I'd just washed my dishes when Oscar's car pulled up in front of the house.

"Hey," I said, opening the door. "What are you doing here?"

Instead of answering, he carefully scanned the parlor before walking over to the kitchen.

"She's not here," I said. "And by the way, Louise does the same thing whenever she comes by."

"I can't say I blame her," he said with a shrug.

"What's happening here falls into the category of weirdest things ever."

"You didn't answer my question," I said.

"Your phone is off," he said. "It's been going straight to voicemail."

"Really? I texted you this morning."

I went to check, and sure enough, the screen was dead. I could have sworn I'd charged it the night before, but then again, it might just have been another inexplicable coincidence, like the power blowing out when I'd tried to kiss Wren. These days, who knew? I plugged it in.

"I got us an appointment with Dax at noon," Oscar announced.

"How did you do that?"

"I reached out to the Mercy Center director and told him that a donation would be forthcoming. When he suggested we get together, I said I wanted to meet with someone who saw patients, and that I'd heard good things about Dax."

"He's not going to be happy when he finds out why we're really there," I remarked. "Nor is Dax."

"I still intend to make the donation," Oscar said with a breezy wave. "Did you get lucky and dig up anything more?"

"Actually, I did," I said. I fetched the files and the letter. He took a seat on the sofa and studied them.

I also filled him in on what Wren had told me

the day before and sensed his thoughts paralleling my own: while the letter was suspicious, it was no smoking gun. He handed the papers back to me.

"Last night, I figured out something that's been bothering me about the night that Wren died," Oscar said.

"What's that?"

"I've been wondering why she didn't seem to recognize her killer," he said. "That part didn't make sense to me until Dugan told me she died the first night of the festival."

I followed his train of thought. "You think the killer might have been wearing a mask?"

He nodded before looking at me square on. "I have to ask you something else, though, Tate."

I straightened at his tone. "Yes?"

Oscar's eyes bored into me. "What if we never know who did it?"

"What do you mean?"

"I'm just wondering how long you're going to keep going with this. Are you planning to cook, play games, and read poetry with Wren indefinitely?"

"I haven't thought that far ahead."

"Okay, how about this? What happens if you're right, and in a short while, scary Wren is the only one remaining? Are you still going to stay here?"

Probably.

"I don't know," I hedged.

"What if Aldrich decides to close the house again?"

The concern behind his questions was obvious, and I shifted uncomfortably.

"In that case, I guess I would have to buy the property," I joked. At the sight of his shocked expression, I added, "Just kidding."

"Are you?" Oscar blew out his cheeks. "Because right now, I'm not so sure. You do understand she's not real, don't you?"

"She's real—"

"She died," he said, cutting me off. When I didn't respond, he went on. "We both know that whether we solve this or not, there's only one ending to all of this." He leaned forward, his expression earnest. "I don't want you going down the rabbit hole again, Tate. As your friend, I'm telling you to guard your heart."

I merely nodded, because my throat was too tight to speak.

• • •

Shortly before noon, a doorbell chime announced our arrival at Mercy Center.

There was no receptionist in the small waiting area, which featured plastic chairs set along the walls, inexpensive art prints, and a cork bulletin board with flyers listing schedules for AA, NA, Al-Anon, and Narc-Anon meetings. The blue carpet was threadbare, and a single wilting plant languished in a pot near the door. Although Mercy Center shared a similar mission with the hospital where I'd stayed, the contrast was not lost on me.

Less than a minute after we entered, a paunchy, middle-aged man in a sports jacket emerged from the back. Smiling and extending his hand to both of us, he introduced himself as Dr. Singer, the director.

Dr. Singer responded with eagerness to Oscar's questions about the center: how many people they treated, whether they provided mental health care for low-income residents, what kinds of therapeutic interventions they offered, and so on. I found myself impressed by his thorough and compassionate answers. Mercy Center may not have had the resources or luxurious appointments of my hospital in Connecticut, but it seemed to be serving its community with integrity and surprising sophistication.

After ushering us to the back, Dr. Singer pointed out an office bearing the name Rene Joblin, encouraging us to meet with her as well. As we reached Dax's office, he offered his card to each of us, inviting us to call him with questions about the center at any time.

Dax's office door stood open, revealing a thin man with a sparse mustache sitting behind a desk, unpacking the contents of a brown paper bag. His dun-colored hair was parted neatly on the side, and he wore a pressed, collared shirt without a tie. Looking up, he waved at the two vinyl armchairs facing his desk.

"I hope you don't mind if I eat," he said, licking a squirt of mayonnaise off his thumb. "My appointments this morning started at seven and are back-to-back all day until after six. I have to run to a meeting after that, so it's a full day."

"Don't let us stop you," Oscar said. "We're grateful you were able to meet on such short notice."

We took our seats as Dax carefully unwrapped his sandwich and cut open a small package of Fritos with a pair of desk scissors. "My wife packed this for me," he said.

"Tessa?"

He glanced up, startled. "Yes. Do you know her?"

"We've never met," I said, "but it's a small town."

"Of course," Dax replied. He took a small bite of his sandwich, chewing thoroughly and chasing it with a swallow of coffee from a mug that read **Emotional Support Human—Do Not Pet** before focusing his attention on Oscar. "Dr. Singer mentioned that you bought property here in town? And that you'd like to make a donation to the center?"

Oscar nodded, and for a few minutes we made desultory small talk about Mercy Center. When Dax segued into a question about what Oscar hoped to accomplish with his donation, Oscar held up his hand.

"Before we get to that, I was curious if any family or friends come to you with their problems. It has to be awkward, although pretty common, no?"

Dax stroked his mustache. "I try to avoid those scenarios," he said, raising his chin. "While it's okay to offer advice on small things, psychologists shouldn't counsel family members for the same reason a surgeon shouldn't operate on his wife or child."

"But it happens?"

"I do my best to avoid that kind of situation," he repeated.

Oscar gave me a sidelong glance before leaning forward, his elbows on his knees. "That's not what we've heard."

Dax blinked. "Excuse me?"

"We're referring to Wren," I clarified.

Dax grew silent, his gaze shifting from me to Oscar and back again before his eyes narrowed. "You didn't come here to discuss a donation to the Mercy Center, did you?"

"As a friend of Wren's, I'm fully aware of how your obsession with her escalated to stalking, which required police intervention."

Dax's expression hardened, although he didn't betray any signs of anxiety. "I see that I misjudged the purpose of your desire to meet with me, so I'll have to ask you to leave—"

"In a minute," I interrupted. "Just tell us this: where were you on the night that Wren was murdered?"

"I don't have to answer your questions," he said with a trace of contempt.

"It's obvious you couldn't let her go," I said, feeling

a prickle of anger at his smugness. "Did you go to her house that night to try to convince her to run away with you? And maybe things escalated when she refused?"

Something flashed in Dax's eyes, and he got to his feet. "If you even whisper that accusation, I'll sue you for defamation," he said in an icy voice that I was sure his patients never heard. "My father is a criminal defense attorney who knows lots of lawyers who'd be more than happy to bankrupt you."

Though Wren had said Dax's dad was an attorney, she hadn't mentioned his specialty.

"It's only defamation if we know it to be untrue," Oscar countered with commendable insouciance.

"You don't know what you're talking about," Dax said after a tense moment, taking a seat once more. When he continued, his words were deliberate, his gaze at once calculating and assured. "Yes, Wren sought me out. We were friends, and I wanted to help her. But she ended up trying to seduce me." He gave a tight-lipped smile. "She was a beautiful woman, and I admit that I responded when she kissed me, but it went no further than that."

I kept my expression impassive as he went on. "Unfortunately, once I put an end to her overtures, she became hysterical. A day or two later, she called me, claiming she was suicidal, so I rushed over to her house. As soon as I got there, she called the police and claimed I'd been stalking her, which was ridiculous since **she** came on to **me.** The police know all of this, which is why I wasn't charged."

The words sounded practiced, and I wondered how many times he'd recited this tale. I pulled the letter from my pocket, displaying it for him.

"Then you probably won't mind if we show the police the letter you wrote to Wren not long before she was killed," I said.

It took him a beat to recognize what I was holding, and for the first time, I detected a tiny crack in his composure.

"Where did you get that?" he asked.

"Wren left it for me," I said.

"Where?"

"At her house. I've been staying there."

"That's impossible."

I sat back and folded my hands in my lap. "I'm guessing this letter will be enough for the police to reconsider the stalking charges. I'm also fairly certain that stalking, in addition to being a suspect in a murder case, could derail your career. I wouldn't be surprised if your license is suspended, if not revoked entirely."

"And what will Tessa think?" Oscar added, spreading his hands out. "Or the rest of the town?"

Dax swallowed, trying to maintain his composure, but his mind was clearly racing.

"Why are you here?" He cleared his throat with some difficulty. "What do you want?"

I slid the letter back into my pocket. "I want you to tell us where you were between nine and midnight on the night that Wren was killed," I said.

Dax ran a hand through his thinning hair. "I've already told the police all of this."

"We'd like to hear it from you."

"I was at home."

"Can anyone verify that?"

"I was alone. Tessa and her sister Lauren were at the festival."

"Why didn't you go with them?"

"I wasn't invited," he said through pinched lips. "Tessa and I were going through a rocky patch at the time."

"So, no one can vouch for you that night?" I pressed.

"Not for most of it. Lauren dropped Tessa off at half past eleven."

"And you had access to a car?"

He crossed his arms and leveled a defiant gaze at us. "I didn't drive. I'd been drinking that night."

"Drinking is known to lower inhibition," Oscar observed.

"I didn't go to Wren's, if that's what you're implying."

I studied him. "Did you know that the medical examiner considered Wren's death suspicious, not accidental?"

Dax gave an impatient snort. "All that means is

that the accident couldn't be perfectly reconstructed. Many deaths are regarded as suspicious before the investigation is concluded."

"You sound very well versed in the police investigation," I noted.

He sighed. "I already told you, my dad is a criminal defense lawyer."

"What if I told you that someone spotted your car in the area that night?" I bluffed.

"I'd say you're lying."

We stared at each other before a smirk slowly spread across his face.

"We're done here," he said, sounding almost bored.

"Then I'll be bringing this letter to the police."

He cocked his head, seemingly unperturbed. "And I'll tell them that I didn't write it."

I raised an eyebrow at his brazenness. "Did you just think of that?"

"It's the truth."

"I wonder if your wife will agree once she sees the handwriting."

At this, Dax stiffened. "The fact that you're trying to sabotage all the hard work we've put into our marriage is beyond contemptible."

"Tell us something we don't know about Wren's murder, or I'm going to show the police and Tessa the letter next week. And I'll make sure your boss and the state licensing board receive copies as well."

We stood and left the center, the doorbell chiming behind us.

As we approached his Escalade, Oscar whistled and said, “That guy was as slippery as they come.”

“You think his dad prepped his story for the cops?”

“Could be.” Oscar shrugged. “In any case, it’s clear that he’s willing to lie, and if he lies about one thing . . .”

He didn’t finish, but then again, he didn’t have to.

• • •

That evening, I settled down at my computer to commence the schematic designs for Oscar and Lorena’s house. I worked steadily for a couple of hours but found myself distracted, my senses constantly attuned to any signals heralding Wren’s appearance, even though it was long past sunset. I wasn’t surprised when she never showed up. Restless, I eventually texted Mike, asking him to forward the final video from my sister.

It arrived within ten minutes, and after a quick exchange of texts, I poured myself a glass of wine before settling down to watch. My sister’s face appeared in the hospital setting that was by now all too familiar.

Hi Tate,

This is my last message to you, and I’m sure it comes as no surprise that I want to talk about love. I know I've told you that if you truly open yourself up to someone, anything is possible. But I never mentioned the corollary to that truth: that love can also be frightening.

Let me tell you a story. You know that Mike proposed to me while we were in Positano. I texted you the photos right after it happened, and I still use one of them as my screen saver, because it remains one of the happiest days of my life. What you don't know is that it was the third time Mike had proposed to me, because I'd said no the first two times.

Until now, I've kept that part of the story to myself, not because I was embarrassed, but because of my love for Mike. I didn't want people to think I considered him unworthy, or that my instincts were telling me I was making a mistake—I couldn't do that to the man I loved. So why did I say no, not once but twice?

All relationships entail risk because happy endings are never guaranteed. But marrying me? A tragic ending, sooner rather than later, was all but a certainty, and because I loved him, I was afraid for him. I didn't want him to experience the pain of losing his wife. He accepted both my rejections with astounding humility and grace. But when he asked me the third time, just as the sun was setting over the Mediterranean, he said this:

I'd rather be married to you for a single day than live a hundred lifetimes without you.

Well, we both know how that story ends. We had some blissful years together, but now I have only a handful of days left, and the prospect of being separated from this good man, who loves me with every fiber of his soul, devastates me more than the loss of my own life. Thinking about his grief and suffering in the aftermath of my passing fills me with anguish. But listen when I say this to you, Tate: despite all the pain we're facing, and the terror I feel at the loss of our life together, it is infinitely scarier to go through life never having loved at all. Because without him, what would my life have meant?

I love you fiercely, little brother. Someday, like all of us, you'll face your own end. And more than anything, I hope that you will look back, as I am now, on a life made worthy by the only thing that matters: love. Take care of yourself, and believe me when I tell you that I'm going to be watching over you from the other side.

She ended the video by blowing me a kiss. I watched it over and over, missing Sylvia more with every viewing. It also left me with an unexpected feeling of kinship with Mike. Like me, he'd given himself fully to love, despite the knowledge that it would end all too soon. But I now understood that the limited time he spent with Sylvia only distilled and intensified his feelings into something more precious, because he'd loved her knowing that every moment together could be their last.

CHAPTER 24

The next morning, I was examining the sketch of Wren in the parlor while savoring my first cup of coffee when I noticed a flurry of movement near the kitchen.

"Wren?" I called, striding toward it. When I reached the kitchen, she was standing in front of the sink, staring out the window. She was dressed in the same outfit as the first time I'd seen her. Despite the rays of morning light seeping through her, I felt a surge of relief. She turned to look over her shoulder at me.

"This doesn't feel right," she said, bewildered. "Does it feel right to you?"

"I'm not sure what you mean."

"Where's my car?" she asked. "Where's breakfast? Where are the guests?" With every question, the colors of her clothing and hair grew duller. "None of this makes any sense to me. I should probably go over and ask Louise what's going on, but somehow the thought of it feels overwhelming." She looked at me uncertainly. "I can't seem to mobilize myself to actually do it."

"I like the quiet." I shrugged, forcing myself to respond in a steady, almost soothing tone. "Good morning, by the way."

"I'm sorry. Good morning. And I apologize for babbling." She frowned. "My mind is so fuzzy lately. It feels like it's wrapped in gauze."

"It's okay," I said. "We all have days when the synapses aren't firing the way they're supposed to." Then, casually, I said, "Hey, I finished the drawing if you'd like to see it."

"Maybe in a few minutes," she said, clocking the change in subject. She tilted her head. "I hope you made me look prettier than I really am."

"I'm not sure that's possible."

At that, her appearance brightened, like a peacock flashing its feathers.

"You know what else I was thinking as I was zoning out just now?" she asked.

"Tell me."

"I was thinking about Brian and how sad I was when he moved away."

"Why do you suppose that came to mind?"

She wrapped her arms around her body, as if chilled. "I think it's because I know you're going to be leaving, too."

"I've already told you that I'll be coming back."

"I know." Her gaze dipped. "But what if something changes before then?"

"Like what?"

"What if you get home and realize the truth about me?"

"What truth?" I felt my heart begin to race.

"That I'm ordinary." Her voice was so tentative, I had to strain to hear it.

"I didn't go to Exeter or Yale or grow up in New York City. I'm a small-town girl, and when you get back to the city, you're going to realize how different we are. I'm afraid that all of this—whatever it is to you—will be either remembered like a dream or forgotten."

"You're not ordinary," I insisted. "And I promise that I'll never forget you."

Her eyes told me she longed to believe me. "You know what else I was wondering this morning? Before you came down?"

"I'm almost afraid to ask."

"I was wondering about Sylvia and Mike," she said. "When did you know they were in love?"

"When Sylvia told me."

"Not before?"

I squinted, trying to recall the early days of their courtship. "I think I might have begun to suspect it a few months after they started dating. I met them for dinner one night, and I noticed how she kept looking at him whenever he spoke—as if he were the most captivating human she'd ever met. Which was a little disconcerting to me, since I'd never seen her look at a man that way before."

"Do you think you'll ever look at a woman that way?"

I held her gaze. "I'm pretty sure I already have."

She studied me, the silence crackling between us, before she offered a shy smile. "I think I'd like to see that drawing now."

In the parlor, I retrieved the sketchbook from the sofa and held it up for her to examine.

"Ah," she sighed. "Just what I thought. You drew the new and improved version of me."

"I just draw what I see."

"I'm not this beautiful."

"Yes," I said. "You are."

She looked at me wordlessly. Beyond the window, a flock of starlings broke from the branches, flooding the sky with their beating wings. Standing close, I caught the scent of her perfume, something floral and rich, like rose petals. In that moment, I felt the weight of our shared confessions, and the carefree joy of our laughter, and wondered whether my time with Wren had somehow been preordained, every decision I'd made in my life leading me to her without my knowing it.

"Wren—" I began. But before I could say anything else, my phone rang, and the woman who'd already marked my life forever was gone.

• • •

Reluctantly, I answered my phone. Oscar caught my tone.

"Let me guess. She's there?"

Background noise made it difficult to hear him. "Not anymore."

"I'm sorry."

"You didn't know," I said. "Where are you?"

"At the diner. I was calling to see if you wanted to get breakfast, but seeing as I ruined your morning, maybe you're not in the mood."

"I'm not really hungry."

"Figures." He snorted. "Anyway, there's a few things you should know. First, I just found out I have Zoom meetings all day tomorrow, so you'll be on your own. Today, though, we'll be meeting Griffin at eleven at the fairground, and I'll be picking you up, so be ready. I also found out that Griffin was arrested seven months ago for—get this—being too rough with a woman he's dating. Her name is Sandra Hall. Supposedly, he used her as a punching bag one night, but Sandra decided not to press charges."

"Who told you that?"

"The waitress," he said. "She remembered seeing me talking to Griffin the other day, and Sandra is one of her friends. Apparently, Sandra and Griffin have been seeing each other on and off for years."

"Even when he was married to Wren?"

"Before the marriage and again after Wren died," Oscar said. "According to the waitress, Sandra is stunning and could get any man she wants, but she has this weird addiction to Griffin."

"She told you all of this?"

"Why not? I'm a friendly guy. I also finally received a call back from Aldrich. He's at a conference in Boston, and he wasn't comfortable discussing the trust on the phone, but he promised to touch base as soon as he gets back tomorrow night. I should be done with my meetings by then, so I'll keep you informed."

"He's getting back on the opening night of the festival."

"I doubt he'll be going. He's not the type."

"That's not what I meant."

"I know you were thinking about Wren," he said. "It feels like things are coming to a head, doesn't it?"

"Yeah," I said. "It does."

• • •

I worked a bit more on the schematics for the house, mainly to kill time, and while I was hunched over the computer, I heard a knock at the door. I opened it to find Louise and Reece standing on the porch. As earlier in the week, Louise carried a basket of cleaning supplies and a laundry bag of clean linens. Beside her, Reece gripped his toolbox.

"The parts I ordered came in," Reece said. "Would

it be okay to repair the fuses now? Some of them are overloaded, and I don't want to continue straining the system any longer than I have to."

"I figured I might as well clean at the same time," Louise added.

"Of course. I'll be leaving in fifteen minutes anyway."

Reece edged past me, toward the cellar. Meanwhile, Louise eyed her surroundings, her gaze settling on the sketchbook, which still lay open on the parlor sofa.

Without a word, I went over and brought it to her. She set the basket and linen bag on the floor. She bit her lip as she stared at the drawing of Wren.

"When did you last see her?"

"This morning."

"I still don't understand." She took a step back, as if eager to put distance between herself and Wren's image. "I've thought and thought about what you told me, but you're wrong about what happened to her. She was alone in the house that night."

"You sound sure of that."

"Reece and I were in the cottage. Wren came home around half past eight, but no one else arrived until well after midnight. We would have seen any cars pull up because the headlights flash right through our living room window."

"Maybe you fell asleep."

"We didn't," she said, expelling a breath. "People who come for the festival are not always the most conscientious of guests. They'll throw parties after they return in the middle of the night, or they've been drinking and they damage things. Sometimes they get wild ideas, like starting a bonfire out back. We always keep a close eye on the place, but especially during that weekend."

I considered what she'd said. "Maybe whoever killed her parked on the road and walked up to the house."

"He would have needed a room key to get in the front door."

"Is it possible that someone could have made a copy?"

"I guess," she said, sounding skeptical. "It's true that we haven't changed the locks as often as we should. But what's going to happen if Mr. Aldrich keeps the house open? Are other guests going to see her, too? Or what if word gets out, and loony ghost hunters start to show up?"

"I don't know."

"Does Mr. Aldrich know what's going on in the house?"

"I haven't said anything to him."

"Should I?"

"That's up to you."

"But I haven't seen her," she protested. "No one's seen her but you."

There was nothing I could say to that. Instead I asked, "Why are the photos of Wren in the shed?"

Louise looked startled. "How do you know about that?"

"They were in a cardboard box of her belongings, and I'm just curious why you didn't keep any of them."

"We did keep them." She shrugged. "Obviously, you found them."

I said nothing, watching as she picked up the bag of linens.

"They were in Wren's room," she said, "along with the rest of her things. Mr. Aldrich suggested we box up everything because at that time, he hadn't yet decided what he was going to do about the bed-and-breakfast, and it wasn't appropriate to keep them in the room if he intended to rent it out. Why were you in the shed?"

"I thought I saw something," I answered.

She glanced away before her gaze drifted back to the drawing. "Is this the way she looks to you?" she asked, sounding weary.

Sometimes, but not always . . .

"It is," I said.

Louise was quiet for a moment. When she spoke, her voice was so soft I could barely make it out. "I wish she still looked like this to me, but I'm never going to forget the way I found her."

• • •

Oscar arrived on schedule, and in the car, I reviewed with him the list of Griffin's transgressions that Wren had compiled for her lawyer.

A few minutes later, we pulled into the festival's

dirt parking lot and wound our way between haphazardly parked trucks and vans of every size, looking for a place to park. Oscar opted for a spot off to the side, where the Escalade was unlikely to get dinged by other vehicles.

A banner that read HEATHERINGTON LIVE 2025—IT'S ALL ABOUT THE MUSIC hung over the main gate. Inside the fenced perimeter, makeshift stages were scattered throughout the grounds, surrounded by bleachers and plastic folding chairs. Food and drink concessions dominated the center of the grounds, along with restroom facilities and huge white tents selling merchandise. Everywhere I looked, roadies were unloading vans and pickup trucks or arranging speakers on stages, tech personnel were climbing scaffolding and hanging lights, and other workers were delivering concessions.

"Where are we supposed to meet him?" I asked Oscar, surveying the swarm of activity.

"He said that we should start in the office, but that he'd be running around all day," Oscar answered. "He was plainly annoyed by my request, but eventually agreed to give us ten minutes if we could track him down."

"That's only because he still wants your money."

"He's not going to get it," Oscar said. "The masks make me feel like I need to keep my hands on my wallet to keep from getting robbed."

"That's a little paranoid, don't you think?"

"Yeah, well, if you ever see a man enter the bank

wearing a Halloween mask, you might change your mind."

Griffin wasn't in the office, but an employee directed us to one of the stages, where a harried-looking guy with a clipboard pointed toward a nearby staff parking lot. We finally located Griffin talking to what looked like several band members whose makeup, piercings, and tattoos made it difficult to determine their ages. We waited on the periphery until Griffin signaled that he'd be with us soon. Red-faced, he was exhorting the band members about some point, gesticulating emphatically while they looked on with obvious boredom. When they slunk away, Griffin wiped his forehead with the sleeve of his shirt and approached us.

"Sorry about that," he said. "I was just explaining to them that they wouldn't be able to set off the fireworks they'd planned. They wanted it to be part of the show, but there's no way the fire marshal will allow that so close to the audience."

"It looks like you still have a lot to do before tomorrow night," Oscar observed.

"It's always chaos toward the end," he said. "No matter how many deadlines I set, the work always seems to happen at the last minute. But somehow, I manage to pull it off," he said. "This year's lineup is the best yet."

"Will there be a band called Monkey Tears?" I asked.

"Not this year," he said with a curious look. "Why? You a fan?"

I shrugged.

"They're from Providence and were last here two years ago. It was an all-female band, and they had a fan base among young women. I invited them back last year, but they'd broken up and gone their separate ways by then. It happens." He looked from me to Oscar. "As you can see, I'm beyond swamped today, so what can I do for you?"

"We wanted to talk to you about someone you used to know."

He cocked his head. "You told me it was urgent."

"It is," Oscar said.

"All right, fine. But I only have a few minutes. I'm supposed to be meeting the sound guys on Stage Five right now."

"We won't keep you," Oscar said. "What can you tell us about your ex-wife?"

"You came here to talk to me about Wren?" Griffin's face registered his disbelief.

"I'm curious as to why she left you," I said.

"None of your business," he snapped.

"I'm also curious as to why you lied to us about her wanting to get back together."

"I didn't lie . . ."

"Wren kept a record of your drug and alcohol abuse—as well as your violent episodes at home." I watched as Griffin's shock turned to fury, a flush creeping up his neck. "Tell me, Griffin—did you ever hit her, like you did Sandra Hall?"

Griffin whirled toward Oscar, his hands clenched. "Seriously, Oscar? You came here to pull this kind of stunt? What the hell's wrong with you?"

"Her death came at the perfect time for you," I added, "since you're now claiming ownership of her property."

"I'm not talking to you!" he shouted, before snarling at Oscar over his shoulder. "What the hell's going on? Who is this guy?"

"Tate is a friend of Wren's," Oscar said. "And according to the police, you're one of the prime suspects in her murder."

"What police? The investigation's over!"

Like Dax, he didn't seem surprised by the word "murder." "Not anymore," Oscar stated. "New information has come to light."

"Yeah, well, I'm not talking to this guy," Griffin said, jerking his thumb at me. "And I'm not talking to you either."

"The police will want to know your whereabouts on the night Wren was killed."

"Where the hell do you think I was?" Griffin shouted, drawing glances from passersby. "I'm overseeing a thousand different things while the festival's going on. I was here, there, everywhere!"

"And who can vouch for you between nine and midnight?" I asked.

"How should I remember that?" he demanded

before breaking off. He turned, looking as though he'd just figured out something important. An ugly sneer spread across his face. "Oh, I get it. You're working for those other attorneys, right? And you're trying to smear my reputation?" He leaned toward me. "I'll say it again: Wren begged me to take her back and I agreed to call off the divorce. Which means half of that property is mine. So get the hell out of here before I call some guys over to throw you out. You're trespassing, and believe me when I say I'll press charges. So. Get. The. Hell. Out. Of. My. Face."

He punctuated each word by stabbing his forefinger at me. I wished I could have gotten more from him, but at Oscar's signal we turned to leave. I took a step before turning back around.

"If, as you say, you were in a lot of different places that night, that also means there's no one who can vouch for you the whole time, is there? You could have driven up to the house and killed her." I allowed myself a tight smile. "You had all the motive in the world, and soon, the whole town, and the police, are going to be thinking exactly the same thing."

Griffin erupted and lunged toward me, spewing a string of curses, but Oscar was quicker and immediately put his hands up, keeping us separated. He then grabbed me and, before the situation could escalate, pushed me back toward the entrance.

We climbed into the Escalade, neither of us speaking until we reached downtown.

As he pulled into a parking space a few blocks off Pleasant Street, Oscar turned toward me and said the last thing I expected.

"We're being followed."

• • •

We got out of the SUV and surveyed our surroundings. Up the block, I saw a blue car, double-parked. A stream of people passed through the intersection behind it, while musicians played on all four corners.

Oscar nodded toward the car. "I couldn't make out the driver in the rearview mirror, but whoever that is followed us from your place to the fairground, then waited for us, and followed us again."

"Who is it, do you think?" I asked, trying to get a better look.

"Could be Nash, since you pissed him off a couple days ago. Or Dax, since it's clear he hates your guts, too. Or, of course, it could be one of their friends, some jacked-up dude who wears his keys on a chain and has a skull or a spider tattooed on his neck."

"I didn't get the sense that either Nash or Dax would have friends like that."

"They might be murderers, but they can't have dangerous friends?" Oscar scoffed. "By the way, have you even considered the possibility that any of the people we've talked to might have hired someone else to kill Wren?"

"Why didn't you suggest that idea earlier?"

"Because I just thought of it!" Oscar answered,

throwing up his hands. "It's not every day that I play cold case investigator!"

The small foreign hatchback idling down the block didn't strike me as the kind of car that someone dangerous might drive, but what did I know?

"What do you want to do? Get back in the Escalade?"

"No. I really don't want whoever it is to follow me back to my place. They know how to find you but not me, and I'd like to keep it that way."

"Thanks."

"Don't worry about it," he said. "I doubt we're in any danger here, though. Too many witnesses. I think we need to see who it is and what he wants."

Because Oscar had better streetwise instincts than I did, I nodded and reluctantly followed along. Nonetheless, my stomach flip-flopped as we approached the car. Just as we drew parallel, the driver's side door swung open. A high-heeled boot stepped out, and I realized with surprise that it was a woman. Like Wren, she had dark hair and green eyes, though she was shorter.

"I'm Tessa," the woman said, closing the door behind her. She glared at each of us in turn. "My husband told me you're trying to dredge up the past."

Dax's wife.

"We're looking into Wren's death—" I began.

"Why?" she interrupted, putting her hands on her hips. "It was an accident."

"It wasn't," I said.

"Yeah, well, even if she was killed by someone, she deserved it. The world's a better place without her."

I fell silent, noting Oscar's shocked expression as well. Tessa smirked, as though proud that her remark had had its intended effect.

"You know what she did, right?" she demanded.

"We know that she confided in your husband about her problems with Griffin."

She gave a bitter laugh. "Is that what you're claiming she told you?" She narrowed her eyes at me. "Dax told me all about your little meeting, but unlike my husband, I think you're lying about knowing Wren. Wren never mentioned you to Dax, and she would have. It would have been part of the whole woe-is-me web of lies that she'd been weaving ever since she was a little girl. And trust me, I should know, because Wren and I used to be friends. But I really don't care about your little crusade. What I do care about is the way you threatened my husband and our marriage."

I wondered whether Dax had told her about the letter but doubted it. "We're just trying to find out what really happened," I said in a level voice.

"What happened was that Wren made a pass at my husband," she said, color rising in her cheeks. "She called him, sobbing, and he went to her house. But, of course when he got there, she'd been drinking and was all over him, claiming that he was 'the only man who really cared' about her. Then she kissed him. He pushed her away, because he didn't want to take advantage of her, and because he loves me. But the rejection pissed her off, so the next time he went over, she called the police and made up some sick story about him being obsessed with her."

The letter in my pocket almost seemed to be vibrating, though I knew it was my imagination.

I tried to keep my voice matter-of-fact. "Obviously, your version of events differs from what I know to be true."

"You don't know anything about Wren," she hissed, eyes glowing with rage. "If you did, you'd know this wasn't the first time she went after someone who was already in a relationship. There was a reason people around here didn't like her."

My mind flashed to what Wren had told me about Brian and Tessa, but I kept my expression steady.

"Did you know that Griffin is seeing a woman named Sandra Hall?" she asked, jutting out her chin.

"Yes."

"Did you know they were engaged before Wren set her sights on Griffin?"

This time, I couldn't hide my surprise, and she pounced, her tone almost victorious. "Oh, I guess no one told you that, huh? Yeah, Sandra and Griffin were engaged when Wren fixated on him. She'd known Sandra as long as she'd known me. She met with Griffin on the sly, flirting and sneaking around with him at night, even giving him a copy of the key to her house. And sure enough, Griffin fell head over heels for her, and he dumped Sandra.

Eventually Griffin was dumb enough to put a ring on her finger, but as soon as the chase was over, she got bored."

"Look—" I started, a little thrown and offended by the picture she was painting of Wren.

Her mouth curled into a snarl as she interrupted me. "That's when she went after my husband! Because that's what she did! If she needed counseling, she could have talked to Rene Joblin at the Mercy Center, but she didn't! She could have spoken to Leslie Sloan, another psychologist here in town. Hell, she could have talked to Ethel Lampier in the park, but she didn't do that either! Instead, she chose Dax **because** he was married. She got off by manipulating men in relationships into falling for her!"

Her gaze ricocheted between Oscar and me, daring us to contradict her, but we remained silent.

"If you really were a friend of Wren's, you would know she was a sociopath."

She turned and got back into her car without a second glance. We watched in silence as the engine roared to life and Tessa made a quick U-turn, back toward Pleasant Street. At the corner, she turned and accelerated, her car disappearing.

CHAPTER 25

At the diner, I picked at my BLT as Oscar and I rehashed the conversation. Sorting the lies from the truth felt impossible because all of it was tangled up in hurt feelings and small-town historics. I also reminded myself that no one could resist casting themselves as the wronged but noble hero of their own story.

I didn't want to admit that Wren may have lied to me, even by omission, but I couldn't deny the possibility. I also knew that Oscar had his own doubts about Wren, though he was kind enough not to double down on them now. Instead, he pointed out the waitress he'd spoken with and asked if I wanted to confirm that Griffin and Sandra had once been engaged, but I shook my head. I already suspected that part to be true.

But what about the rest of it? Did Wren have a

history of falling for men who were already in relationships? She'd put a sympathetic spin on her history with her high school boyfriend but mentioned nothing about Griffin and Sandra. By omitting that part, had she been trying to present herself in a better light, or did Tessa's account fall apart when other important truths were added to the story? Griffin, for instance, might have pursued Wren, not the other way around; he seemed the type who would have recognized her vulnerability after the death of her grandma. But again, it was impossible to know for sure.

After we finished, neither Oscar nor I wanted to walk. I think both of us were ready to be alone, so he drove me home after reminding me again that he'd be tied up most of the following day. Reece was digging in the garden while Louise was snapping green beans on the front porch of the cottage as I stepped into the house.

With my thoughts circling, I was again drawn to the bookshelves in the parlor. I waited for a sign to guide me, but when nothing materialized, I pulled down a book at random and flipped through the pages, stopping at the first highlighted passage.

It was by Emily Dickinson:

Tell all the Truth, but tell it slant—

I looked up, nodding in recognition: **Yes,** I thought, **that's exactly how it is.**

So much of what I'd been told felt **slanted.** The final lines captured my confusion as I'd groped my way through the investigation without much success.

The Truth must dazzle gradually
Or every man be blind—

On the opposite page was another short poem by Dickinson that Wren had not only highlighted but underlined as well.

As subtle as tomorrow
That never came,
A warrant, a conviction,
Yet but a name.

In the margin, she had written, **Believe!**

I smiled, thinking that perhaps my search for the truth wouldn't be in vain after all.

• • •

Later, I glanced out the window and saw Reece loading gardening implements into the wheelbarrow. I strolled out to the porch, struck by the beauty of the afternoon. There was just enough breeze to move the leaves, and the sky above was an unbroken expanse of blue. Inhaling the scent of freshly cut grass and a trace of the sea, I meandered down the steps.

Reece had just lifted the handles of the wheelbarrow

and begun to push when he saw me approaching. He stopped, lowering it back to the ground before reaching for a red bandanna in his back pocket and wiping his brow.

I stopped a few feet away, feeling his wary gaze. "Did the repair go okay this morning?"

"It did," he said. "But I wouldn't be surprised if another fuse blows soon. It's an old system. I'm sure that you didn't come out here to talk to me about the fuses, though."

"No, I didn't."

"You want to know about Wren." He tucked the bandanna back into his pocket. "My wife's been telling me about all the stuff you've been saying to her."

"I know it's probably hard to believe," I said.

"There's no ghost in that house," he said. "Louise and I have been inside hundreds of times. Earlier in the spring, I sanded and restained the floors in the entire place. Upstairs and down. I must have spent forty hours in the house that week, and nothing happened. I think either you're seeing things or you came here with that story ready to go."

"Why would I do that?"

He leaned over and pretended to adjust the gardening implements, as if buying time to find the words he wanted.

"I looked you up when I was in town," he said, straightening. "On the computer at the library. You're smart, you've got money, and maybe you think that this story you're telling will help you buy this property for less than it's worth. Then you can turn around and sell it for even more. That's how rich people stay rich." There was a suspicious light in his eyes as his gaze swept over me from head to toe.

I didn't take the bait.

"Your wife believes that I've seen and spoken to Wren."

"I know she does. She pointed out the drawing you made after I finished the repairs. We weren't snooping. It was on the sofa, and I couldn't help but see it."

"What can you tell me about Wren?"

He shrugged. "Nothing that my wife hasn't already told you."

"Why did no one find her until Monday?"

"Guests on that particular weekend left the house early and got home late because of the festival. No one wants to take a bath in the middle of the night, and frankly that bathroom isn't used all that much the rest of the year either. Wren used the tub more than anyone."

I tucked a hand in my pocket. "What did you think of Wren as a person?"

He shrugged. "She seemed like a good kid, but Louise knew her better than I did. I was always too busy working to spend much time with her. I'd see her coming and going, but that was about it."

"Did you ever see her business partner, Nash, here at the house?"

"Sure," he said. "They were friendly when they

were in high school, I think. And then they opened that store downtown together. So yeah, I saw him from time to time, but I don't really know him."

"And Griffin—he visited the house?"

Reece scowled at the name. "Yeah, he came around. Not after they were married, but before. He used to drive up in his Porsche at all hours of the night, always acting like the world owed him favors."

"You don't like him."

"No."

I didn't bother asking about Dax, since I already knew the answer. "Was Wren acting strange on the Friday she died? Was she upset about anything?"

"I didn't see her at all that day. I was in the woods, cutting up a fallen tree to use for firewood. If I'd known it was the last day she'd be alive, of course . . ."

I nodded after he trailed off. "I guess that's it. I appreciate your time."

I turned to leave when I heard his voice again.

"You really think someone killed her?"

"I do."

"Who?"

"I'm not sure yet."

"You think she knows who did it?" His expression was skeptical as he studied me, but I also detected a faint air of curiosity.

I considered the question. "I think she knows something important that will lead me to the answer."

"Why hasn't she told you yet?"

"I don't think she's ready."

"What's she waiting for?"

I remembered the poem I'd just read.

"Tomorrow," I said. "I think she's waiting for tomorrow."

CHAPTER 26

Friday dawned bright and clear. Taking advantage of the beautiful weather, I went for a run, had a light breakfast, and feeling virtuous, started a load of laundry. I tried to do a little work on the schematics while sitting on the porch, but I couldn't concentrate and put my computer aside.

Getting up, I decided to walk the property, hoping that my absence from the house might entice Wren to return. I took a seat on the bench on the edge of the bluff. Wren was right, I thought with a smile. Its location really was a bit diabolical. There was nothing to see but water and sky, and it was easy to imagine Wren's misery at being confined to this desolate spot for hours on end.

On the way back, I spotted Louise and Reece heading to their truck, but they didn't see me. They were dressed up; Louise was in a pleated dress with a lace collar, while Reece sported a dated blazer and white shirt. Their impending absence triggered an idea that I hoped might lure Wren back from wherever she was. As their truck disappeared down the drive, I returned to the small shed where I'd found her things.

Pulling down the box I needed, I found the recipe box and brought it back to the house. I thumbed through the cards, hoping to find something appealing that wasn't beyond my capabilities.

I finally selected a recipe for coq au vin—Google informed me that the literal translation was "rooster in wine." I drove into town to buy the ingredients, doing my best to dodge the crowds. By the time I got back, it was early afternoon, and recalling what Wren had taught me, I measured out ingredients into ramekins and bowls, chopped the vegetables and herbs, and laid out all my implements and cookware. Then I began crisping the bacon and browning the chicken. The only tricky part was igniting the cognac, but I felt like a culinary hero when it all worked out and my eyebrows remained intact. Before putting on the lid, I added the remaining ingredients, except the mushrooms, which, according to her recipe, I was supposed to add later.

As Wren had also taught me, I put the ingredients away, cleaned the counters, and washed what I'd used. I had just begun to dry my hands when I heard her.

"Are you making coq au vin?"

Her voice was coming from the parlor, and I exhaled, releasing tension that I didn't know I'd been holding. Suddenly nervous, I refolded the dish towel and ran a quick hand through my hair before she appeared in the kitchen doorway.

She was dressed for a night on the town: faded jeans, a green, sleeveless, V-necked top, glittery sandals, red fingernail polish, her hair pinned up, and small gold hoop earrings that matched a distressed-looking heart-shaped locket around her neck. A touch of lip gloss brought out the fullness of her mouth, and dark mascara accentuated the unusual shape and color of her eyes. She was extraordinarily beautiful, and I had to clear my throat before I was able to speak.

"I am. And you look dressed to kill," I told her and whistled.

"Oh, please," she said, rolling her eyes.

"I'm serious," I said. "I love the locket, too. Is it an antique?"

She absently reached for it. "It was my grandma's. When I wear it, I always think of her, and I feel like I'm going to need a bit of her strength today."

"Big plans?"

She shrugged without answering before breathing in deeply. "Nothing smells better than coq au vin. I used to make it a lot. It was one of the meals my grandma actually enjoyed."

I smiled, pleased that she was exhibiting none of the confusion of the previous day. "It was a meal

I thought I could pull off without your help," I told her.

"Is it my recipe? From the box in the cupboard? Or did you find it online?"

"Yours," I answered, pointing to the recipe box. "I hope you don't mind."

"Not at all," she said. "It's in the cupboard for the same reason the books are in the parlor. But I'm pretty sure you're the first guest to take advantage of my stash of favorites."

"The beef bourguignon was so delicious, I couldn't resist."

"Did you remember to add the bay leaf?"

"I did," I said. "Chopped it up until it looked like oregano." When her eyes widened, I laughed. "I'm kidding. I also made sure to get the stock from Let's Meat."

"Good for you," she said. "But I'm kind of surprised to find you here. I figured you'd be working today."

"Oscar has other things to do," I said, "so thc day's all mine. How about you? I'm guessing that you'll be heading into town?"

"Later," she said. "I'm going to the festival tonight."

"Are you meeting anyone there?" I asked, trying to sound casual.

"Why?" She lifted an eyebrow. "Do you want to come?"

If you could leave the house, then I'd love to . . .

"It's not really my thing," I demurred.

She laughed. "I'm going by myself, but I won't be

staying long. A band I like is playing at seven-thirty. I should be home early."

"Monkey Tears?"

She did a double take. "Oh, that's right," she said, her face clearing. "You saw me wearing their jacket. They're great, and I still can't figure out how Griffin managed to get them to come."

I hooked a thumb toward the pot on the stove. "This still has to cook a little while. Do you want to sit in the parlor? Until you have to leave?"

"Sure," she said. "And while I'll admit that I'm impressed you're trying your hand in the kitchen again, I'm afraid you've already forgotten the most important step."

"A glass of wine?"

"Get yourself some and I'll meet you on the sofa."

By the time I entered the parlor, wine in hand, Wren was sitting with her own glass of wine. She tucked a leg up and turned as I sat down beside her.

"I love that you're learning how to prepare your own meals," she said.

"I also started a load of laundry this morning."

"It sounds like you're finally growing up."

"That's what Oscar said."

She smiled before growing serious. "I feel a little better today. Less **off** than I've been lately."

"I'm glad to hear that," I said, resisting the impulse to move a strand of hair that had fallen out of her loose chignon.

"I'm sorry that I've been preoccupied with all the

stuff I told you about. It's been hard to relax, but talking to you has helped a lot."

"Happy to help," I said. "And don't worry about it. Are you looking forward to tonight?"

"I think it'll be good for me to get out. And then, as soon as I get back, I'm going to pour myself another glass of wine, take a nice, warm bath, and get a good night's sleep. It's just what I need to keep the blues away."

I felt a twist in my gut and glanced away, realizing again that she had no inkling of what was coming. She must have noticed something in my expression because she leaned toward me.

"What's wrong? Did I say something that upset you?"

"No," I said. "I was just reminded of something else. But I was wondering if you're nervous about attending the festival alone."

"Because of Griffin, you mean?"

"Dax and Nash, too."

"Not really. There are going to be thousands of people there, so I think I can get in and out without running into any of them. But even if I do, I doubt that any of them will make a scene."

"Do you think Dax will keep his distance? Since the police warned him to stay away?"

"I hope so." She tucked a lock of hair behind her ear before going on. "I didn't mention it to you, but not too long ago, he left a letter in my bike basket, when I was in town running errands."

"Did you tell the police?"

"No," she answered. "I didn't discover it until I was already home, and I crumpled it up and tossed it. I'm sure it's still in the shed somewhere if I change my mind about showing it to the police, but right now, I'm just focusing on putting all of this behind me."

"I don't like him."

"You haven't even met him."

"It doesn't matter," I said, not bothering to correct her. "I'm on your side."

"I wish more people were these days," she said.

She shimmered, the outline of her shoulders and legs losing some definition. I was reminded that she could vanish at any moment. Her last visit had ended long before sunset, and recalling how Oscar's call had made her disappear, I set my glass on the coffee table.

"Hold on for a second," I said, reaching into my back pocket and turning off my phone. I stood up to make sure my computer was off as well.

"What are you doing?"

"I don't want us to be disturbed," I said, sitting next to her again. "Technology can be intrusive."

Looking around the house as if seeing it for the last time, she was suddenly pensive. "It's going to be sad when I sell this place. It's the only home I've ever known. On the other hand, it will mean that I won't have to scrimp and save the way I've had to my whole life." She sighed. "I'm sure I'm still going to check prices compulsively and shop at thrift stores. Old habits, you know. I saved my babysitting money, then money I earned at the drugstore for two years to buy my first car."

"Your grandma didn't help?"

"Are you kidding? Not a chance. She was the kind of woman who would bring items to the register and demand that the manager discount them on the spot. As a child, I was mortified by it, but I suppose it taught me to be careful with money. And no one believed in the value of financial independence more than my grandma did. When I sell this place, I don't want to end up like one of those lottery winners who have to declare bankruptcy a few years after they collect their prize."

You won't, I thought. **You'll never get the chance.**

When I didn't respond, she stared at me, her brows knit together. "You just got that look again."

"I must be tired. I slept in this morning, but I guess it wasn't enough."

I wasn't sure she believed me, but she let it pass. "I do have a favor to ask. It feels a little weird, though, and you can of course say no."

"What is it?"

She toyed with one of her earrings, as if hesitating over the right way to frame her request. "I know that you're not only rich, but superrich," she said. "The stories about your upbringing made that plain as day, so I was wondering if I could call you if I ever need financial advice. Or talk to you about the best way to manage the money from the sale of this property. I don't want to make mistakes, but I don't even know what I don't know about all this."

"I'll gladly talk to you forever about anything you'd like."

She smiled. "Do you want to play a game?"

"Charades? Boggle?"

"I was thinking about a drinking game instead," she said, a mischievous gleam in her eyes.

"I played some of those in college. Which one?"

"Two Truths and a Lie," she said. "It'll help us get to know each other even better."

"Do you really think that's possible?"

"Trust me," she said with a provocative wink. "There's still a lot you don't know."

I felt my heart skip a beat. "Can you remind me how to play?"

"It's easy. You make three statements about yourself, but one of them has to be untrue. I try to guess which one is a lie. If I'm wrong, I drink, but if I'm right, you drink. Then it's my turn. You can go first."

I thought about it and said the first things that came to mind. "I'm an architect, I live in Manhattan, and I competed in 4-H as a child."

"Too easy," she chided. "Try again. And make each statement believable but interesting. It's more fun that way."

"Why don't you go first? So I have time to think about it."

"Sure," she said. I watched as she moistened her lips before starting. "I once climbed so high in a tree that a fireman had to help me down. I French-kissed a girl named Susan in tenth grade. I had so much pumpkin pie at Thanksgiving when I was nine that I threw up at the table."

I squinted, trying to read her as she lifted an eyebrow. "I'm going to say the first one. Firemen don't do that."

"Drink," she said. "That one is true. I was seven years old and we were at the park. When I froze in the top branches of the tree, Bill Henderson, the fire chief, helped me down. He happened to be at the park with his family."

I dutifully swallowed a mouthful of wine. "Which one was the lie?"

"Wouldn't you like to know?" she said with a smirk. "Your turn."

It took me a minute to come up with credible scenarios. "I've been to Greece. I've met Meryl Streep. I saw **Hamilton** before it premiered on Broadway."

The speed of her answer stunned me. "You've never been to Greece."

"How did you know?"

"Because you would have mentioned it when we talked about my dream of traveling abroad, or when you were telling me about your sister's trips. Drink."

I took another gulp of wine. When she spoke again, her voice was solemn. "I lost my virginity at eighteen. When I was nine, I got on the riding mower and drove myself to town. I am allergic to penicillin."

I considered the choices. "I'm going to say that you're lying about being allergic to penicillin."

"Drink," she said. "Aside from hay fever, it's my only known allergy."

I drained my glass, wondering again which of her other statements was true.

"A drawing I made of the Eiffel Tower hangs on the wall in my bedroom. I was thirteen when I kissed a girl for the first time. I went fishing one summer in Long Island and caught a shark."

She stared at me with an appraising eye. "This one's tougher. But I'm going to say there's no framed Eiffel Tower drawing." She nodded at my empty glass. "Better pour yourself a refill."

I opened my mouth in shock. "Do I have a tell? You can't possibly be right all the time."

"What can I say? I'm good at this game."

I opened my hands. "Of course you are."

• • •

We played for another twenty minutes, until it was time to add the mushrooms to the coq au vin.

Wren followed me into the kitchen and leaned against the counter, watching as I tasted it, added a little more salt and pepper, and removed it from the burner.

"Good?"

"Delicious," I answered. "But I forgot to put the bread in the oven."

"It happens when you've been drinking."

I laughed, wishing we could eat together, but refraining from suggesting it in case it caused her to withdraw. "I think I'll put it in later. I'm not hungry yet, so I'll reheat this for dinner."

"You sure?"

"I'd rather keep playing. And you were right. I did learn some new things about you, even if I still don't know which statements were true and which were false."

"It's a good game to play early in a relationship."

"Is that what we have?" I asked softly.

She met my eyes and held them. "I'd like to think so."

I desperately wanted to kiss her, and it took everything I had to hold back. The afternoon sun had already peaked, and I knew that our time together would soon be coming to an end.

This time, maybe forever.

"Then you're late to the party," I said. "I've known it for a while now."

She looked away and absently fiddled with her locket. "This isn't a good idea," she said quietly. "For either of us."

"I know," I said.

"We should stop."

"I know that, too. But I don't want to."

Our eyes met again, and in that moment, I was

certain Wren had come into my life for a reason. If nothing else, she'd made me feel alive, as if for all the long years before, I'd been sleepwalking through my existence. I could hardly remember the man I'd been before I arrived here, and it struck me that she'd turned me into the kind of person I'd always wanted to be.

"I love you," I whispered. I'd never said the words to a lover before, but now they seemed as natural and undeniable as the rising sun.

"Come with me," she murmured in response, the sound more seductive than anything I'd ever heard. "I want you to do something for me."

She pushed off the counter and slowly walked to the bottom of the stairs. Then, turning to face me, she slipped off one sandal, then the other. I thought she would stop there, but instead, she nodded toward my shoes.

I removed my loafers and socks, and for a moment, we simply stared at each other. Holding my gaze, she unsnapped the top button of her jeans, making it difficult for me to breathe. She peeked at me over her shoulder as she unhurriedly climbed the steps.

I trailed behind her as if under a spell, noticing the sensual sway and shape of her hips. When she reached the top, she turned to make sure I was following her before moving deliberately toward the open door of my bedroom.

My senses were on fire as I tracked the dark waterfall of her hair when she released it from its confining hairpins; I heard the gentle padding of her footsteps and inhaled the scent of her perfume.

After entering my bedroom, she turned and faced me while I closed the door behind me. Sunlight streamed through the windows, and when she glanced toward them, I knew instinctively what she wanted me to do. I crossed the room and pulled the curtains. Then I slowly approached her, stopping when I was close.

She looked up at me. "Do you remember the rules?" she whispered.

I nodded, watching as she took a small step backward.

With casual grace she reached for the bottom of her blouse and pulled it over her head before dropping it onto the floor. I saw the outline of her breasts through her bra as I unbuttoned my shirt and allowed that to fall free as well. I could feel my rapid breath as she slowly ran her finger over the waistline of her jeans, stopping when she reached the zipper. I could almost hear my own heartbeat as she pulled the zipper down, loosening the jeans before shimmying out of them and kicking them aside.

I took her in, knowing I'd never seen anyone so beautiful. Desire flooded every nerve in my body. More than anything, I wanted to take her in my arms. Instead, I forced myself to steady my breathing and took off my pants, leaving me standing before her in my boxers. I thought she would stop there, but she didn't. Instead, she reached behind her back and with a quick twist, loosened her lacy bra before she let it drop. Her panties came next, and I knew then it was my turn.

I stood naked, taking in all of her, suddenly feeling the overwhelming heat of our connection. She stepped closer then, and closer still, until I could feel the heat of her body mingling with my own.

She reached up, nearly caressing my face, and though I couldn't feel it, the sensation was nonetheless exquisite, as though she was really touching me. When it was my turn, I used a finger, starting at her chin and jaw before tracing down to the area between her breasts and then lower, to her navel, before stopping.

Her eyes were heavy-lidded with desire as she moved her hands over my chest and waist, and I did the same to her in return. She was breathing rapidly, and when I had to lick my lips because my mouth had gone dry, she stood on her toes and moved her lips so close to mine that I imagined I could taste her. My eyes closed in pleasure as I felt her breath on mine.

"I love you, too," she whispered, the words flowing with her breath, and I suddenly understood everything that Sylvia had ever wanted for me, just as I knew I'd been waiting for Wren all along.

• • •

We ended up lying in the bed, sometimes exchanging heated whispers and gasps of pleasure, but other times saying nothing at all. I marveled at the depth of my feelings for her, wishing fervently for the afternoon to stretch on forever.

But inevitably, as the sun dipped toward the horizon, her presence began to stutter and blink out, losing its density and sensual detail. In the last minutes we were together, she was virtually translucent, and I felt my stomach begin to contract, making it hard to speak.

"Tell me what I need to do," I begged. "Tell me what I need to know."

She stared at me, bemused. "What are you talking about?"

"I need to know how to help you."

She smiled, her green-gold eyes liquid as she stared over at me. "All you need to do is come back to me."

I had just opened my mouth to press for more when she vanished completely.

• • •

I lay there for a long time afterward, replaying those hours together. But as the fading light leaked through the curtains, I forced myself from the bed and pulled open the drapes, staring out at the bruise-colored sky of dusk. I dressed and went downstairs, finding Paulie pacing from the parlor to the kitchen and back again. I checked her water, thinking she might be thirsty, but she ignored the bowl. Deciding to try feeding her, I opened a can and scooped the food into her bowl, but when I put it down, she sniffed at it and walked away, only to continue her pacing.

I turned on my phone and realized Oscar had called. Thinking I could call him back after dinner, I hit the switch on the stove light, pausing when it didn't turn on. I tried the lights in the kitchen, only to see they were out as well. It didn't take long to realize that while I'd been upstairs with Wren, the power had blown again.

Annoyed, I thought about traipsing over to the cottage to seek Reece's help, but I wasn't sure whether he and Louise had returned. More than that, I wasn't in the mood to talk to anyone, so I pulled up YouTube on my phone, quickly finding a video on how to reset a breaker. If restoring power required anything beyond that, I knew I'd have to solicit Reece's help. But as Wren had pointed out, there was something worthy in learning to be self-sufficient.

Paulie made a funny sound behind me, not quite her normal meow.

"Oh, hush, Paulie. I can do this," I mumbled over my shoulder.

I looked for the flashlight in the pantry, but oddly it was missing. I turned on my phone flashlight instead and pulled open the cellar door. The stairs descended into cave-like darkness. Spooky, but I reminded myself of the layout of the cellar and braced myself for the descent.

I heard Paulie snarl in the same instant I heard footsteps behind me. I didn't have time to turn before I felt a hard shove at my back, and all at once I was falling. I hit the stairs below hard and felt momentum flip me over. I came to a stop on the cellar floor, reeling in darkness. As if from a distance, I heard someone groaning, only to realize that the sound was my own before I lost consciousness.

CHAPTER 27

I must have blacked out for only a few seconds, because when I opened my eyes, I saw a blurry figure backlit at the top of the stairs. My body, especially my knee, was exploding in coronas of pain, but fear took over as the figure began to descend the steps.

Someone is trying to kill me.

Adrenaline surged through me. I'd never been a fighter, but I instinctively understood that I had to get up. I rolled onto my stomach, absolute panic overwhelming the pain, and got on all fours. I started to inch away, but by then the figure had reached me, and I felt a sudden blow to my back, the impact excruciating.

Whatever hit me was hard and heavy, and it left me wheezing for breath. The darkness was complete, and I could see nothing at all. Nonetheless I lurched forward on all fours. Another blow struck my shoulder, pain electrifying the length of my arm, leaving my fingers tingling, but I somehow lunged again.

My head collided with the washing machine, and I reached up and pulled, trying to get to my feet. Another blow glanced off my upper back as I was rising, but I spun to the side, smashing into the laundry table. The next blow narrowly missed me, and I heard the crash of wood on the metal washer, darkness finally aiding me. **That one would have killed me,** I registered dully. Turning, I grabbed for anything I could find. It was the box of laundry detergent, and I heaved it, hearing a thud as it connected with the attacker, but it did little to slow whoever it was. I heaved the bottle of bleach next in a frantic motion before I latched onto the iron.

I turned and swung, the iron colliding into flesh. I stepped forward, swinging wildly again, feeling a sudden fury combined with a primal will to survive. Another one of the swings landed hard, and I heard a yelp, followed by the sound of something wooden hitting the concrete. I surged forward to press my advantage, swinging the iron and ignoring the agonizing pain in my knee. My foot kicked something. Judging by the sound as it bounced and rolled across the concrete, it might have been a baseball bat.

It was then that the attacker must have turned away; an instant later, I barely made out a figure fleeing up the steps. I staggered after, my knee on fire, but by the time I reached the staircase, I could see no one. Gasping, I used the railing to pull myself up the stairs. In the pantry, I anticipated another attack, but it was empty.

I limped through a house now dimmed by dusk and reached the front door. Limping onto the porch, I looked around frantically, just in time to spot a distant figure disappearing into the shadow of the woods, toward the road.

With my knee, I knew there was no way I could catch whoever it was, not to mention survive another confrontation.

• • •

I dragged myself back to the kitchen, my body trembling with adrenaline, and put a hand on the counter to steady myself. Pain radiated from my back and shoulder, where the blows had landed, spreading fire all the way to my organs, and I could barely put any weight on my knee. I must have wrenched it badly in my tumble. After a long time, my breath began to stabilize and my mind cleared, but I remained shaky. I tentatively stretched out my arms and winced as I rolled my shoulders, wondering if anything was broken. I gently touched my ribs, and while my entire side throbbed, nothing protruded, and the pain, although sharp, was bearable.

I needed my phone to call the police, but it was lost somewhere in the cellar. I considered lighting one of the candles Louise had left in the foyer, but

I didn't think I could navigate the steps with it in my hand.

But even if I had my phone, what would I tell them?

That I was pushed down the stairs and attacked but had no idea who'd done it; at best, I could only offer my hunches. I thought of Nash, Dax, and Griffin, realizing if I could find them—if I knew with certainty where each of them was at this very moment—I might know who'd attacked me. Whoever it was still had to be in the vicinity. I didn't have time to waste talking to the police. The killer had just been here.

It was a better idea to call Oscar, and a quick glance out the window let me know that Reece and Louise had returned. But I also needed a weapon in case the attacker had doubled back for a second run at me. I thought about grabbing a butcher knife but wasn't sure I was steady or strong enough for another close-in encounter. Instead, I staggered to the parlor and scanned the room, ultimately seizing the poker from the fireplace, along with my wallet and keys. I clung to the railing with both hands as I descended the porch steps, the poker beneath my armpit. I could feel my knee growing stiffer as I hobbled across the lawn toward the lights of the cottage. The first stars had begun to appear in the nighttime sky. At the front door of the cottage, I knocked, then pounded. It took a few moments, but Louise pulled open the door, still wearing the fancy dress I'd seen her in earlier, though she'd topped it with an apron.

"Oh my God!" she cried, her eyes widening. "You're bleeding! Are you all right?"

I reached up, the blood in my hair staining my fingers, thinking, **I've gotten more head wounds in Heatherington than I've had in the rest of my life combined.**

"I need to borrow your phone," I rasped through dry lips, but she was barely listening. She looked terrified.

"We just got back—what happened to you?"

Behind her, I heard Reece call out, "Who is it, Louise?"

"Will you please get the phone?" I urged.

"Are you calling the police?" Her voice trembled. "Maybe Reece can help—"

"Please!" I snapped, holding out my hand. I watched as her eyes flashed to the poker.

"Louise?" Reece's voice sounded impatient.

"It's Tate," she called over her shoulder before pulling out an old-fashioned flip phone from the pocket of her apron.

Without a word, I took it and moved away from the door so I wouldn't be overheard. I called Oscar, quickly explaining what had happened and what I needed.

When he realized that I wasn't going to listen to his pleas to go straight to the hospital or the police, he reluctantly agreed to my requests.

• • •

Back in the house, I stood before the mirror in the foyer and saw how I'd appeared to Louise. There was blood in my hair and on my cheek, which I hurriedly used a dish towel to remove. My scalp was tender to the touch, but like my previous head wound, it seemed manageable. The throbbing in my back and shoulder had settled into a dull but constant ache, but my knee was a different matter. With every step I took, pain shot through my body like an electric jolt.

Still, I knew what I had to do, and I limped to my car, the fireplace poker still in hand. The roads were quiet, but as I neared the fairground, the traffic picked up, and half a mile out, cars and trucks were parked on both sides of the road. Hoping I'd find someplace closer to park, I continued to the lot, where I was waved off by an attendant wearing an orange vest. Forced to return the way I'd just come, I eventually found a spot near the other late arrivals, a long way from the entrance.

I slowly hobbled toward the fairground, the sound of thumping music and microphone feedback gradually growing louder. My knee was swelling with every step, but I gritted my teeth, forcing myself forward. Oscar's SUV eventually drew up alongside me; he was no doubt looking for a place to park just as I had. He must have recognized me because his brake lights flashed, and after a moment

I arduously climbed into the Escalade, hoisting my bad leg after me.

"I warned you," he said as soon as I closed the door. "I literally warned you that it wasn't a good idea to threaten a murderer, didn't I?"

"If I hadn't confronted them, we wouldn't be closing in on them now."

"Do you still think you can suss out which one of them was at the house tonight?"

"Hopefully, the innocent will tell us where they've been or who they've been with, meaning they'll have alibis."

"This really is something for the police to handle."

"We went over this on the phone already."

"You're making a mistake. Even if we do find Griffin or Dax or Nash, what makes you think they'll answer your questions? You'll be lucky if you're not attacked again."

He had a point, but I was unmoved. We'd been given an opening, and I had to pursue it.

"Drop me off as close as you can," I said. "I'll wait for you."

He pulled over near the entrance to the parking area, and I opened the door. Then, remembering, I asked, "Why did you call me earlier today?"

"To let you know that Aldrich pushed our meeting to tomorrow," he said. "I'll park and be back as soon as I can."

After I got out, Oscar turned the Escalade around

and drove back the way we'd come. Time seemed to slow, minutes passing like hours, before he reappeared.

"I feel like I had to park in Florida," he said, panting. "I think everyone from the Cape is here. How the hell are we going to find these guys?"

"I have some ideas," I answered.

I limped alongside Oscar, eyeing the scores of people waiting in line for tickets. Oscar pointed toward the VIP area.

"Let me see if Griffin left us the passes he promised. I know we pissed him off, but he might have forgotten to cancel them."

At the VIP table, I watched as Oscar showed his ID. A minute later, he was walking toward me, digging through an envelope and then pulling out a couple of wristbands. "Not that you care, but there are lanyards for backstage passes, too."

I put the wristband on, and the two of us made our way toward the entrance.

• • •

The fairground teemed with boisterous festivalgoers, many of them holding Solo cups full of beer and wearing masks.

"Where to?" Oscar asked.

"The office," I said. "Someone has to know where Griffin is."

We wove our way through the raucous crowds,

eventually reaching the office. Immediately upon entering, I saw a young woman in a red T-shirt and jeans, shouting on speakerphone at what sounded like Griffin's voice while frantically digging through a file cabinet. She cried, "Got them!" before disconnecting the call with a stab of her finger. She pulled out a set of blueprints and turned, finally spotting us.

"Get out," she barked, pocketing her phone. "You can't be in here. The office is closed."

"We're trying to find Griffin—" I began.

She tucked the blueprints under her arm as she strode toward the door. "Did you hear me? I said, 'Get out!' I have to lock up!"

"We're happy to leave," I said. "Just tell us where Griffin is."

"Stage Five," she said, reaching around me to the door handle. "Where the hell else would he be?"

"Why Stage Five?"

"Because the generator went out!" she shouted, opening the door to reveal the milling crowds outside. "He needs these specs, and he's not going to have time to talk to you. He's got to figure out a way to get the power on again."

We followed her out as she jammed a key into the handle to lock the door.

"How long has he been there?"

"Since it blew out in the middle of the five o'clock show!"

"Are you sure?"

"Yeah, I'm sure! I just came from there! Now get the hell out of my way. I don't have time for you right now."

She rushed off, leaving us behind. Oscar turned toward me.

"I think we can safely assume it wasn't Griffin at the house tonight."

I nodded, disappointed, realizing that I'd suspected him more than anyone.

• • •

As we approached the food and drink concessions, I knew there was no way we'd be able to track down Nash or Dax in these crowds. The fairground was too large, and given that so many attendees were wearing masks, I might not recognize them even if they were standing next to me.

Staring out at the hordes of people, I said, "I think we should have Nash find us."

"What do you mean?" Oscar asked.

"Let me borrow your phone."

I dug through my wallet for Nash's business card and flipped it over to find the cellphone number he had scrawled on the back. Oscar handed me his phone and I dialed. After several rings he answered, sounding uncertain.

"Hey, Nash . . . this is Steve!" I shouted over the din.

"Who?"

"I just saw some dude scrape the hell out of your Prius! Tore your side mirror completely off!"

"Wait . . . what?"

"Your car!" I shouted. "Some dude just sideswiped your Prius! You gotta get out here fast! I'm trying to keep him here until you can deal with it . . ."

"Someone hit my car?"

"Just get out here!" I shouted before disconnecting. When the phone rang a moment later, I didn't bother to answer. Oscar and I hurried back to the entrance.

Within minutes, Nash and a burly friend were striding in our direction. A clown mask was pushed back on Nash's head, revealing his worried expression. They passed us without a glance and hustled to the gravel lot.

We followed, waiting until we were deep into the grid of closely parked cars before I called out his name.

He stopped and turned, but in the darkness, he didn't seem to recognize me until we closed the distance between us. When he did recognize us, he waved us off and kept going.

"Go away! I don't have time to talk right now! I have to deal with my car."

"Your car is fine," I called out. "We were the ones who called you."

He slowed to a full stop before turning around, bewildered. "You called me?"

"We just need to know where you were earlier tonight," I said.

"What? Why?" Nash frowned before confusion began to give way to anger.

"Tell us or tell the police," I bluffed. "They're already on their way."

Nash paled. He opened his mouth to respond, but nothing came out.

His friend cut in, stepping in front of Nash. "Who? Us?"

"Nash was seen fleeing the scene of an assault earlier tonight . . ." I bluffed again.

"Whoa, whoa, whoa . . ." the friend interjected. "It wasn't Nash. We've both been here the whole time. We're with friends. We have witnesses."

"What time did you get here?"

"Before five." The guy bristled, crossing his thick arms. "He picked me up from work at the warehouse at four-thirty. I don't know what's going on here . . ."

"And neither of you left the festival since then?"

"We've been here the whole time," he reiterated, before narrowing his eyes at me. "What the hell is going on?"

I knew instinctively he was telling the truth, and I tuned the rest of it out, even as his inquiries grew more belligerent. Exchanging glances, Oscar and I turned and walked off, leaving Nash and his companion behind.

• • •

"Dax," Oscar said. "If the others were here, it has to be him."

I hesitated, recalling the calculated quality of his responses during our meeting with him.

"Has to be," I agreed, although it was hard to reconcile his weaselly affect with the rage-filled attack against me.

"How do we prove it, though?" Oscar asked. "I doubt that he's going to confess, and you said yourself you didn't see who it was."

"I'm not sure," I said. "Maybe when I hit him with the iron, it left some kind of mark."

As Oscar seemed to think about my answer, I suddenly sensed more than saw a familiar movement at the edge of my vision, almost like the flash of a mirror's reflection. As I stared straight ahead, the flickering solidified into something I recognized, and I tracked it as it slowly moved toward the road leading out of the fairground. I could feel it beginning to tug at me.

All at once, the flickering vanished, then reappeared where I'd first seen it and tracked toward the road again, like a scene on repeat. Again, I felt its pull, but as I watched, I noticed a second flickering in the opposite direction, hovering in the sky above the festival. I'd never seen simultaneous flickering in opposite directions, and as I tried to understand what it meant, I realized the pulsing over the festival seemed less intense, less urgent, somehow. The one leading up the road seemed to demand that I follow, but the other one . . .

"Are you seeing something again?" Oscar asked, breaking into my thoughts.

"And feeling something."

As though in a time loop, the flickering on the road vanished and reappeared again, its beckoning even stronger now, the pull impossible to resist. The one over the festival, however, remained soft and steady, and while I continued to watch it, Wren's final words came rushing back to me, almost as though she was whispering in my ear. My eyes widened, and suddenly knowing what I was supposed to do, I began staggering toward the road, moving as fast as I could.

"Where are you going?" Oscar asked, hurrying after me.

"I have to go back to the house."

"Now? Why?"

"Because Wren told me to," I said, glancing over at him. "The last thing she said to me was that if I wanted to help her, all I needed to do was come back."

"I'm not sure that's a good idea," Oscar said. "What if Dax is waiting for you?"

"I'll be careful."

"Then I'll come, too."

I shook my head.

"No," I said. "I need to go alone, or Wren won't

appear. But I think another part of the answer is still here at the festival. I need you to stay here and look for them."

"Them?" he asked. "Don't you mean Dax?"

I continued to stare at him. "And Tessa," I said. "You need to find both of them."

CHAPTER 28

The house was still dark as I pulled up the drive. I'd lost sight of the flickering when I reached the main road, but when I climbed out of the car, I noticed an intermittent glimmer dancing above the house, more motion than light. Turning toward the blank windows and empty porch, I felt a prickle of foreboding. Had Reece come by to check the fuse box and been unable to repair it? Was he even aware that the house had lost power? In my frantic haste, I had forgotten to tell him, and the lights were on at the cottage, so perhaps not.

I checked my watch, noting that it was eight-thirty. Wren had arrived home at this exact hour on the first night of the festival two years earlier, and it felt like an omen.

Limping to the door, I unlocked it and groped around on the table in the foyer for the candles and matches Louise had left there. I tore open the package, shoving two candles into my back pocket and lighting the third. The flame cast long shadows as I circled the parlor, turning the normally cheery room into a silent, desolate stage.

"Wren?" I called out.

Only one version of her had ever appeared in darkness, and I didn't expect to see her outside the bathroom but wanted to make sure. Holding the burning candle before me, I carefully inspected each of the main-floor rooms. Pausing in the kitchen, I thought about removing the lid of the Dutch oven on the stove and fanning the aroma. Earlier today, the scent had been enough to lure Wren to my side, but because the meal had been unrefrigerated, I wasn't sure whether it had gone bad, so the lid remained in place.

I opened the cellar door and thought again about trying to rescue my phone. But the candle's weak light barely penetrated the inky depths of the stairwell. When I peered down, the complete darkness beneath the house evoked a gaping hole, and for a moment, I couldn't summon the courage I needed to descend.

I jumped as something brushed my leg, but it was only Paulie, purring as she rubbed against me. I reached down to stroke her, wincing as my knee bent. **Forget it,** I said to myself. **I'll look for the phone later.** Besides, I needed to save my strength to get upstairs, where I had a feeling the answers I was seeking would be found.

I closed the cellar door and hobbled out to the main staircase. Leaning on the railing with my elbow while trying to hold the candle, I winced with every step. At the top, I slowly navigated the hall, stopping before the hallway bathroom. Finding it empty, I went to my room and alternately pushed and pulled the bench into the hallway, indifferent to the scratches I was no doubt leaving on the wooden plank floors. After maneuvering it into place, I collapsed on the bench. I dripped wax onto the floor and set the candle in the puddle until it hardened into a makeshift holder. Paulie watched with interest, then jumped up on the bench beside me.

I tried to reconstruct Wren's time line that night. How long after her return had she lingered downstairs before coming up to take her bath?

I absently stroked Paulie's back, waiting and watching. Finally, I let out a long exhale and closed my eyes. "I'm here, Wren," I whispered into the dark. "Tell me how to help."

The house creaked and settled around me, its timbers cracking like human joints. There was still no sound from the bathroom. I waited and watched some more.

Then, after what felt like hours but was probably only several minutes, I heard the squeak of hinges. The sign hanging on the doorknob tapped against the wood as the door swung open, and the pipes began to squeal.

Suddenly, I heard water starting to fill the tub.

• • •

I freed the candle and held it before me as I limped to the bathroom, steeling myself for whatever might happen next. Like the light on my camera, the candle's illumination dimmed in the suffocating dark. I pulled out the second candle and lit that one with the first, but it did little to make the bathroom brighter. I held one candle in each fist as I circled the room, feeling the hairs on my neck rise when I slowly began to approach the tub.

Wren was dead. She was naked, lying face up in a shallow pool of water that was murky with bodily fluids. Her skin was gray and swollen, encasing her like a grotesque wrapper; her eyes were open but cloudy and blank. When I glanced at the faucet, I saw dried blood encrusted with fragments of flesh and hair. I felt bile rise in my throat as I wondered why this was being shown to me.

At the same time, I could see why the medical examiner had labeled the death suspicious. The scene just didn't make sense. The faucet was too low, protruding into the hollow of the tub and making it impossible to lie with one's head at that end. What the medical examiner and Dugan didn't know, but I did, was that Wren **had** been using a towel that night; I'd seen one wrapped around her. But there was no towel on the floor near the tub, nor was it draped over the side of the tub.

So where was it?

Swinging the candles around, I located a stack of folded towels on the shelf beneath the sink. But now, there was a tall glass of wine on one side of the sink and a pile of clothes on the other. A pair of sandals was on the floor. I assumed I was looking at the scene when Wren had been discovered by Louise, but if that was true, the question came again: why was I meant to see it?

I forced myself to look over at the tub a second time. Seeing Wren in this state felt especially cruel after the afternoon we'd just spent together, and I didn't want to remember her like this. I understood why Louise had said she'd never forget finding Wren this way, and I closed my eyes, knowing that it would be impossible for me to forget as well.

It was then that I heard the faint sound of humming and realized someone was coming up the stairs. When I turned toward the tub again, Wren had vanished, and the bathtub was dry. The wineglass, clothes, and sandals near the sink were gone as well.

As the humming grew louder, I recognized the tune I'd heard from the kitchen on my first day in the house. I knew it was Wren even before she entered the bathroom, and though she automatically hit the light switch, she didn't seem to notice when it didn't come on. Nor did she see me; instead, her eyes swept over me without registering any sign of my presence. In that instant, I understood I would be only a spectator to all that would happen next.

I immediately recognized her outfit: she was wearing the same faded jeans, green top, and glittery sandals I'd seen earlier, the same clothing she'd worn to the festival two years ago. I noticed the same gold hoop earrings and the distressed, heart-shaped locket around her neck. In her hand, she held a glass of white wine. Setting it on the counter next to the sink, she crossed to the tub and bent over to start the flow of water. She ran her hand under the water, testing the temperature before inserting the old-fashioned rubber plug to seal the drain.

She crossed the room to close and lock the door. Then, standing in front of the sink, she took a sip of wine and stared at herself in the mirror. She made a series of funny faces—puffing out her cheeks, crossing her eyes, and puckering up her lips in an exaggerated kiss—before heaving a sigh and looking away. I felt uncomfortable spying on her private moment, but she looked so vibrant in her spontaneity that I couldn't turn away.

She stepped out of her sandals before unbuttoning her jeans and pulling them down over her hips, then all the way off. I watched as she casually folded and set them on the counter; she then removed her blouse, folded it in quarters, and set it on top of her jeans. Her bra and panties came off last.

Looking in the mirror, she removed her earrings, laying them on top of her clothing. I thought she'd take off the locket next. Instead, she fiddled briefly with the clasp before deciding to leave it on. She took another sip from her glass and peered over at the tub to check on the water level. Humming under her breath, she reached below the sink for a towel to wrap around her before taking a seat on the side of the tub.

She seemed lost in a daydream, one foot swinging to an imaginary beat as the tub continued to fill. Suddenly she turned toward the door, an expression of annoyance forming on her face. Following her gaze, I saw the doorknob turning.

"I'm in here," she called out. "And I'll probably be here for a while!"

Though there was no answer, the knob stopped turning. After a moment she relaxed, leaning down to run her hand through the water in the tub. Standing, she reached over to turn off the faucet.

Her back was still to the door when it suddenly burst open. She jumped—I did, too, almost dropping the candles—as a shadowlike figure rushed toward her. In the chaos that ensued, I couldn't make out much about the blurry figure except for the mask; it was a cheap plastic model of a happy face emoji.

She shouted the words I'd heard Nighttime Wren scream before:

What are you doing in here?
Who are you?
Get out, get out, get out, get out . . .

But he was on her fast, seizing a chunk of her hair and yanking her head back and forth as he pulled backward. One more violent jerk, then her feet went out from under her and the towel flew off. As she scrambled to stand again, he dragged her closer to the tub. With a final heave, he jerked her head hard toward the faucet, her lower body slamming against the tub in the same moment. I heard a sickening crunch as her skull punched the ornate faucet, and all at once she ceased moving.

The killer stood panting over Wren's body. She lay half in the tub, her legs splayed awkwardly on the floor, her body bent at an unnatural angle. I watched as he lifted her legs and tipped them into the water with a splash.

I blinked and saw that there were now **two** figures standing over the tub. Trembling, I raised the candles higher, straining to make sure I wasn't mistaken, but the two distinct figures remained in place. They each took a seat on the lip of the tub, and I watched as the first, larger figure bent over, using both hands to push Wren's body beneath the water. The second figure joined in, both holding fast for what felt like an agonizing eternity.

Eventually they both leaned back. For a moment they sat silent on the edge of the tub, breathing heavily. Then the smaller figure reached into the tub with both hands a second time. This person seemed to be fiddling with something, and then all at once, the figures were gone, and so was the discarded towel.

The air in the bathroom grew cold. In my shaking hands, the candles' flames diminished, casting a yellow, eerie glow. I knew instinctively that Wren had died, but I slowly crept to the side of the tub.

She stared up at me with unseeing eyes, a cloud of blood blossoming in the water near her head, but otherwise looking exactly like the Wren I'd come to know. This, I knew, was how she'd looked only moments after her death.

I forced myself to draw a breath. **Think,** I told myself. **Wren wanted me to see this for a reason.**

Gazing at her figure, I had to choke back a sob as I tried to figure it out. I flashed back to the faces she'd made in the mirror; in my mind, the scene continued to unfold, and I saw her undress and remove her earrings. I remembered, too, the way she'd fiddled with the clasp on the chain that held the locket—

I froze, my breath strangled as if I'd been punched in the stomach.

She'd been wearing the locket when she was attacked.

Focusing on her unmoving shape, I confirmed what I already knew: the chain and locket were gone. I searched the floor around the tub, then aimed the candles' sparse light into each corner of the room, thinking the necklace might have been torn off and skidded away in the struggle. But it was nowhere to be seen.

And then, like something dreadful arising from the depths of a murky lake, I remembered the second figure reaching into the tub with both hands and seeming to fiddle with something, the truth hitting me with a force I hadn't expected.

I knew then that one of the killers had taken the locket from Wren. And with chilling clarity, I also recalled where I had seen it before. Not on Wren, but on someone else.

In shock, I pushed the bathroom door open and staggered toward the stairs. But just as I reached them, I heard the scuff of footsteps behind me. Turning, I glimpsed a familiar face looming out of the darkness.

"You—" I started to say, before something struck the side of my head with blinding force, and for a split second, I felt myself falling and tumbling before the world went dark.

CHAPTER 29

Wren stood in front of the bathroom mirror, wondering where her glass of wine had gone. She could remember bringing it upstairs and setting it next to the sink; she could even recall taking a sip, so where was it? She scanned the area around the tub, thinking she'd perhaps set it on the floor while she was adjusting the water temperature, but it wasn't there. And why wasn't the water running?

I must be losing my mind, she thought. She supposed she'd left the glass of wine in the kitchen, but when she concentrated, even the memory of pouring it seemed hazy. Odd, given that she had no problem recalling every detail of her afternoon with Tate, and afterward she'd gone to the festival . . .

Hadn't she?

The more she tried to revisit the evening, the more slippery her memories became. Much of the last few hours was blank, and the images that she managed to dredge up were static, like snapshots in their brevity. At the Monkey Tears show, she'd seen the petite lead singer clutching the microphone with both hands; she could picture the dreadlocked guitarist hunched over her shiny red Fender during her solo; she could even remember a brief sighting of Griffin striding toward the stage; but that was it. Stranger yet, those three recollections had a fuzzy quality, as if they had happened not tonight but rather long ago.

She really wished that Tate had come with her to the festival, because talking with him might help fill in the blanks. She hadn't seen him downstairs; his bedroom door stood open, and she wondered where he was. Perhaps he'd gone off with Oscar somewhere.

She wanted to apologize to him for the way she'd left. Except, right now, she couldn't exactly remember how their afternoon together had ended. One minute, they were lying in bed, but the next, there was nothing. She couldn't recall saying goodbye or getting dressed, or even driving to the festival. Come to think of it, she couldn't remember the drive back home either.

She frowned, raising a hand to massage her temples. Everything felt so jumbled right now. Not just her memories from earlier tonight, she realized, but even those from the recent past. Only Tate stood out with clarity. Her conversation with him about his sister, and his peculiar expression while he watched her search for the puzzle piece, were indelibly etched in her mind. She could easily reconstruct every game they'd played and the laughs they'd shared when she taught him to cook. Every moment of their soul-baring discussions in the parlor was within reach, but if you asked her what else she'd done lately, she'd be hard-pressed to describe anything at all. Right now, she wasn't even sure if she really had spoken to Nash the other day, because that, too, felt like eons ago. For that matter, when was the last time she'd seen Reece or Louise? Or any of the other guests?

A prickling sensation interrupted her reverie, and as the hairs on the back of her neck began to rise, she had the uncanny feeling that she was no longer alone in the bathroom. Whirling around, she saw nothing, but her heart continued to race. When she looked down, she saw that her glass of wine had magically reappeared on the counter; directly opposite lay the clothing she'd just been wearing. She was now naked with only a towel wrapped around her.

This isn't real. This can't be happening—

But she knew she wasn't dreaming. If anything, she felt intensely awake, more lucid and alert at this moment than she'd felt in a long time. In the mirror, she caught a reflection of the bathtub, and the hairs on her arms began to rise.

Come see . . .

The bathtub beckoned to her. Indistinct whispers urged her forward, and despite the dread seeping through her limbs, she couldn't stop herself. She took a step toward the deep well of the tub, dread turning to fear as she lurched toward it against her will. Leaning over the edge of the basin, she saw legs and gasped. Her eyes traveled up the length of the torso, and she knew at once there was something wrong with the body. It was gray and mottled and swollen, and when her gaze finally reached the face, recognition slammed her like a closed fist. She stumbled backward in shock.

Oh my God, oh my God, oh my God . . .

The back of her head exploded in pain, and she screamed, instinctively reaching for the wound. Doubling over, she stared at the viscous slick of blood on her fingers. She screamed again.

Then, inexplicably, the pain evaporated, and her fingers were clean, as though it had all been nothing more than a momentary nightmare. The towel was gone, and she was once again fully dressed. Only the terrifying corpse remained, and despite her revulsion, she found it difficult to look away. An unsettling curiosity arose within her, drawing her gaze back to the battered figure. Her eyes roamed over the distended limbs and bluish lips. While she stared at the body, new memories began trickling in. Initially, a few disjointed flashes, like rivulets through a crack in a dam; then a growing stream of terrible sequences, chaotic and loud; and finally, a deluge of violent scenes, each more brutal and horrifying than the last as they built toward a sickening conclusion.

I died—

She felt like retching, but even her reflexes were frozen in shock.

She stood unmoving as the truth began to take hold, settling like a blanket of snow on a shattered landscape. Time stretched out, suspended while she tentatively explored this new reality, examining it from every angle. As she began to reconcile the dissonance and agitation she'd been experiencing, a glimmer of understanding emerged. She hadn't been able to name the restless, out-of-kilter sensation that had plagued her for so long, or understand why the intertwining of past and present had felt so confusing, so **wrong.** Now, the answer to all her questions was clear. As astonishing as it was, it somehow made sense.

I'm here, but I'm not really here.

And Tate, sweet Tate. Had he known all along? She thought back on his careful overtures, the times he had held back when she could tell he wanted to do and say more. She had thought him merely a gentleman in word and deed. She understood now that his deference signaled what he knew, but he'd been trying to protect her from the knowledge.

When she looked in the mirror, there was no surprise now at her lack of a reflection. Gone, too, were the waves of confusion and panic; in their place was a shadow of wistfulness, if not yet grief. **There was still so much I wanted to do,** she thought. **I'll never visit the great cities of the world.**

She took a seat on the edge of the tub, no longer afraid of or repulsed by the cloudy-eyed body in the water. As she studied the details of her physical remains—the tendrils of hair spreading like seagrass around her shoulders, the crooked left pinkie toe she'd broken while riding her bike, even the chipped red nail polish on her index finger—she tried to picture that self, undamaged and whole, strolling down the winding streets of Paris. She realized that lately in her fantasies, she had unconsciously pictured Tate by her side, holding her hand as they meandered together.

There would be no journeys with Tate, and somehow, that realization hurt almost as much as everything else she had lost combined. **He was supposed to be The One,** she thought. The One for her.

Looking around the bathroom, she sighed. Some part of her had been trapped in this room, the part she'd closed off from herself, the keeper of the terrible memories of what had happened to her that night. As she stared down at the bruised, bloody figure in the tub, Wren knew that this being was a part of her as well, and that it was time for them to leave this place behind—their memories, impulses, emotions dark and light—reunited at last.

She closed her eyes, and Tennyson's words came to her like an elegy:

Twilight and evening bell,
And after that the dark!

And may there be no sadness of farewell,
When I embark.

When she opened her eyes, the figure in the water was gone, the tub dry and pristine.

Standing, she moved to the door without looking back.

• • •

As she stood at the top of the staircase, she caught the unmistakable smell of smoke, and she wondered if Tate had returned and burned something on the stove.

When she strained to see into the darkness of the foyer below, she saw the walls lit with an eerie, orangish glow. She watched as shadows leapt and lengthened against a rapidly brightening backdrop, and with cold dread, she knew at once that the smoke was not the product of a cooking mishap. The house was on fire.

Her first thought was of Tate. **Please let him be somewhere safe,** she prayed, and as she rushed down the stairs, frantically peering into the darkened rooms on the main floor, a growing sense of panic engulfed her. When she looked out the window near the front door, her worst fears were confirmed: Tate's car was parked out front.

He was somewhere in the house. But where?

Smoke was beginning to billow out of the kitchen, and Wren turned, plunging through the stinging clouds, afraid to find Tate battling the fire, or worse, overcome by smoke. She skidded to a stop in the kitchen, confused. Standing over a flaming cast-iron pan, its contents ablaze as he waved it below the kitchen cupboards, was . . .

Reece?

She watched in speechless horror as Reece uncorked a bottle of cognac with one hand and doused the lower cabinets with alcohol. Now the cabinets on the far side were burning, the flames reaching toward the ceiling.

"Stop!" she screamed. "Reece! What are you doing?"

He could neither see nor hear her, and when she rushed at him, trying to seize the flaming pan from his grip, her blows passed through him, unnoticed. **I can't stop him,** she realized with frustration and rage. **I can't do anything.**

Whirling around, she ran into the dining room, the light of the fire behind her illuminating the smoky confines. **Tate.** She had to find Tate. Reece was burning the house down and she couldn't escape the sickening sensation that he'd done something to Tate as well.

She frantically circled the dining room table and looked beneath it, finding nothing; she rushed to the parlor, stumbling toward the bookshelves, then fell to all fours in front of the fireplace to peer through the acrid smoke. Crawling blindly over the Oriental carpet, she finally found him near the sofa, lying on his side, his eyes closed. She called to him, but there was no response. She tried to shake him, but her hands passed through him without effect. When she glanced over her shoulder toward the kitchen, flames were already licking the dining room walls.

The thudding of her heartbeat had almost drowned out the roar of the fire when headlights flashed across the windows. Someone was coming up the drive.

Reece must have seen the headlights as well, because she heard the pan clank against the stovetop before he raced out of the kitchen toward the front door. He hesitated only long enough to kick Tate's inert form, satisfying himself that Tate was still unconscious. As he flung open the front door, the flames in the house seemed to explode, filling the entirety of the dining room in an instant and reaching like tentacles into the parlor. Slamming the door behind him, he darted down the porch steps. Wren scrambled to the window just in time to see him disappear around the corner of the house.

The headlights were closing in fast, and Wren watched as a huge black SUV fishtailed to a stop in front of the house. A dark-haired man jumped out then staggered backward as he took in the inferno.

He reached for his phone and quickly punched in a number; a few seconds later, he pressed one finger to his ear, jamming the receiver against the other. He shouted into the phone while staring at the burning house with an expression of horror. He hung up, shoving the phone back in his pocket.

"Tate! Are you in there?" she heard him yell.

Oscar.

Behind her, the heat was like an implacable wall, moving ever closer. On the floor, Tate didn't move. Desperate, she pressed the length of her body against the parlor window. **Look at me, Oscar,** she begged. **See me.**

Slowly, Oscar turned to look up at the window. He froze.

Meeting his eyes, Wren mouthed, **He's here! Tate is here.** Frantically, she began waving him in, gesturing at the floor behind her.

She watched in frustration as Oscar hesitated before swiping at his eyes in obvious disbelief. All around her, the house was creaking and crackling as if it were being devoured. **Tate is here,** she mouthed again, beckoning him toward her with increasing panic.

Through the glass, she finally saw something shift in Oscar's face as he stared at her—comprehension dawning, then fear. Galvanized, he ran up the porch steps. The front doorknob rattled in vain, and she cursed her inability to unlock it. A moment later, she watched Oscar turn on his heel and sprint for the SUV.

As Oscar flung open the hatchback, pulling out a bulky child's car seat, she saw Louise bolt out of the cottage. For a moment Louise stood as if paralyzed, her mouth open in shock. In the window, Wren shouted and waved her arms at Louise, hoping that the woman would somehow sense her entreaties to help Oscar. Inexplicably, instead of racing to Oscar's aid, Louise ran instead to Reece's truck, climbing into the cab.

Lugging the car seat in his arms, Oscar had started for the porch, clearly intending to smash through the parlor window. Wren's confusion changed to horror as Reece's truck roared to life and surged toward Oscar. She saw Oscar look over his shoulder and catch sight of Louise behind the wheel, her expression deranged as she floored the accelerator. The truck smashed into Oscar with a sickening thud, the car seat bouncing across the gravel.

It must have been a glancing blow because Oscar managed to get onto all fours and look up, squinting in shock at the taillights of the truck as it skidded to a stop. He scrambled toward the corner of the house. Before he could get there, the truck reoriented itself and accelerated in reverse, flinging Oscar's body to the side like a broken toy.

• • •

The fire was rapidly swallowing the house, one side nearly destroyed already. Inside, the air was so blisteringly hot that when Wren squatted down next to him, she could see that Tate's skin had begun to turn a dangerous shade of red. A deafening roar erupted as part of the second floor collapsed into the kitchen.

Terrified, Wren crouched next to his body, shouting and screaming, but Tate showed no sign of waking. Had she not seen the slight rise and fall of his chest, she would have believed that he was already dead.

She could feel tears stream down her face as she leaned toward his ear.

"You have to get out of here," she pleaded. "It's not your time. Please. You have to hear me."

Again, there was no response. Closing her eyes, she summoned every shred of willpower, concentrating like never before on a single impassioned wish.

"I love you, Tate," she whispered, "and if you love me, you have to wake up now."

Nothing happened.

On the verge of despair, she let out a broken sob . . . and, like a miracle, Tate began to cough, his eyes finally fluttering open.

CHAPTER 30

I awakened to coughing spasms so deep and raw that my chest and stomach felt like they were tearing apart. When I tried to draw breath, there was little oxygen to be had, and my skin felt as though I had been plunged in boiling water. Blinking back burning tears, I struggled to comprehend what was happening.

Another round of coughing seized me, and I could feel myself beginning to black out again when Wren's face materialized inches from mine.

"Tate!" she screamed. "Stay with me! You've got to get up." I could barely hear her amid the roar that seemed to be coming from all around us.

I tried to respond, but my throat felt as though I'd swallowed hot charcoal. It was Wren's panicked expression that roused me more than anything.

"Wren?" I croaked.

"The house is on fire!" she shouted. "You have to get out!"

Before I could answer, another bout of violent coughing racked my body. Tears streamed from my eyes, their salt stinging my inflamed skin.

"Please, Tate! You have to get out of the house! You have to save Oscar!"

I drew an agonized breath. "Oscar?"

"Louise hit him with the truck!" She gestured frantically toward the driveway. "He's hurt!"

It took a moment for me to make sense of her words, but her distress spurred me to action. I forced myself to roll over onto my stomach. Choking on the thick black smoke, I rose to all fours, dragging my upper torso onto the sofa cushions. Then I hoisted myself into a standing position, triggering an explosion of agony in my knee that momentarily turned my world black again.

Meanwhile, Wren continued to shadow me, yelling encouragement and urging me toward the front door.

"Keep going! You're almost there! You've got to leave **now.**"

Looking over my shoulder, I felt a wave of terror. Where the kitchen and dining room had been, an inferno raged, and every wall of the parlor was on fire. Flames mounted the staircase in giant bounds, their long tongues stretching toward the ceiling.

I lurched for the door. My hand erupted in pain as I turned the scorching knob, disengaging the lock. I yanked open the door in time to see a gray-and-white blur dash across my feet as Paulie fled for safety outdoors. With the sound of a bomb detonating, the parlor exploded behind me, flinging me down the porch steps. I landed hard, straining for breath as I stared up at the orange-tinted sky, even as Wren's words came back to me.

You have to save Oscar . . .

Rolling over to my side, I was forced into a fetal position by another excruciating coughing spasm, but I eventually managed to get onto my hands and knees. My eyes watered as I strained to make out my surroundings. Looking around, I spotted a child's car seat lying in the grass; beyond that, in the drive, stood Oscar's Escalade. Sparks were beginning to shower down into the yard as I pushed myself to my feet.

"Oscar!" I shouted, my voice drowned out by the hurricane force of the fire.

I staggered across the yard, ignoring the white-hot bolts of pain in my knee as I peered into the shadows. It wasn't until I reached the corner of the house that I finally saw a figure sprawled in the grass, unmoving. I hobbled toward it, recognizing Oscar's familiar form just as part of the second floor gave way, crashing down in a geyser of flames.

"Why won't you just die?"

The enraged voice came from behind me, and I turned. The blazing light made Reece look demonic. In his hand, he held a crowbar, and I felt a surge of dread and fear. As he advanced toward me, my knee buckled, and I fell on my side. I watched in terror as he raised the crowbar, knowing there was no escape from the blow that was coming. In the seconds before Reece was upon me, I closed my eyes, sensing with sudden intensity Wren's presence hovering over me.

In that instant, the house exploded from within. A deafening boom shook the ground beneath me, and every window along the front of the house blew out. The force of the blast washed over me like a wave, and I stared at the conflagration. Chunks of debris rained down. Flames were pouring through every window, and another part of the roof began to cave in; the parlor where Wren had been standing was a blazing furnace. In the distance, I heard the faint wail of sirens.

Reece—

I struggled to my feet, my limbs numb and my ears ringing. I turned in a circle, expecting to see Reece rising to finish me off. But I didn't see him, not right away. Scanning the area where he had stood just moments ago, I saw the crowbar first, lying in the grass. And then, a few steps away, the bulky outline of his figure, prone, his head an almost unrecognizable pulp of blood and brain matter. A slab of heavy oak debris the width of a man's torso lay blackened and smoking on the ground nearby.

Turning away, I felt close to vomiting before I remembered that Oscar needed me. I wheeled in the direction where I'd seen him last and felt a wave of relief that he was in the same place as before, miraculously shielded from the explosion by the porch. But the porch was now on fire, the flames snaking ever closer to his unmoving body. I scrambled over to him, bracing myself against the searing temperature. I reached for one of his arms and, straining with all I had left, I began to slowly drag him away from the inferno. He grew heavier with each step, my every movement unleashing a burst of agony. Sweat poured into my eyes.

Steadily we inched farther from the house, the blast force of heat gradually diminishing. I continued to pull until my strength gave out and I collapsed beside him. As I lay gasping, I heard Oscar moan, and I almost shouted with joy that he was still alive.

Lifting myself up on my elbow, I peered across the yard. Louise was hunched over Reece's disfigured form, her shirt and hands soaked with blood. I watched as she let out a wail that rose into the rippling waves of superheated air.

As if sensing my gaze, she turned toward me, her expression of anguish giving way to one of murderous rage. In slow motion, I saw her stand, her eyes alighting on the crowbar in the grass.

Staring at me with implacable hatred, she lunged for it.

• • •

The sirens were louder now, and flashing lights raced up the bottom of the drive.

Louise stood with the crowbar in hand, but I couldn't push myself to my feet. My body was utterly spent, my legs unable to bear weight. I slumped back to the ground, wheezing. With a sense of terrible resignation, I watched her break into a run. Raising an arm to shield myself as she lifted the crowbar into the air, I barely registered the sound of spraying gravel and doors flying open behind me.

"Freeze! Put it down! **Now!**"

I risked a glance over my shoulder to see two police officers advancing toward us, guns drawn.

I turned toward Louise and our eyes locked. Shadows danced madly across her face while embers drifted around us. I was certain she was going to slam the crowbar down on my huddled figure. And then something dimmed in her maniacal gaze.

"Drop the weapon now!" the officers shouted, stepping around Oscar and me to surround her in tense formation.

Inch by inch, she lowered her arms and released the crowbar. She looked over at the police officers, dazed.

"It wasn't supposed to happen like this," she said, sinking to her knees.

CHAPTER 31

Last night I dreamed of Wren.

We were walking on a beach near Heatherington on an overcast day, wintry air distilling our breath into cloudy puffs. She wore a turtleneck sweater beneath a forest-green coat, her hands hidden deep in her pockets. About a mile up the beach, I saw a carnival, complete with a slowly rotating Ferris wheel, and understood that we were making our way toward it.

The dream jumped forward, and we were riding the Ferris wheel. Wren sat beside me, our fingers intertwined. Cold wind blew over my face as we stared out at the slate-colored expanse of the ocean.

"Why did you bring me back to Heatherington, Tate?" she asked.

"Don't you like it here?"

"I do, but we could have gone anywhere. You're dreaming."

"I am?"

She nodded, sweeping her wind-whipped hair out of her face. "We could be at a bistro in Paris or on a beach in the South Pacific, or on a safari watching lions, like Sylvia and Mike." Her eyes lit up. "Or we could go somewhere else, and I could finally teach you to dance."

"I'd go anywhere with you."

The dream shifted again, and we were now on the beach behind my family's home in the Hamptons. It was a balmy summer night, and a full moon rode high in the sky. The murmur of cocktail party conversation and the lively sounds of a swing band drifted over the dunes. Wren stood before me in a strapless white dress that flared below the waist, reaching to just above her knees. I wore white linen, and both of us were barefoot.

"Are you ready?" she asked, offering me her hand.

I took it, marveling at my first ever feel of her skin, as I slipped my arm around her lower back. I tugged gently, savoring the press of her body against mine. The cloud of her musky perfume enveloped us as we rotated in slow circles.

"What am I supposed to do?" I asked.

She looked up at me with a contented smile.

"You're doing it," she answered. "We're dancing."

"I'm not doing anything special."

"You don't have to."

"Fred Astaire does."

"I don't want you to be him," she said. "All I've ever wanted is for you to be you."

She leaned into me, resting her head on my chest, and we continued to sway. The song ended and another began, a romantic number in a minor key.

"Thank you for saving me, Tate," she murmured.

"I could say the same thing to you."

"Will you come and say goodbye?"

"I don't want to say goodbye."

"Please," she said, raising her face to mine.

When I nodded, she kissed me tenderly on the lips.

• • •

As my eyes opened, I struggled to make sense of my surroundings. The dream continued to feel vivid and tangible; I could still smell Wren's perfume and hear the melody that played as we danced. Then I saw my bandaged knee in a brace, stretched out on an institutional white bed beneath fluorescent lights, and I remembered where I was.

I'd been in the hospital since Friday night. The doctors had diagnosed me with a severe concussion, and though I'd managed to avoid any intracranial hemorrhaging, the swelling had only yesterday begun to subside.

The prognosis for my knee was cloudier. Due to extensive swelling, it would be a week or two before scans could yield an accurate picture of the injuries.

But I'd already been in touch with an orthopedic surgeon at New York-Presbyterian, as well as my neurologist, and made appointments for a full workup as soon as I was home.

I got out of the bed and used nearby crutches to hobble to the bathroom. Catching sight of myself in the mirror, I noted that I still looked like hell, covered in bruises and pale with bone-deep exhaustion. I thought again how lucky I was to have survived all that had happened.

When I left the bathroom, I was surprised to see Oscar sitting in the chair next to my bed.

"Hey, stranger," he said with a grin.

"Hey, yourself," I answered.

Though we'd been treated at the same hospital, I hadn't seen Oscar since the night of the fire. Lorena had told me that Oscar, too, had suffered a concussion and that his arm had been broken. He now wore a brightly colored cast signed and decorated by his kids with drawings of the sun, rockets, and hearts.

He rose and offered me a one-armed hug, careful not to disturb my crutches.

"Have you been released?" I asked, scrutinizing him for further injuries.

"I got out yesterday," he answered. "And I slept like a baby last night. They really need more comfortable beds in this place."

I smiled. "How's Paulie?"

"I knew that was going to be your next question," he said with a smile. "She's fine. Lorena said that as soon as she got to the property and called for her, Paulie dashed out of the woods and jumped straight into the SUV. I think she's still a little wigged-out from spending the night outside. Lorena said that every time she sits down, Paulie immediately hops into her lap."

"Poor Paulie. Tell Lorena thank you."

"You'll tell her later when you pick up your cat," he said, waving it off. "Besides, she loves Paulie. I think she was more worried about her than about me."

"I doubt it."

"You didn't see her expression when I asked her to find the little thing. She couldn't get to the house fast enough. Fortunately, I hear you're getting out of here today."

"Three days is quite enough for me, thank you," I said. "Are you going to stay in Chatham for a while?"

"No, we're driving home tonight. I think I need a break from Heatherington, at least for a little while. We'll be back when school's finished, though. And you'll be heading back to the city, I assume?"

"I have to." I explained my upcoming doctors' appointments, motioning him into the chair while I gingerly sat on the edge of the bed.

"All right," he said, propping his cast on the armrest. "Catch me up. Chief Dugan gave me the official brief when he came to see me, but I want the real story."

It took a while to relate everything that had happened on Friday evening. At times, the events felt surreal even to me. It was astonishing how Oscar and I had managed to embroil ourselves in such harrowing events.

"How did you know I was in trouble?" I asked.

"I didn't," he answered with a shrug. "I came to the house to tell you that I found Dax and Tessa at the festival. Like Nash and Griffin, they'd clearly been there for hours."

"How did you find them?"

"I picked a spot where I could keep an eye on the bathrooms. They walked up twenty minutes after you left, almost like they'd been paged."

Perhaps, I thought as I remembered the pulsing light over the festival, **they had been.**

"I can't believe they were willing to talk to you."

"I think Dax was terrified I was going to whip out the letter in front of the wife." He smirked. "I assume Chief Dugan came to see you here as well?"

"He stopped by twice, actually."

"And?"

I shrugged. "He was mainly interested in the events of Friday night, even though I couldn't shed any light on how the fire started. I'm just glad the officers showed up when they did. Of course, he kept pressing, so I eventually told him almost everything. Let's just say he wasn't amused by our 'citizens' investigation.' "

"He scolded me, too," Oscar admitted. "But when you say 'almost everything,' do you mean you told him about Wren?"

I gave a sheepish nod. "As predicted, he thinks I'm certifiable."

"It **is** a little crazy."

"Yeah," I agreed. "Did he end up revealing anything about their investigation into the fire?"

"He's still playing things close to the vest, but he's fairly certain arson was involved. Dogs picked up traces of accelerant where the kitchen used to be, and they recovered an empty bottle of liquor. Reece also had alcohol on his clothing, so they suspect he started it."

I thought of the cognac I'd purchased for the coq au vin.

"Does he know how I ended up by the sofa? The last thing I remember is tumbling down the stairs."

"Either you somehow dragged yourself and don't remember it, or Reece dragged you over there. Maybe he wasn't sure whether the whole house would burn, but he wanted you in a spot he knew you wouldn't survive."

I nodded, realizing I would likely never know. "What about Louise?"

"Things aren't looking good for her. Her bail has been set at an astronomical figure."

"Because she had Wren's locket?"

"Because she ran me down with the truck before going after you with a crowbar. Dugan said the prosecutor intends to charge her with attempted murder. I don't know that they have enough evidence to charge her with Wren's murder."

"So she'll get away with it?"

"She'll end up in prison," he said. "Even though Reece is dead, it's clear by her actions on Friday that she and Reece were in it together. Not only did you see him attack you after you left the bathroom only to have Louise try to finish the job, but Reece had injuries consistent with that iron you swung at him. Most important, it turns out that both Reece and Louise had a very strong motive to eliminate Wren."

"What do you mean?"

"Aldrich came by my place in Chatham this morning."

"And?"

"Apparently the trust documents governing the property were poorly drafted. As Wren told you, she was the primary beneficiary, and if nothing had happened to her, the house and property would have passed to her. Because she died before distribution, however, the trust required that the proceeds be split among the secondary beneficiaries, and that's where the problem came in. The property was supposed to be split among surviving family, the town, and the conservation trust. But the trust had failed to specify any percentages—hence the litigation. Reece was the only remaining blood relative, and he was fighting for a bigger share. Still, even if he only received a quarter or a third of the value of the property, it would have been millions."

I vaguely recalled Wren mentioning to me that Reece was the only family she had left.

"So who's going to get the property now? Griffin?"

Oscar shook his head. "Aldrich suspects it'll be split between the town and the conservation trust. He doubts Griffin will receive anything at all: Wren's divorce attorney is adamant that Wren and Griffin weren't getting back together, and he's willing to testify to that fact. Massachusetts law is also clear that inheritances that haven't been received aren't considered marital property, and because Wren died before the trust was distributed, the property never actually transferred to her."

"Griffin won't be happy about that."

"Who cares?" Oscar snorted. "Oh, and for what it's worth, Aldrich claims to have had suspicions about Reece and Louise all along, just not enough evidence to do anything about it."

I raised an eyebrow. "Had Aldrich been in touch earlier in the week, it would have saved us a lot of trouble."

"That's assuming he would have told us. I think the only reason he mentioned it this morning was because Reece is dead, and Louise is behind bars. But that reminds me: what do you want to do about Nash, Griffin, and Dax?"

I'd been thinking about that on and off in the hospital. "Nothing," I finally answered. "They might have been awful to Wren, but they didn't kill her."

"You don't care that Nash is a thief or that the last thing Dax should be doing is counseling people?"

"I think it's best if I try to put all this behind me.

More important, you'll be living here, and you don't need enemies."

"Okay," he said, scratching the skin at the upper end of his cast. He glanced away before turning back to me. "I saw her, you know. Wren, I mean. When I came to the house, I saw her through the window. She let me know you were trapped inside."

"And?"

"It made me realize that even though I mostly believed you, there was a tiny part of me that didn't. But actually seeing her . . ." He hesitated. "It's like having the rug pulled out from under you, because it reveals how little we know about existence. And it makes me wonder about the big questions in life: Is there a God? What else is out there? Where do we go when we die?"

I nodded. "She saved my life, you know. She woke me up when I was unconscious. Without her, I wouldn't have made it."

For a moment we stayed quiet before he leaned toward me. "How are you doing? Now that you've had a little time to process everything?"

Remembering the dream, I avoided his gaze. "I miss her."

"Maybe you'll see her again."

I stared out the window, focusing on a lone cloud in the bright blue sky beyond. "Maybe."

• • •

I was discharged later that day and immediately called an Uber to take me to the property. Among other things, I needed to pick up my car, the keys having fortunately been in my pocket when I'd dragged myself from the house.

After being dropped off, I took in the site where the house had been. Little was left except the skeletal, charred structure and mountains of ash. Aside from the concrete cellar and the chimney, only a blackened fragment of the corner wall near the bookshelves remained, overhung by a small wedge of the second floor. This was the place where Wren had lived and died and lived again, and the destruction triggered a new wave of sadness.

I maneuvered through the debris, my crutches sinking into sodden piles of ash. I examined the remnants for signs of smoldering, but the firefighters had done their job well. No other structures on the property had been damaged, and even the nearby trees seemed unaffected.

I shuffled to the corner of the house that was still standing, moving with care to avoid disturbing the precarious structure. The walls had nearly burned through, and the struts looked as though they'd dissipate in the slightest breeze. Sunlight streamed through the gaps in the blackened masonry. I had the strange feeling that Wren had preserved this part of the house for me, and I stopped short of the overhang.

"I'm here, Wren," I said.

I waited, but there was nothing. Searching for a place to sit, I took a step toward a nearby lump of concrete when I heard her voice.

"Hello, Tate," she said from behind me.

I turned. She was wearing the white dress from my dream. She was as beautiful as I remembered, and yet I detected a new aura of peace about her, heightening her loveliness. Her gold-flecked eyes, once troubled and plagued by self-doubt, now held only grace.

"I knew you'd come," I said.

She tilted her head. "I could say the same thing," she said, her gaze traveling over me. A frown creased her forehead as she took in my crutches and ugly bruises. "You're injured."

"I'll be okay," I said, thinking the change in her was remarkable. There was a quality of ease about her now, as if all her questions had been answered.

"Do you know?" I ventured in a tentative voice.

"Yes," she answered. "I know what Reece and Louise did to me."

"I wish I could have stopped it."

She shook her head. "You didn't know me then."

In the hospital, I'd rehearsed everything I wanted to say to her, but in her presence, it was impossible to recall the words. Instead, I could only blurt out the obvious. "I don't want you to go. I want you to remain here with me."

Her eyes brimmed with regret. "I can't stay."

"But I love you."

"And I love you," she responded. "I think I loved you from the moment we met."

I felt a part of me begin to disintegrate, a slow landslide beneath my feet. "What is there left for me without you?"

"Everything," she answered. "It's all waiting for you, Tate." She took a step toward me, her expression tender. "I want you to live well and love deeply. Look for reasons to be grateful. Treasure your friends. Embark on wonderful adventures. Honor the gifts you've been given."

"I want to do those things with you," I said, already feeling defeated.

"If you really love me, you'll do them anyway."

"I don't know how."

"You will," she promised. She smiled before raising an eyebrow. "Your sister feels certain that you can."

"Sylvia? You and she . . ."

"Yes. You made her sound so delicate, but she's a force of nature," Wren observed. "She's sweet and funny but **determined.** And she still worries about you and Mike. She watches over both of you."

"Will you watch over me, too?"

"Always."

"Will I be able to sense you?"

"Only in memory."

I was quiet again, trying and failing to imagine a future in which I could no longer reach out for her. "I dreamed about you."

"I know. I wanted to dance with you. I wanted

to finally feel your arms around me. I wanted to kiss you."

"Will I dream about you again?"

"Perhaps. But I won't be there with you."

I could feel despair seeping into me like water leaking into the foundation of a house. "I don't think I can love anyone else."

Her green eyes softened. "Oh, Tate," she whispered, "loving another is a gift that you give to yourself. Haven't you learned that yet?"

I had no answer. Stirring the ashes underfoot with the tip of one of my crutches, I asked instead, "How long can you stay with me?" My voice cracked.

"Not long now," she said. "It's almost time."

"Can I ask a question?"

"You can ask me anything."

"Why me? Was it because of Sylvia? Because she gave me her gift?"

"Sylvia might have opened the door, but in the end, it could only have been you."

"I don't understand."

"Yes," she said with an enigmatic smile. "You do."

Staring into her eyes, I suddenly realized she was right. When I'd arrived in Heatherington, I was a man held prisoner by my past; Wren, too, had been locked in a cage of her own making. Falling in love—and truly loving each other—had been the only way to free and save us both.

She smiled as though she'd heard me. Somehow, I knew that Sylvia, too, was smiling in agreement, and

I watched as Wren slowly brought her hands toward me. She gently cradled my face, without touching me, and when she was finished, I responded by tracing a finger along her cheekbones and lips, committing every line to memory. She took a small step backward then, and I could feel her eyes on mine as the outline of her image began to fade.

"Wait! Wren!"

She paused, wavering like a mirage in the desert heat.

"I have to know. Did you make the house explode? When Reece was about to hit me with the crowbar? To stop him?"

She tilted her head. "What do you believe?"

For a moment she hovered before me, translucent, before she raised an eyebrow and began to fade again. And then, all at once, she was gone.

I don't know how long I stood in the ruins of the house, tears streaming unchecked down my face. When the ache in my knee brought me back to reality, I wiped my eyes before carefully picking my way back through the ashes.

Opening my car door, I took one last glance over my shoulder, just in time to see the ruined overhang crash to the ground with a thunderclap. The walls followed in an avalanche of ashy dust, until nothing remained at all.

EPILOGUE

EIGHT MONTHS LATER

I awakened this morning to find the city covered in snow. Looking down on Central Park from my bedroom window, I am delighted as always by the sight of the pristine white blanket obscuring all of New York's blemishes. Soon it will turn a slushy, dirty gray, but for now, the scene inspires the same sense of wonder it has since I was a child.

I returned last night from Newton, where I met again with Oscar and Lorena. The schematics are finished, and I showed them a complete 3D walk-through of their future summer home. The presentation enthralled them; they can hardly wait for the groundbreaking, scheduled for this spring. The lot has already been cleared. I've been working in lock-step with the general contractor to ensure that the project proceeds smoothly through construction.

Paulie squeaks, and glancing over my shoulder, I

smile at the sight of her leaping onto the bed. She is as sweet a companion as ever, apparently no worse for wear after her night in the wild outdoors while Wren's house burned to the ground.

My knee has recovered, though it took longer than expected. I escaped surgery but spent months in physical therapy, only recently returning to running again. These days I make my usual loop around the park, albeit at a slower pace. I also took up yoga, dropping in to classes on Wednesday nights at a studio near my apartment. It's done wonders for my rehabilitation and even more for my peace of mind.

I've visited Oscar's building site in Heatherington numerous times, though like Oscar and his family, I now stay in Chatham, sometimes in a hotel, other times at an Airbnb. It's easier that way. Heatherington still holds too many memories, and I'd prefer to avoid Nash, Dax, and Griffin, who surely still harbor grudges against me.

I've also visited Wren's property twice, once about a month after the fire and again a few weeks ago. By that second visit, all the debris had been cleared away. On neither visit did I sense Wren's presence, nor did I expect to; I knew her spirit had been linked to the house. Her absence left me feeling hollow, even though I knew she had moved on to the place she was supposed to be.

The property remains mired in litigation, but with Aldrich's permission, I visited the smaller of the storage sheds and took the photographs. I removed the pictures from their frames and placed them in an album that I keep in the drawer of my nightstand. Sometimes late at night, I'll flip through the pages, but I don't often feel the urge to do so. The Wren in those photographs was someone I didn't yet know, and I prefer to remember the Wren I came to love. The drawing of her, like everything else I kept at the house aside from my keys and wallet, burned up in the fire.

Oscar informed me a few months after we left Heatherington that Louise pleaded guilty to attempted murder in a bid for leniency. Her plea forestalled any further investigation into her and Reece's role in Wren's death. Oscar monitored my reaction carefully as he passed along this news, having continued to keep a close eye on my mental state. I think he was worried that I'd fall into the same kind of depression that befell me after Sylvia died, but his fears did not come to pass. Though I shed some tears on a few lonely nights, in the mornings I always awoke knowing that I would disappoint Wren if I failed to take her admonitions to heart. I took a lot of long walks in the park and reconnected with some college friends. Mike and I also now meet for dinner at least once a month, and it's been good for both of us. There's an unforced kindness to him that inspires trust, and I eventually told him about Wren. Surprising me, he accepted my story at face value, but then again, he was married to my sister, which probably explained it.

Work on Oscar and Lorena's house has kept me centered as well. I've also been approached about projects by two former clients, one for a renovation in the Hamptons and the other for a new estate in Greenwich, Connecticut. I'm careful, though, not to fall back into my old workaholic routines. I'm committed to living a fuller life these days, making time for some enjoyable pastimes in addition to running and yoga: a juggling workshop and cooking lessons at the International Culinary Center. I make myself dinner at least once a week, and I think Wren would be pleased, even if I still send my laundry out.

As promised, I checked in with Dr. Rollins upon my return and began meeting with a new psychiatrist named Amy Westover every other week. She's good, but as with Dr. Rollins, I wasn't comfortable telling her everything, and we agreed to part ways last month. We had decided early in the fall to wean me off my antidepressants, which went fine. Since then, I haven't looked back.

I've also been on a few dates, though it still feels strange. The first three women had their charms, but the chemistry simply wasn't there. In October, however, I went out with a woman named Rachel, with whom Mike set me up. She graduated from NYU and works as a PA with a cardiac surgeon who has an office not far from my apartment. She's pretty and has a quirky sense of humor; on our second date, when we played Two Truths and a Lie, I liked what I learned about her. I wouldn't say I'm in love with her, but we have fun, and I remain open to the possibility that I will love again, maybe with her, or with someone else down the road. I have a feeling that Wren and Sylvia are watching my progress with approval, wherever they are.

Because that's the thing. Even if I can never recreate what I had with Wren, I realized in the wake of all that happened that I want my life to be filled with love. I still miss her, and I know I'll always cherish her. More than anything, she taught me to believe in the idea that love will find me when I least expect it, but that it's up to me to be ready to receive it.

• • •

For the past three days, I've been watching a young boy in the park. He must be seven or eight, and he's wearing jeans, white sneakers, and a red T-shirt with a Nike logo. He races back and forth from a park bench, over a grassy mound, to an oak tree that must be more than a hundred years old. At first, I wondered why he wasn't wearing a jacket, where his parents were, and why he wasn't in school. But in the city, there are exceptions to every rule, so I figured it was really none of my business. Now, however, as I watch him plowing through the snowdrifts in his sneakers, I accept what I am seeing and recall Wren's words to me the last time we spoke.

Honor the gifts you've been given.

At the time, I wasn't sure what she meant, but

when I turn from the window, I recognize a familiar flickering in my peripheral vision in the same spot I'd seen the young boy. And I see that the boy, still without a jacket despite the frigid temperature, isn't leaving any footprints in the snow.

I don't know why he has chosen to show himself to me. I don't know what he wants or if there will be anything I can do to help him. The last thing I need is an encounter that I'm ill-equipped to handle, but what choice do I have?

He's only a child.

I bend down to rub Paulie's back before walking to the closet in the hallway. I put on boots, scarf, hat, gloves, and a heavy jacket before descending to the lobby.

I've known Adam, the doorman, since I moved into this building after college. He was elderly then, and is now positively stooped, with white hair, deep wrinkles, and jowls like a basset hound.

"The sidewalks are icy," he warns me. "Be careful out there."

I nod, thinking, **If only you knew.**

OCTOBER 12, 2024–JANUARY 29, 2025

when I turn from the window, I recognize [illegible] at my [illegible] in the [illegible] I'd seen the young boy, and I see that the boy still [illegible] despite the bright [illegible] leaving any footprints in the snow.

[illegible] he has entered a new [illegible] I don't know [illegible] anything I could do to help him. [illegible] encountered [illegible] have.

He's only a child.

I head down to the [illegible] the hallway [illegible] descending to the lobby.

[illegible]

The sidewalks [illegible] warm [illegible]

I nod, thinking [illegible] only you know.

OCTOBER 12, 2024–JANUARY 29, 2025

ACKNOWLEDGMENTS

Many people are surprised to discover that I've been a huge fan of the supernatural genre since I was a child—not only was my first attempt at writing a horror novel, but I havc an encyclopedic knowledge of horror films dating back to the 1950s and have avidly watched every episode of TV series like **The Twilight Zone** and **Supernatural.** I devour every new film and TV series in this category, including foreign releases (I'm a particular fan of the incredible work being produced in Japan and Korea these days). However, it was only when my longtime film agent Howie Sanders introduced me to the great writer/director M. Night Shyamalan that I considered writing a fully realized supernatural love story like **Remain.**

I've been a great admirer of Night's remarkable films, which epitomize how supernatural stories can thrill us, move us, and inspire us to ponder universal mysteries of the human experience. From the first conversation when we conceived the story that would become **Remain,** through every discussion about world-building and characters, and then at last to the transformation of those early ideas into works for the page and screen, this collaboration has been a highlight of my career. Night, thank you. I feel lucky to be working with someone I admire so deeply, and whom I am now proud to call a friend. I am grateful we are telling this story together.

To the team at Park, Fine & Brower: Thank you for your expertise and care. You always set the bar high for yourselves and everyone around you, and then you raise it higher once again. For Celeste Fine, my agent, I'd be remiss if I didn't thank you not only for the many thought-provoking phone calls and brilliant insights you offered while working through the manuscript, but for the friendship and tireless professionalism you've always offered me. Regarding Andrea Mai, Emily Sweet, and Abigail Koons, I am forever grateful for your creative and tireless efforts to reach readers around the world in new ways. Book publishing is always in flux, and not only are you steadfast in the face of change, you stay gracefully ahead of the curve. Alex Greene, I feel fortunate to benefit from your legal expertise, even as you embark on new adventures. Haley Garrison, John Maas, Charlotte Sunderland, Angela Lee, and Ben Kaslow-Zieve: I am appreciative of each of your contributions. Finally, a special welcome to Kimberly Brower; it has been exciting to watch Park, Fine, and now Brower grow into the kind of literary agency that maintains and builds on the tradition of excellence and integrity I myself have known for decades.

I am pleased to work again with the stellar team at Random House. Jennifer Hershey, thank you for understanding and championing this book from day one. Your editorial guidance helped me see new possibilities in Tate's and Wren's stories and your influence shines brightly on these pages. President Kara Welsh and Deputy Publisher Kim Hovey, thank you for marshaling the many people and resources that are required to get a book into the world, and especially for doing it always with such class, creativity, and grace. I am thankful to each of the three of you for exemplary leadership and boundless vision. My heartfelt gratitude also goes out to every member of the wider team. To Jaci Updike, Cynthia Lasky, and the rest of the sales force, thank you for everything you do to support the many wonderful booksellers and librarians who put this book into the hands of readers. Jeanne Reina, thank you for your skilled art direction. Kelly Chian, Susan Brown, Maggie Hart, Caroline Cunningham, and the rest of the production team: Thank you for taking words on a page and transforming them into a stunning book. Denise Lee, Ellen Folan, Nicole McArdle, and Donna Passannante in the audio department: Thank you for bringing those same words to life as narration. Kate Gomer, thank you for juggling so many moving pieces on the editorial side. Karen Fink and Chelsea Woodward in publicity, thank you for stewarding an effective campaign. Taylor Noel, Emma Thomasch, and Megan Whalen in marketing, thank you for helping this book find its audience.

An extra-special note of appreciation goes to Flag, my cover designer and friend. We have known each other for a long time, and I am grateful that you always have an innate and unmatched sense for the perfect illustration to convey emotion, character, and story. I couldn't imagine this book without your work on the cover.

One of the most exciting aspects of my collaboration with Night has been the opportunity to witness his unique creative process as he built a film around the premise and characters we jointly dreamed up. At his production company, Blinding Edge Pictures, his producing partner Ashwin Rajan was tasked with executing much of Night's vision while also liaising with my film and publishing teams. We've collectively enjoyed teaming up with Ashwin, who is as amiable as he is able. At Blinding Edge, we've also had the pleasure of working with hardworking Creative Executive Shuni Chopra Dhar, Grace Winters, Scott Friend, Adam Leach, and Steph Tullis. Many thanks to Tanya Cohen and Rich Cook at Range Media, attorneys Greg Slewett and Deb Lintz, and Katherine Rowe and Lindsay Stevens at

Rowe PR for making our many points of coordination and creativity so seamless and productive.

The master of all my film and TV endeavors has always been my longtime agent and close friend, Howie Sanders. Thank you, Howie, for dreaming up this groundbreaking collaboration with Night and for continuing to advance my career with finesse and out-of-the-box thinking. Howie's right-hand person and resourceful assistant Rachel Duboff always keeps Howie's overwhelming obligations in order; Rachel, thank you for your work on **Remain** and also for your emergency cat-sitting!

My longtime entertainment attorney, Scott Schwimer, remains my on-call hero for all matters, personal and professional. He's also one of my closest friends, whose support and advice I've relied on for thirty years. Scottie, I'm grateful for everything you've done for me and am thrilled to see you living your best life these days.

And of course, my former literary agent Theresa Park, who remains my producing partner on all of my film and TV endeavors, is my most trusted creative collaborator and one of my very best friends. Theresa, I'm excited for your new independent ventures with Per Capita Productions and know that they will also enrich the many films we are working on together. Our journey together continues, albeit in a slightly different configuration! To Charlotte Gillies, Theresa's longtime assistant and now Creative Executive at Per Capita, thank you for supporting both my publishing and film endeavors over the past several years with such professionalism and care.

Thank you to my publicist, Jill Fritzo, and her colleagues Michael Geiser and Stephen Fertelmes, who have a gift for navigating the media landscape and envisioning new ways for me to share stories with the world. Thank you to LaQuishe Wright ("Q"), whose patience and good spirit keep me up-to-date on the always-shifting world of social media—and even make it enjoyable. Mollie Smith, thank you for giving my books an online home. I could not reach readers without you. To my accountants Pam Pope and Oscara Stevick: Thank you for your years of guidance.

Tia Scott-Shaver, Jeannie Armentrout, Andy Sommers, and Hannah Mensch deserve my heartfelt thanks for ensuring that the moving pieces of everyday life, big and small, come together seamlessly.

And to my family and friends: Thank you for adding love, joy, and meaning to my life. I pray for all of you daily, with gratitude.

ABOUT THE AUTHORS

NICHOLAS SPARKS is the author of twenty-six books, including **Counting Miracles** and **Dreamland.** His books have been published across more than fifty languages with over 150 million copies sold worldwide, and eleven have been adapted into films. He is also the founder of the Nicholas Sparks Foundation, a nonprofit that provides educational scholarships to underprivileged children. He lives in North Carolina.

nicholassparks.com

M. NIGHT SHYAMALAN is an internationally acclaimed director, screenwriter, and producer who has written and produced films such as **The Sixth Sense, Signs,** and **Trap.** His movies have grossed over $3.3 billion globally, and he's best known for creating psychological thrillers with supernatural themes. He is the founder of the film and television production company Blinding Edge Pictures. Shyamalan lives in Pennsylvania.